The End of Me

The Single Lady Spy Series

Tara Brown

Copyright © 2013 Tara Brown

All rights reserved.

ISBN-10: 0991841166
ISBN-13: 978-0991841165

For Triple M and Totally Booked
Thank you for the laughs and dirty pictures.

Thank you so much to my cover artist Steph, at Once Upon a Time Covers. You are always on call and manage to make my visions come to life.

Thank you to my editors, Blue Butterfly and Andrea Burns!! Thanks to my street team, the Nators. You girls are awesome and I love you to bits.

Thank you to my husband, I am not sure how you tolerate this all but I love you and am grateful for you.

Thank you to the bloggers and reviewers who make my job what it is. Being the kooky writer is the easy part I think.

The End of Me

"The more identities a man has, the more they express the person they conceal."
— John le Carré, *Tinker, Tailor, Soldier, Spy*

Chapter One

Not quite the end of me

"Mom...Jules spilled her juice."

I looked in the rearview for a second and clenched my jaw. The thousands of errands didn't go away. The thousands of obligations felt like they had doubled. Nothing was ever going to be small again. This wasn't the plan, not that there had ever been one.

I sighed and turned around. "Mitch, clean it up for her," I said trying not to be angry. She was five and my temper was short fused.

He gave me the look his father always gave and rolled his eyes, "With what?" The shitty-tween attitude was the icing on the cake of doom, that I was currently being force-fed.

The traffic slowed, giving me a chance to reach around in my yoga bag for the sweaty towel, I still had not taken out of the van. I flung it over the seat at him.

"Jules, no spilling. Mommy can't stop." I could, but I was scared of what would happen if I stopped the van and thought, for even a second. Stopping had been bad, thinking had been worse.

She smiled her bright face and nodded, "Uhmkay." It was more of a sound and less of a word, but she was five and sounds were still huge for her.

Her bright-blue eyes, and the way she looked up at me through her lashes, the way he used to, brought it on. The tightening of the chest was first. The tears were unstoppable. The minivan didn't feel as big as it actually was. I was sure it was closing in on me.

He hadn't loved me. That also hadn't ever been part of the plan. I knew we had taken a risk getting married, but the fact he hadn't loved me, never crossed my mind.

My body pulled forward, as the need to rock filled me.

My broken heart wouldn't stay hidden much longer; it wouldn't let me be okay in front of them. It forced its way, bursting tears from me and ripping at my chest. A sob slipped from my pressed lips. Everything felt like an avalanche of bad things, and all I could do was watch, as they rolled down the hill and buried me.

I made the mistake I feared making. I stopped moving. I swerved the van into a motel parking lot on the side of the road and collapsed into the steering wheel. The moving van was keeping my mind moving.

No sounds escaped my lips. The tears blinded me; at least the van was stopped.

I heaved, but managed to hold back the noises. Slight whimpers slipped past the hold I had, that trembled like a twig about to snap.

"Mommy, you said you couldn't stop," her squeaky voice broke the silence.

I moaned slightly as I pressed the button for the music. Philip Philips sang loud and clear, filling the van with fun and fast music.

I shook for the second I needed and wiped my face. Mitch never looked up from his iPod and Julie colored on her tray, nodding her head to the music. I rocked, ever so slightly.

I was struggling to get some semblance of control as my body fought for gasps of air. I wiped my face clean and agreed with my brain's demand of alcohol. I needed a drink.

The End of Me

I needed so many things... too many.

I drove back toward the road in silence. The song ended and when a new one came on, I braved a glance at them. Mitch's bright-blue eyes caught mine. He frowned, but I shook my head and smiled at him. Nothing could hide the breakdown, I was about to have. Nothing would make any of it better. I just needed to be alone and let the dam break.

He had cheated our family, and instead of facing the music like a man, he had died. He didn't even have the consideration to let me find out, the way I deserved. He had made me the object of gossip. He had made me a fool.

The funeral home looked exactly how it should. I drove into the parking lot and looked back at Mitch, "Be right back, okay?"

He nodded. I locked the van and handed him my cell phone. My parenting skills were slowly diminishing. They too, were being smothered by the avalanche of bad things.

I walked up to the funeral home door where a man with dark hair and dull eyes answered the door, "Mrs. Evans, I presume?"

I nodded. He glanced back at the kids in the van and smiled. It didn't improve the lifelessness in his dark stare, "They are more than welcome to come in."

I shook my head and walked past him, "Do you have an office that I can sit in a window and watch them?"

He held a hand out, "Of course we do. This way." I walked the way he was pointing and turned to the right, past the doorway.

He opened the door to an office just past the main area with the pews and podium. I walked in and sat in a small wooden chair. From the window, I could watch my minivan. This wasn't going to be a habit. I was going to be a better parent than that. Once I buried him and he was gone and I crawled out from under the rubble, I would try harder to be better.

"I'm so sorry about your husband," he said pleasantly, as he sat in the chair across from me. His way of speaking made me uncomfortable; how many times a day did he have cause for that sentence? How many apologies did he hand out? If he had known about the type of husband I had had, would he still offer condolences, or would I be getting the glass of wine I wanted?

"How are they taking it?" he glanced over his shoulder at the silver van.

I shook my head blankly, "They're sad, but it's just regular sad." It was true. They were no sadder than they would have been, if it had been Ralph, our cat. James had always worked away a lot. It wasn't anything new for them. It made me sadder they accepted it so easily. In the eight weeks since we had learned of his death, they had completed all of their stages of grief. I had to repeat all of mine, when I had found out about the other things.

I had been the grieving widow for a few days and then the angry ex-wife. Now I was somewhere in the middle, making me a terrible combination of both.

He nodded, "Of course they are. How old are they?"

I answered him. I didn't want to, but my mouth wanted to move. I wanted someone to know about my sadness. "Ten and five. He was having an affair." There they were... those words. They slipped out before I could stop them.

His eyes lifted but he didn't miss a beat, "I'm so sorry. That's a tragedy to lose a father so young."

I hated that word. Lose. I didn't lose him. They didn't lose him. He wasn't lost, he was dead and so was I.

I would never be whole again. James and the kids had been my everything, because I made them that way. I believed his lies and drank the Kool-Aid, and not even the funeral director would pay attention to the pain that I had laid out for him so clearly. He moved past it, like he didn't hear it, but we both still felt it there in the air where I had left it. James was having an affair and no one cared.

"The kids bounce back faster than we do," he said softly, letting that be his comment on the subject.

But I was having a sickeningly hard time, making my kids be my everything or the focus. Their pain had somehow taken a serious backseat to the betrayal, I had let overcome me.

Being a mom used to be the easy part, but my pity and shame had gotten bigger than I could handle. They had joined the avalanche and I was buried.

"Do you have any questions?" he asked.

I snapped back, "Costs mostly." I felt hollow and dead.

Somehow the director of the funeral home was calming with his general lack of personality. He made me numb, as if I were dead inside like him. His dark hair had no sheen and his dark eyes were lifeless. He was surrounded by so much death that he actually seemed dead. He was a vacuum that pulled all of my emotions away, leaving us both hollow shells.

He clasped his hands, "Of course. Well, the military covers some of the funeral costs for a man like him, but the remaining balance will be yours. The VA only covers about three hundred dollars of our bill for a person not on active duty, at the time of death. The remaining few thousand will have to be covered by you." He didn't sugarcoat it. I didn't mind that. I think I preferred the fact he was dead inside too.

"Can I write you a cheque?" I asked calmly.

He nodded and put his cold pale hands on his cherry-wood desk, "Of course. The service is planned for Sunday, still?"

I nodded and shivered and fought the dark places my brain wanted to go, "It is. They finally cleared the body." The military had been slow to transport him home and even slower to release his remains.

He slid a document to me and passed me a pen. I took it and signed where the red lines were. My fingers shook, making my name look different than it ever had. It wasn't my name, not really. It was the name of a lady who was married to a guy named James Evans. A man who loved his family, worked hard, and made his wife feel like she was safe.

That lady was gone and I was left in her stead. I didn't know what my next move was, but the safety was gone, and the love was entirely based on his being with me. The love and warmth left with him.

I was stuck living behind the wall of bullshit he had built around us. The wall I never bothered to try to climb and see the world for what it really was.

I choked out a sob and stood up quickly, "Thank you." I scribbled on a cheque and left it on the desk. I turned and ran to the van, clicking the unlock button like it was broken.

Inside the van, I wanted to lose it. I wanted to let myself slip into it, but they were watching me. I wiped my face and smiled, "MacDonald's?"

Mitch wrinkled his nose and shook his head, "Grandma took us there yesterday. Can you just make eggs like Dad used to, with the hole in the bread?"

My heart broke and my lip quivered as the tears flooded my face. The sounds coming from me were evidence of the struggle I was facing. I nodded, "Yeah," and started the van.

Julie started to cry, "Mommy. Mommy." She sobbed with me, wiggling in her seat. She always cried when I did. Mitch wiped his eyes and looked down. I unbuckled my seatbelt and jumped from the van. I opened the sliding door with a savage jerk and ripped her from the chair, smothering her with my love, trying not to get any of my self-pity on her. The smell of raspberry shampoo in her golden curls seeped into my bones. I sobbed into her neck and waved at Mitch to come to me. He climbed forward. I grabbed his arm and dragged him to me. I wrapped myself around them as much as I could. I needed to shield them. They didn't deserve the fate they got, and they didn't need to know what all was in the package deal. They didn't need to know about the wall of bullshit.

The heaving, yet silent cries tearing from me, were painful. They made a sickening ache inside of me. It was like they were bouncing around in the hollowed walls that were once my chest.

My head and neck were soaked from their tears as wails of the word "Mommy" filled my dark hair.

We moved like an ocean of misery, rocking and swaying into each other, like we rode painful torrents of heartache. The blinding pain inside of me would never go away. Betrayal was a terrible feeling; it overshadowed the grief tenfold.

"I love you, babies," I whispered when I ran out of tears.

"I love you too. Can we go home and have eggs?" Jules asked and wiped her little chubby cheeks. She was so matter-of-fact. I laughed and wiped my face. I could at least be grateful, their pain was never going to be as bad as mine was. I would guarantee they would be spared the details.

We sniffled and smiled and tried to be strong the whole ride home. I parked the van in the driveway and looked at my house. It was nice—fancy even. We lived a good life. I was grateful at least all of that would still be there... our life that we built together. We were two crazy military intelligence officers who fell in love and got pregnant and then married. We were happy against all of the odds that everyone believed would destroy our marriage. No one believed I could be capable of being a housewife.

We had been cocky in our ability to make a marriage out of nothing; it had been easy.

Of course, that was because it was a façade.

His smile was gone forever, but it still broke my heart every time I saw it in my mind. The fake him with the fake smile would have to live on in our children. My heart was no longer going to allow him to take up space.

I had to shut him out of it. I had to let him and his filth die together.

I climbed out of the van and looked at the ringette and hockey gear against the other door. How would I afford it all? The money from the insurance was going to have to last the year until Jules started school full-time and then the rest would have to go to their schooling.

I stared at the gear and shook my head. Baseball, soccer, dancing, skating, ringette, swimming and hockey. Two kids who played two sports a season. It never felt like too much before, but that was before I needed time scheduled for my daily dose of self-pity and a nap. I closed the van and added it to the list of shit I still didn't have a plan for, which was everything. I wasn't going to make it past his funeral, I was sure of that.

My mom opened the door and smiled at me. She hugged Jules and rubbed Mitch's head. She was my godsend. I wished Dad were there for the second I had to watch them embracing. Her eyes were sweet and kind, soft brown and gentle, but they looked worried. She nodded at me, "There is a man in the office. A Mr. Wilkes. He was James' attorney."

I swallowed and cringed inwardly. I didn't want to see anyone. I wanted a hot bath and a glass of red and to be left with my tears and my plans.

"I don't know a Mr. Wilkes," I said softly.

"Well, he's in the office. I'll make them some supper." She pulled the kids in the house and smiled at me.

"Thanks," I called after her.

She laughed and walked away, "Worry about the important stuff, Evie." She walked into the kitchen and started making noise. The kid's spoke to her about their day, she made things normal.

I placed my coat down and walked down the hall to the office. I swallowed and opened the door to the study. An older man with glasses and a wrinkled face put his fingers to his lips, like he was pretending to scratch, "Mrs. Evans, it's so nice to see you again."

I didn't understand, but I went along with it and nodded, "Yes. How are you?" The question felt forced and awkward. I hadn't played this game in a long time, and just the thought of it made my insides ache.

He smiled gently and placed a package in my hands. He leaned in and whispered softly, "Meet me outside in five minutes. We can take a walk. Don't bring the package. Leave it in here."

My stomach sunk.

He pulled back and spoke in a loud voice, "Everything you need is in the package; the instructions are there. Everything is explained. Have a nice evening." He nodded and walked from the room. He was the first person not to tell me he was sorry for my loss.

He closed the door and I took a deep breath. I looked around the room and wondered what he was whispering for, who he was, and what on earth I was holding? Was I being brought back in? Could they do that? Could I do it? It would solve my money issues, but I needed to be a mom for my children.

I sighed and sat in the chair behind me; the government could do anything they wanted.

His whispering and telling me not to bring the envelope, made me wonder if it was bugged. I could only assume if it was bugged, I was being brought back in.

I felt sickness rolling around inside of me, as I slid my finger along the taped edge and braced myself for it.

I stared down into the huge envelope. It contained three small things; a phone, a Visa card, and a smaller envelope. The name on the Visa was an old name I had used once in Bangladesh, on a mission.

My world spun. I felt as if I were outside of myself looking in. I stared at the name so long, my eyes fuzzed out on the letter. Macy Green...she was a dead travel agent.

The door opened, making me jump up as I placed the envelope on the shelf next to me.

"You want dinner too?" Mom asked, giving me a weird smile. She looked around the room.

I shook my head and walked past her, "I need some air." I walked down the hall and grabbed my coat. I pulled it on and looked back at her, "Be right back."

She tilted her head and watched me for a second, before her kind look returned. She knew the routine. I could see it in her eyes. She had played this game for a long time too.

I leaned in and kissed her cheek, "Thanks." What I didn't say was thanks for not asking and not needing to know. She never did, even when it had been my dad with the secrets and lies. She smiled and pretended everything was fine. She trusted. I couldn't help but wonder, which parent had been right. The blind one who smiled through it all, or the one building the wall of bullshit. Having been on both sides, I preferred to know what I was facing.

Her hands wrapped around my head, squeezing and holding me there, with a tremble. She whispered, "Hurry back. I'll keep a plate warm for you."

I pulled back and walked through the front door. Mr. Wilkes waited across the street.

Dressed in a trench coat and dark slacks, he looked like a lawyer, but I didn't know what to expect from him. He could be one of them.

My arms crept across my body, wrapping around me before I could even stop myself. I was holding myself together. I was vulnerable. I didn't need to hide it; he already knew it, if he had been watching me.

"You're in a situation," his bold words stunned me.

I stopped and watched his face for a sign of anger or violence. I would have to run, I was pretty sure I couldn't fight anymore.

He waited for me to hear his words and process them before he continued, "I'm not sure what your husband did for a living, beyond his day job. I'm not sure what you know, but I am sure you're in a terrible bind." He started walking away from me but continued talking as he walked, "He has left you a rather large pile to clean up."

I jogged and caught up, "What do you mean?" Am I not being brought back in?

He shook his head, "I can't say, but I do know that there is a man who requested that package be delivered to you. Your husband owed him everything."

I swallowed hard and tried to imagine how that was possible. Had he been gambling? After the other deeds I had learned about, gambling seemed like a rather small thing.

He looked at me with emotions filling his stare, "The man who now owns you...is trouble." He looked around us, nervously.

I scowled, "No one owns me, Mr. Wilkes."

He ignored me and continued, "He is the worst of the worst. He owns your house, your van, your life. He has information on you, crucial information. He can make it look like you have done things. I have seen it."

I stopped walking. The words wouldn't sink in, I wouldn't let them. I didn't have any responses. I was already over my head in the debris my marriage had created.

He glanced back at me casually, "Do you understand me?"

I shook my head.

He looked at my neighbor's houses and turned around, "Your husband did something. I don't know what. But the man who sent that package, is the one who now owns your life. You're alive because he says it's okay for you to be alive." He looked wicked in the gloomy, dim light of dusk, as it fell upon my lush and rich neighborhood. It felt clandestine—something I had not felt in a long time.

I frowned, "What?" Of course, I had heard of it. People disappearing because of the intel they had or being tried as traitors for crimes we all knew they hadn't committed. It was like the military's version of a ghost story. "Is the man military?" I asked. I could be tried as a traitor for the things I had done before.

He nodded, "I would imagine something along those lines, or drugs, or weaponry. I am guessing, but I'm just a lawyer and a messenger." His words remained cold, but his eyes warmed to me. He took a step forward and put his hands on my arms. He gripped and looked into my eyes deeply, "You are in danger. Your husband is dead and his debt is now yours. Do you understand me?"

My military training slowly crept back in. I nodded, like a good soldier.

He smiled, but I could see the panic in his eyes, "You have tonight to run. Take your kids and your mother and run. Be fast and silent and find a new life. You know how to do it. You know how to disappear. As of Sunday, they're coming for you. You will be contacted either by that phone or by messenger at your dead husband's funeral."

I took a step back, "What am I going to do?" My heart was in my throat.

He shook his head and I watched him shut the emotion off, "I wanted to warn you. I knew your father. He was a good man and because of him, I wanted you to have the chance to run. I know very little of the details. What I do know is, if you get wrapped up in this, it will be bad for you. You and your kids and your dear mother."

The momma bear anger lashed out. I shoved him back, "You leave my fucking kids out of this. You tell your boss to go fuck himself. Whatever James did, he did on his own. I had no hand in it."

He put his hands in the air, "I am the messenger, I didn't have to warn you. I wanted to warn you. You have to run, Mrs. Evans. Run and never look back."

I looked down at my feet, still keeping my eyes on him and shook my head, "You have to be mistaken. You have to be at the wrong house. My husband may have been a lot of things, but he wouldn't endanger his children."

The emotion crept back into his eyes, "He obviously didn't think he had a choice, and I think if you stay, you'll see that you don't either. Knowing my employers, James did what he did to keep you and the kids safe."

I scowled and walked back toward my house, "He died." It was bullshit, somehow it had to be.

He called after me, "He did. His usefulness must have run out." He snatched my hand lightning fast and pulled me back to him, "No matter what, if you stay, don't let your usefulness run out."

I looked at the severity in his eyes and jerked my hand free. I jogged back to my driveway. I turned and watched him climb into his Saab and drive away. The empty cold inside of me grew as I wondered what the fuck had just happened, and what the even-bigger fuck James had done to me? Was I really that stupid? Had I really been that blind?

Chapter Two

The Con job

The phone rang from inside of the package as I sat on the bed and stared at his pillow. I wanted to burn the damned pillow in the outdoor fireplace, but I was scared of the smell and the possibility it would get out of control and burn the house to the ground. Ideas flashed through my head as I wondered if we could fake our deaths? I knew how, but I needed documents and passports and things I didn't even know where to get anymore.

I looked at my Lulu yoga pants crumpled on the floor in a pile, next to my PTA binder and laughed. Who was I kidding? I hadn't worked in too long to remember how to do any of it. I grabbed his pillow and threw it across the room. The smell of him wafted in the air. I gagged but it turned into a sob. The ringing of the phone in the package never seemed to stop. It was trying to drive me insane.

We had been partners once. How could he have kept secrets so serious that they endangered his kids and me? I wondered if the bad man knew about the mistresses? Did they know he had affairs? Were they tormenting those women too or just me?

I racked my brain to try to remember a moment from when James spoke of work to me. I needed to try to remember if any of it seemed out of place and would trigger a work memory.

There was nothing. He had kept his work away from the house. I assumed, out of respect for me, the stay-at-home mom who had given up her dreams of being an intelligence officer. I could see that was not the case. Had he talked to me about the cases he was on, perhaps I would have seen the discrepancies in what he was doing. Then I would have known he was corrupt.

The fear grew as I watched the package shudder with the vibration of the ringing phone.

I mentally slapped myself. There was a very strong possibility this was a con. I could be about to be ripped off by hackers. I needed to go to the police like any civilian.

I wasn't an idiot; I wasn't born yesterday. I was a strong ex-military, mother of two. Those traits were far more important than the fact I was now a widow or a cuckolded fool. Could women be cuckolded? It didn't matter—the result was the same.

I lay on my side of the bed and planned my next move. If I didn't answer the constantly-ringing phone, I could pretend it hadn't happened for the next little bit, while I planned. I wasn't going to be the victim of a con artist, set on stealing from lonely widows. Before I could go to the police, I needed to know what I was dealing with. The military was amazing at creating the outcome they desired. If it was a prank, they were messing with the wrong widow. But then again, how did they know about Macy Green? I yawned and all the fight in me slipped away. The tired depression crept back in. I fell asleep with my face in my pillow and denial tucking me in.

I woke to Jules crawling around on the bed, poking me.

"What's this?" she asked. "Mommy." She shook me.

I opened one crusty eye and noticed the phone in her hand. She held it to her face.

"Helloooooooo," she spoke into it exaggeratedly.

I sat up, swaying from the dizziness of the sudden wake up and shook my head, snatching the phone from her hands, "NO!" I shouted. I looked at the screen and jumped when I saw a face.

The End of Me

A young man's face.

He smiled pleasantly, "Hi."

I panicked and wildly tapped at the red button on the bottom of the screen. I dropped the phone in my lap. The face... did I know it? Did I know him? He looked young and seemed polite even. Maybe it was a number she accidentally dialed. She had FaceTime on her iPad. She had done it before with my mom and James when he was off on mission.

I lifted my face from the phone to see her eyes getting red. Her eyes watered but she refused to cry, like I always did when I was her age. The closer I got to forty, the more likely I was to cry at even a commercial.

I pulled her in, "Sorry, Jules. It's not my phone. You can't touch it."

I needed to get the phone to the police. I needed to report the whole thing, before they conned another woman who would buy the whole bullshit. But first, I needed to know if pounds of coke would be found in my underwear drawer, because I didn't play ball. If they knew about Macy Green, they must have known about the things I'd done. If they could hack the system well enough to find out about my alias, then they could hack it for the other things and frame me.

The house phone rang. I almost shouted not to answer it, but Mitch walked into my room, looking sleepy and tossed the phone at me. He turned and walked back out, no doubt going back to bed.

I grabbed the phone and looked at the number before answering, "Hi, Mom," I sighed with relief.

"Honey, I had to leave early this morning, but I wanted to tell you, that nice lady from the flower place called this morning. She said that the cheque you gave her bounced." She sounded confused. I would have been too, had I not spent the morning stressing about a certain con job. They had already stolen my money.

But then a terrifying thought flashed through me—what if it was real, and it was one of two scenarios? One, being my husband, who had not only had affairs on me, but also must have betrayed someone high up, who was bent on getting revenge. Or two—he actually sold secrets. Either way, I was screwed.

My eyes flickered on our daughter on my bed. I couldn't lose it yet. I had to remain calm. I sighed like I was inconvenienced and muttered, "Can you stop by and give her some cash? I'll pay you back."

I heard traffic in the background of her cell phone, "Sure, sweetie. Are you okay?"

"Yeah, I must have used old cheques or something. I don't know where anything is. You know James did everything like that." I was kicking myself as I spoke; how could I have let him have all the power? How could I have trusted that man with everything? How could he leave me with all this to contend with?

"Sure thing. You have some catching up to do then I guess, huh?" Her tone was the mom-tone that still had not accepted the fact I was an adult. Not that my life looked that way. It looked like children were running it. I had more faith in Jules and Mitch, than their father.

I covered my eyes and held my face tightly, as I clicked the phone off and slumped.

"Who was it?" Jules asked in her squeaky voice. I lifted my face and smiled, "Grandma."

She climbed off the bed and ran out of the room. I heard her playing with Monster High dolls, as I fell back to sleep. Denial still felt better than coping.

I woke to a strange sensation. The room was dark, which meant the day was gone. I wasn't certain what my kids had been doing for most of it— okay all of it. I blinked up at the ceiling. Something vibrated under me. I fished the moving thing out from under my butt, when it vibrated again.

The End of Me

I turned it in my hands only to see the same face staring at me. I must have pressed accept to the FaceTime call as I grabbed it.

His voice was pleasant, "You look lovely, Mrs. Evans, those pajamas are becoming on you. You must meet Mr. Cooper in an hour at the Ritz, in the Boston Harbor hotel district. I'll meet you in the lobby." The handsome young face was gone instantly.

My fingers shook as cold sweat covered me. I picked my cell phone up from the bedside table and dialed my mom's cell. Instead of ringing, an automated message spoke, "Nine-ten-three-two—we are sorry but your phone is not activated. Please call to speak to a representative."

I pressed the phone off and looked at it. My phone wasn't active. Chills ran up my spine. Chills caused by memories of taking away people's rights. I had done all of this before to other people. I grabbed the house phone from my bed and pressed it on. A busy signal rang through it.

I scrambled from the bed, throwing on a pair of yoga pants and a sweater. I pulled my hair back into a ponytail and ran from the room pulling on my socks.

"Mitch?" I called. "Mitch, Jules?"

My stomach dropped.

I ran down the stairs screaming, "MITCH!" Oh my God, my kids were gone.

"Mom?" he called from the kitchen. I stumbled in seeing him with a spaghetti noodle across his lips like a mustache and Jules trying to make one with the noodle in her hand. She sat on the counter next to my mom who was stirring a pot.

I took a breath, clutching my chest.

All three wore the same confused face.

I stammered, "Uhm...I-I gave the wrong cheques to everyone. I have to run out and give cash to people."

My mom gave me a look. I shook my head. She sighed and turned back to the pasta. She knew the look on my face. She knew the tone of a well-laid lie.

"Sorry!" I yelled and ran for the garage. I shoved my feet in sneakers, jumped in James' car, and hit the garage door opener. I clutched the phone in my hand and backed out like a madwoman.

"Mr. Cooper?" I muttered while drumming on the steering wheel. The name meant nothing to me, "Who is Mr. Cooper?" I got out onto the 90 and was just passing Auburndale, when I realized how similar it all felt. I had done a job just like this one. I knew there was still a distinct possibility I was being conned, but I was doubting it more with every mile I drove.

I decided to try something and looked at the phone. I picked it up and dialed 9-1-1 with it. Instantly, the young man's face was there, smiling at me on the FaceTime again, "Hi," he said.

I frowned, trying to see behind him in the picture, "What do you want?"

He shook his head, "Just for you to survive all this and not make the same mistake your husband made. You're of use to him alive for now, but you need to remember, that he doesn't care if your sweet old mom takes care of the kids for the rest of their lives."

I gulped, "Why are you doing this to me?" My throat was almost frozen. I felt sickened.

He shook his head again, "I don't know. It isn't me. I'm just the receptionist of sorts."

His blue eyes would be burned into my mind forever.

"Are you hackers?" I asked.

The End of Me

He laughed, "I guess, sort of. Look, just do as he asks. He doesn't do well with insubordination."

Rage filled me, "You aren't even old enough to spell that word, you little shit." My spit hit the screen. He gave me a perplexed look and then he was gone, again. Annoying little dick.

I screamed and threw the phone.

I could drive back and get my kids, but where would I go with no money and no house. My mom's old-age pension and Dad's retirement was great, but it wasn't going to get us all by. Especially, not if we were trying to live off grid and be on the run from the government, trying to control every facet of my life.

I didn't want that. The life we led was something I didn't want to give up. My kids went to the best schools in Weston. The community was amazing. How could I remove them from everything they knew, after everything they'd been through? I could run, but what kind of life was that??

My brain whispered that it was better than death.

I looked at myself in the mirror and shook my head. How had I bought it all? How had I believed all the lies? I was starting to feel like a broken record.

I gripped the steering wheel, as angry tears streamed down my cheeks. I wiped them away and parked a couple blocks from the hotel. I needed the air before I had to face Mr. Cooper.

I strolled up in the damp air of the post-rain evening. The bellhop greeted me with a quizzical brow.

"Good evening, ma'am." He opened the door for me. I smirked at his Boston accent. It always reminded me of Matt Damon.

I entered the lobby and was instantly greeted by the young man I had just raged at on the phone. He walked to me and grinned, "Floor 23, suite 2304." He walked past me like he hadn't meant to speak to me at all, like the kids downtown who offered drugs in muttered words.

I paused and watched, surely covered in confusion, as he left the building. Swallowing my nerves, I turned back to the lobby. It was busy, bustling and moving with people who had no clue about the things happening in front of them. I was being victimized within reach of each of them.

Surely, I could just reach out and touch one of them to explain. Maybe I could cry, I was on the verge of tears again anyway. One of them would help me, would they not?

In the moment I felt like doing it, a woman walked up to me with a patronizing look on her face, "Are you lost?" she asked.

I opened my mouth but nothing came out. The fears of what would happen to my aging mother and two children flashed through my mind. There wouldn't even be enough money to bury me, if everything was really in his name.

I shook my head and walked past her, "Just thought I forgot something."

She nodded and smiled and I wanted to slap the look off her face. It wasn't a rational response, but I didn't think I had any of those left. There was a me that no one had seen in a long time, and I was terrified she would find her way out of me, like a demon.

The elevator doors opened to the bellhop inside smiling at me, "What floor?"

I closed my eyes and stepped inside of the large space, "Twenty-three."

He nodded, "You having a lovely evening?"

The doors closed, sealing my fate. I looked at my reflection in the shiny doors and nodded my head, like a good soldier, "Very lovely."

The End of Me

He smiled back at me, "Excellent."

I had a hard time recognizing the face in the shiny metal. I didn't know her anymore. The dead lifeless look in her eyes was one I had tried to forget about.

The elevator landed smoothly. When I stepped off, I felt a rush of fear and regret. I glanced back at the man inside.

He looked up from the buttons and frowned, "You alright?"

I swallowed the bile in the back of my throat down and nodded, "Have a nice night," I muttered.

The stricken look on my face must have shocked him. He didn't reply. He looked like he wanted to stop the doors from closing but he didn't. I could have reached out for him, and he might have offered me help, but what could he do? What could I do?

I was frozen, staring at the doors and the distorted face of the girl in the brushed-metal door. My breath had frozen somewhere in my chest, trapped by the pounding heartbeat and terror of the unknown.

My legs and arms started to feel numb.

The phone vibrated in my pocket, startling me. I jumped and turned. Pulling the phone out, I looked at the number calling but didn't know it.

I tapped the green button and held it to my ear, "Hello?"

"I put some money in the meter for you, before I realized it's nighttime and the parking was free," the voice of the young man rang into the phone.

I clicked the phone off and walked down the corridor.

He was at my vehicle. He could tamper with the brakes or steering. He could plant a bomb. Is that what happened to James? Did they damage his rental car, killing him? Or did they just kill him, and send those poor men dressed in uniform to my door, to lie to me about how it happened?

When had I become so trusting, that I never even suspected it was a job and not a regular death.

Feelings mixed with fears inside of me, leaving me with sensations even James' death hadn't made me feel. The sickening feeling of being trapped and lost overwhelmed me. It was almost kindred to the feeling of finding out he was fucking everything that moved, on the PTA. Well—at least the two I knew about.

The suite number was directly ahead of me. I took deep breaths to stop the feeling that I would be sick any second. Maybe it would be nothing, just some intel on something I could get quickly. I nodded to myself, but laughed inside. Nothing was ever easy with them and besides, what Intel experience did I have left? It had been ten years since I had worked at all, and James had been very good at keeping the top-secret security clearance information to himself.

I licked my lips, nodding to myself. The least I could do, was hear them out.

But no matter what they had to say, I had to protect my children. They could still be little hacker shits who wanted to steal my identity. I would finish the funeral arrangements and let them have it. Evie Evans was never a great identity anyway.

I knocked once, softly. I didn't have the strength for anything else.

The door opened, swinging slowly. My breath was lodged in my throat. I held it as I stepped into the dimly-lit suite. The back of a man in a dress shirt and slacks walked away from me. He opened the door and turned his back on me? Bizarre? Maybe I knew him.

He had short, dark hair that was styled in a military cut, only slightly longer. That didn't sit well with me. His broad shoulders and thick arms looked the part.

Seeing him made me wish it were just hackers.

"Close the door," his deep voice commanded, not in a bark but more of an arrogant tone. It struck a nerve with me.

He was military.

He could whisper it and my old, long-buried, soldier self would obey.

I closed the door and pressed my back against it. From the darkness of the long corridor I could see a fair amount of the suite. It had a view of the dark night and the city lights. He disappeared around a corner.

"Come in here, Evie," he spoke my first name like I was a child, confirming my fears that he was military. I would bet a limb on it. I gripped the handle of the door and wondered how long it would take him to catch me. His long, strong body would be able to beat me in a foot race, but if I had the advantage of a head start... maybe... no. I was a distance runner not a sprinter. His thick legs said sprinter.

I swallowed and let go of the cold, metal handle, letting the door close and seal my fate. My steps felt thick and hindered by the nerves and fear dumping hormones into my body. Adrenaline, then cortisol, and finally noradrenalin. I was walking with concrete boots, by the time I got moving.

I crept along, unprepared for what I would find, when his deep voice spoke again from around the corner, "I guess we should get right to it then. Your grades in high school were quite good. Your first four years of service were exemplary, getting you into Fort Huachuca easily, after BT and the mandatory four years. You went through the paces and ended up in CI. Your higher-ups had no issues with you in Counter Intelligence, and even recommended you for promotions, which you declined and retired, exactly at the eight-year mark. Sound right?"

A memory attached itself to every single word he said: happy times, hard struggles, James courting me and getting me pregnant, me quitting for the sake of the baby. I entered the room, catching a look on his face in the far corner, where he sat drinking an amber liquid from a rock glass.

His face was incredible looking—young, but incredible. I took a breath when I saw the cold look in his eyes and tensed face.

He was military. Cold steel-blue eyes, square jaw, strong nose, long thick neck, arrogant look on his tanned face. He was military and there was no doubt. That meant I was screwed.

He raised an eyebrow, "Well?"

I nodded.

He pointed at a chair, "Have a seat." It wasn't a question. I walked to the chair and sat on pins and needles.

He sat back, taking me in. A grin crept across his lips. That arrogant smile was part of the kit when you started in CI. He was Intelligence. He was like me.

"Do you have any idea what your husband has been doing the last ten years, while you were having kids and driving them to play dates?" His tone mocked me. I shook my head and looked down. He drank the last of the liquid and stood. He walked to the bar set up in the corner by the window and nodded his head, "James was good at keeping secrets. That was about his only redeeming quality."

I was confused. I wanted to defend James and say he was an amazing father, incredible husband, and kind soul. But I assumed we both knew the truth of all of it.

"James worked for Counter Intelligence. He failed at what he was asked to do. You will have to take it over. You have been named in the intel we have." I could hear the liquid pouring as he spoke the simplest, and yet most complicated words, I'd ever heard.

The End of Me

I lifted my eyes, "Named? What?" It came out before I had a chance at articulating my confusion.

He turned with two drinks. He placed one on the coffee table across from me and sat again, "You only had eight years service, when you went on maternity leave?"

Did he just make finger quotations when he said maternity leave?

He grinned at the look on my face, "So that makes me senior officer here. I think if you want to get snarky, you can add a Sir to the end of that question."

I felt a homicidal look creep across my face.

He shrugged it off, "Or Cooper. When you get to know me better, you can call me Coop." He winked. It was the first playful thing I had seen. It disturbed me, considering we just finished the conversation where he put the finger quotations up for maternity leave, like it wasn't a legit reason to quit.

I reached for the glass. Holding it made me feel better, like it grounded me. I sipped the scotch. I hadn't drunk anything but red wine since I'd joined the mommy brigade. They had rules and liking red wine was one of them. I always assumed it was because Dr. Oz had mentioned it a few times. Those women were nuts for Dr. Oz. He could say smearing your own spit across your forehead was a way to stop cancer and they'd do it.

The scotch burned my throat, but I chugged the whole glass back like I was a sorority girl and placed it back down. He watched me with a half grin. The fact he was still a child himself, made me feel better. He hadn't killed my husband, it had been an accident, and this was an act to try to bully me back to work. I could handle a whippersnapper like him.

I cleared my throat and started, "I am flattered you think I have retained even an ounce of the training I had before. I haven't, but thank you.

That actually made my day. You ruined the rest of it, of course, by bouncing all my cheques and freezing everything. You've terrified me by making me think I had hackers trying to steal my life." I took a breath, "Sweet God. I don't understand why on earth you would want someone like me to help you. I'm under-qualified, under-trained, completely in the dark about the technological advances you've made in the decade I've been off, and I'm really busy as a mom…"

"Stop!" he cut me off. My mouth hung open as he shook his head, "Seriously—I didn't sign up for this shit. It wasn't us freezing accounts. Your name came up in Intel. I'm here to handle you, that's all. I don't want to hear about your bake sales and shit."

I closed my mouth and watched his face change. The playful face and cocky grin were gone. He was back to being senior officer in the room. "James and the man you'll have to get close to, did this to you. We need your help to fix it, but that wasn't us. You need it fixed as much as we do."

Heat crept up my face; I hated the way he controlled the conversation.

I frowned, "That lawyer…"

He laughed cutting me off again, "Wasn't working for us. We jacked the phone they were bringing you, that's all. You think we want you in our employment, no offense, but you're right. You're under-qualified, out of shape, outdated like the suits in the offices, and frankly, you don't seem like you take things seriously. Having to handle you is going to be a fucking nightmare. You'll be expecting to still act like a civi, and I'll have to swoop in and stop everyone from killing you, every minute of the day. Do you even remember any of your training? You are in over your head, but I'm being told this is how it is. I get your dad was a hero, but seriously sweetheart, you are out of your league."

I snapped, "You little shit, I am not out of shape. I ran a marathon three months ago. I ran the Boston Marathon and I got a good time. I…"

The End of Me

"I didn't mean to hurt your feelings." He laughed bitterly, discounting my obvious accomplishments, "But for the job I'm asking you to do, you're outdated. But, we're stuck with you, as much as you're stuck with us. The man your husband double-crossed this country for, killed him. He thinks you know things. The intel is that you're up on the roster as the next piece in his puzzle. He owns you. Are you ready for this?"

I laughed, "I don't know anything."

He shook his head, "As far as my pay grade goes, you have a piece of the puzzle."

I looked at the glass and shook my head. I stood and walked to the bar and poured another glass, drinking it back fast. "No. I don't know anything. He never told me anything. I want protection and to be moved out of the country."

He sighed, "The higher-ups don't want you to hide; they want you to play ball. We've had your house bugged for a few months. We know James never told you anything. We have been watching you." I could hear his footsteps behind me. Suddenly his body was directly behind mine, towering over me. He bent and whispered in my ear softly, "Let me just start by saying, you sing beautifully in the shower."

My eyes bugged open. He poured another drink for us both and carried them back to the table, "This is the plan. You will take the phone call from the man planning on calling you or meeting with you. We will reinstate your wages, at your husband's current salary, and put it in a new account that we will have opened for you. Hopefully, he won't know and you'll be able to continue paying your bills. You will help us to find out what the man wants with you and what your husband told him." He sat down and sipped. I clutched the bar, taking deep breaths.

I turned and walked back to the chair, "What if I can't? What if they just want to kill me too? I can't leave my kids orphaned. You have to get them out."

He watched me, "I think you're a better actress than you give yourself credit for. Act like you might have a secret or two."

His tone told me it was a cheap shot for sure, I just didn't know what for. I clenched my jaw and picked up the glass again, "Why are you my handler? Shouldn't someone with a little experience and age be my handler?" I could play mean too. My philandering husband died two months ago—I deserved to be downright bitchy.

He laughed after a moment. It boomed like a shot in the air. He pointed at me, "You're pissed that I called you old. I get it."

I raised an eyebrow, "No. It's that you're still a Boy Scout. This is my life we're talking about and you've told me nothing. I have no details. And maybe I want to be handled by a man." The scotch was hitting me. The liquid courage was saying things, I wasn't sure I wanted to say.

He smirked, "I'm man enough to handle you, I can assure you." His cold eyes hardened, "I've got this, trust me. You just try not to fuck up your part."

I shook my head, "Have we met before? Have I offended you prior to this meeting? I'm having the rug pulled out from under me and you're acting like a dick."

He sighed, "I've spent the last few months on constant detail, watching you and your family. It feels like we've met a thousand times." Before I could ask anything else, he lifted a cell phone from the couch and dialed. He held it out.

"Good evening, Sir."

"Is she there?" The voice on the other end spoke and I knew it instantly. My stomach clenched as Coop nodded and turned the phone, "She is."

An older man, who I recognized, smiled at me, "Evie, I am so sorry about James." I hated FaceTime, I realized that right then.

The End of Me

I smiled politely, "Thank you, Commander." I felt sick seeing his withered face. God, I was getting old.

He smiled, "You know we need you, right?"

I nodded once. What else was I going to say? He was the commander in charge of the CI unit, I was part of. He was it.

"That's a good girl, your father would be proud of you. Coop will get you outfitted and ready. Our Intel says they'll be calling you tomorrow or contacting you at the funeral. We need to know we can count on you to help fix the situations your husband left us all with." He nodded and then Coop turned the phone back around. "You know your orders!" he barked at Coop, who pressed a button and put the phone down.

I started to laugh, possibly from the scotch and possibly from the ridiculousness of it all. I shook my head and covered my eyes. I understood the threat in the call. If I didn't play ball, they would make sure I fried for his crimes, somehow. The phone call was to ensure I would play ball. I knew it and so did they. I would be guilty of co-conspiring to commit terrorism or God only knew what.

I wondered if they'd already put some coke in my underwear drawer; I could go for a hit.

Tears threatened when I put it all together in a big pile and looked at it. The information, the death, the possibility of working again, all of it. The pile was too big to handle. It was too much to take on.

I stood from the chair and bolted for the door.

Coop moved fast, and as I opened the door, he slammed it shut. He pressed himself against me, shoving me into the door. He wrapped his arms around me, as I cried into my hands.

Chapter Three

The possible end of me

We were silent during the drive home, maybe because he held me when I cried, and it was awkward as ass. I was hoping it was more that he really didn't talk much, unless it was to mock me. Then he seemed like he had tons to say.

I glanced at him, "You drank as much as me. You shouldn't be driving either."

He grinned, "You sound like my mother."

My eyes narrowed, "Well, maybe that's because I'm almost old enough to be your mother."

He laughed, "You're thirty six, I'm twenty-eight."

I frowned, "You look like twenty-two, tops."

He nodded, "Yup. It's good for what I do. I've been doing this a lot longer than you."

I looked back out the window, "You still shouldn't be driving."

His tone changed, "I got this. Don't worry about me. Worry about your kids."

My head snapped back, "What is that supposed to mean?"

He took the exit for Weston, driving far too fast, "It means you need to do this the best you can. I'll be here for you, but all I can do is hope you have the training you'll need for this. The number one skill of any CI officer is belief. You need to believe. 'Cause if you don't, they won't either. Now take this package inside, go over it and then burn it." He pulled the cab onto my street and parked in my driveway with a jerk.

"You drive too fast," I snarled and snatched the package. I jumped out of the car and slammed the door. I ran for my front door, not stealthy like at all.

The house was dark and silent. I slumped when I closed the front door and pressed my back into it. It was too much. It was all too much. I turned the locks and tried to find my peace again.

I could still smell the lingering odor of the spaghetti my mom had made the kids for dinner. I looked up the stairs to where my children were sleeping and made a mental note to change all the locks. Mom and the kids would be on mandatory lockdown.

I had no clue how to protect them. I had never been an agent with a family.

"Fuck!" I whispered into the quiet of the foyer. Looking around, I wondered where they were, the bugs and the cameras?

I grabbed the package and stormed into the powder room, I would hope they hadn't bugged the bathrooms.

But what if they had?

Oh my God, were these people watching my kids shower and use the bathroom?

My stomach sunk farther. Frantically, I rifled the bathroom. When I pulled the fan cover off I found it. A small bug. I ripped it off and tossed it in the toilet. I stuck my hand up farther and found the second one. There was always a decoy. I flushed both and sat down on the lid. I wanted to cry. I wanted it more than I wanted anything, but the tears I had shed in the hotel room had taken all my sadness.

My fingers didn't tremble when I opened the manila envelope. Nothing inside of me was the same as it was when I left the house. In the place of the pain and self-pity, was resentment and a dirty dose of fury.

I shook my head and pulled out the folder, "How could you, James?" I muttered to the folder, "How could you do this to me and the kids?"

The dark-brown folder had one word on the front of it, "Burrow" I didn't know what it meant but I assumed it was something to do with him being a mole. A double agent. How could he? I closed my eyes and repeated the word burrow but it didn't trigger anything.

I twirled the locket on my neck, trying desperately to recall even one thing. The locket made me ashamed. My father had given it to me for my graduation from CI training. He had been commander in charge at the time. He had begged me not to become a CI agent, but when I had ignored him and done amazingly at training he had to be proud. He begged me not to date James when we were discovered. I never understood his hate for him.

I couldn't help but wonder, if my dad had seen the man he would become?

I took a breath and wished I had some red wine to drink as I flipped it open. At first, it was pictures, surveillance photos of buildings I had never seen. No different than what I had looked at a million times in my short career as a CI agent.

I flipped past them, trying to commit them to memory.

Unfortunately, the shows my kids watched everyday had fried my brain somewhat. Well, kids' shows and the many hours I may or may not have spent playing Skyrim. I believed in testing a product before I let my ten-year-old play it. Damn those game makers. They were good. That damned game was addicting, once I got used to the Xbox controls.

My to-do list was balanced in there somewhere, along with the heartbreak that my kids' dad was an idiot. There was no room for surveillance photos.

I closed my eyes and took a deep breath, needing to be the person I once was. I opened them and started to look at the pictures again. Warehouses maybe, factories, trucks parked outside, men walking the yards without guns. The pictures were like looking in over the industrial section of any city. I couldn't even say what country it was. Nothing stood out.

The next pictures were of a man, I thought maybe I knew. The next one was of James and the same man. The man looked to be close to James' age. The black and white photo showed him to be handsome, dark haired, and serious looking.

It wasn't keeping my attention. I needed a snack. I put the papers down and went to the kitchen. I picked my underwear out of my butt, where it got lodged from sitting on the lid to the toilet and then looked around.

"Shit," I whispered.

Coop, or someone, was no doubt watching that. I snarled and opened the freezer. I should have grabbed the plate of food, Mom would have in the fridge for me. Instead, I grabbed the caramel pecan ice cream and a spoon. I raised it like I was toasting whoever was watching me. Fuck Coop and his out of shape comment. He was probably disgusted at the thought of a girl eating ice cream from a container.

I carried it back to the washroom to look at the files again.

Sitting back on the toilet, I spread the photos out on the floor, after I went over each one. The first one was of James and the man talking outside of the warehouse. I knew the man. It was driving me insane where I knew him from, so I blanked my mind, but flashes of Foster's

Home For Imaginary Friends filled it. I loved that show.

I sighed and grabbed the notes.

"Officer Hammond believes Officer Evans to be compromised and possibly committing traitorous acts against the flag."

I reread the sentence and swallowed the lump of cold ice cream. I clenched my face and neck, as a throat burn started from not chewing the ice cream and taking in too large a bite. It happened when I watched Vampire Diaries too. Damn those Original Vampires and their sexiness, they gave me brain freeze and throat burn every time.

The next page was dates. I saw some I recognized as dates he was out of town for work. Others were hockey tournaments and other such competitions for our kids. Some of them, I recalled James being at.

Lastly, was an iPod. I pressed the on button on the top and instantly the screen went to a video. I pressed play.

It was James being filmed from a short distance at night. He stood in a dark corner with someone who I couldn't see, but I could tell it was a woman.

"You think if I had any other choice, I would have let this happen?" he asked the lady.

She put her hands on his jacket, on his chest. I placed the ice cream on the counter and dragged the video back. I watched her hands touch down on his jacket. It was an intimate touch.

My stomach turned, but I forced myself to watch the rest. I was actually being given footage of one of his said infidelities. They knew? They knew and they let me watch the video?

"Heartless bastards," I muttered and looked back at the video.

The lady spoke plainly, "I just want you to be safe. They know about the

Burrow, she knows for sure. There's no way Evie..." I knew her voice.

"Shhhhh," he said and looked around.

My guts burned. Why was my name being mentioned? I knew her voice? Where from?

"James, they know about Evie..." she whispered, just as the camera lost her voice.

I gagged. Of course I knew that voice and the way it whispered my name. It belonged to my best friend in the world. My best friend, who I believed to be on mission and unable to be at my side, as I learned my husband was dead. I waited on pins and needles for the camera to catch her face. If it was her, I was going to have a heart attack.

He grabbed her arms, "I told you not to say that. You don't know who's following us. Just stay out of this and stick to the plan. Meet me in Holland in a week. I have to break this to Evie and the kids. I know she knows, or at least, suspects something. She knows this is coming."

My mouth dropped open. I didn't, in fact, know. I never suspected.

"I hate that she's going to get hurt." She rubbed her hands up and down the front of his body, making mine numb. I felt my lower lip creep out. I was actively praying it wasn't her.

His voice turned soft, "Melanie, I want to be with you. The kids are old enough. It's our turn. Me and you, baby."

My mouth was completely dry, except for the sour taste in my cheeks. I dropped the iPod to the tile floor. My hands covered my mouth, "Fuck." Silent tears streamed my cheeks.

Melanie... Melanie, who sat on the toilet nervously watching me check the pregnancy test. Melanie, the bridesmaid at my wedding. Melanie, who held my hand when I gave birth. Melanie, who I had prayed would get my dozens of desperate emails from the last two months.

She was my best army friend. We had done basic together and Fort Huachuca. We had entered CI together. A million images flashed in my mind. He was fucking her too? The PTA moms weren't enough? He had to take the only thing that was mine—she was mine.

The video was still playing but I couldn't hear anymore. I got up and left the bathroom abruptly.

I needed to be away from the papers.

I paced the hallway. My breath came in rough spurts and panicked half breaths.

I burped the ice cream. It started to creep up my throat. I sat on the stairs; my tears wanted to come but the ice cream was blocking them.

I gagged and ran upstairs to my bathroom, bursting through the door, and running for my toilet. I couldn't go back into the bathroom downstairs, not yet.

I bent over the toilet and gagged for a second before the scotch and ice cream started to flow. My guts retched and my heart broke. Not from his betrayal but from hers. Him, I had started to come to terms with. Hers might kill me.

I finished throwing up and flushed repeatedly. I curled up on the cool floor and pressed my face to the tiles. My silent cries turned to blasting sobs. I let loose the horrors and the pain. I let loose the millions of things I hadn't let myself see. The dam broke and I let the avalanche smother me completely.

Images of things I had not wanted to see, ran like a movie behind my eyes until the movie ended and my eyes went black. But even as I passed out in the bathroom, I dreamt of things I didn't want to see. His hand grazing her thigh, the two of them sneaking off during our wedding, the way he always insisted I invite her along.

I woke to the sound of a man's voice.

"James?" I stirred and wiped the drool from my face.

"No. Come here."

I blinked and saw Coop standing in the doorway. I blinked again and wondered if I was hallucinating.

He had on a hoodie and sweats. I jumped when I realized he was truly there and banged my head on the toilet.

He winced and stepped to me. He lifted me off the floor, "You don't follow orders very well, Evans." He carried me from the bathroom and laid me on my bed, shaking his head, "And your breath stinks."

I started to cry again, rubbing my head. I stammered, "H-h-how could you let-let-let me watch that-that? She was my best friend," I heaved. I wanted so badly for it to be his fault.

He walked to the bathroom and turned the tap on. He came back in with a glass of water, "We saw you find the other evidence. You knew he was a cheater. You've known for a while."

I slapped at him wildly, "Did you plant the other evidence so I would find it? Did you?"

Even in the darkness of my room, I could see the cruelty in his eyes. "Evie, you have hours. I'm not kidding—hours. They are going to come for you or send word about the meeting. You need to remember who you are and shut off the parent act." The words echoed in my mind.

I curled into myself and shook my head when he offered me the water. "She was in my wedding. She was with me when I found out I was pregnant. Her desperately, sad face makes sense now. I thought she was sad 'cause she knew I would leave the army if I had a kid. Fuck, I didn't know. I'm such an idiot. I didn't know, all this time. The PTA moms and Mel. I'm so stupid. I thought he was the lucky one. I was the better catch," I snorted, "How fucking arrogant is that?"

He sat on the end of the bed, the weight of him made me rock back a bit. "You are the catch. He's a dumbass. Luce always called him a douche nozzle. None of us liked him, not even Jack. That takes talent. Jack likes everyone."

I laugh/cried; I didn't even want to know how that was an insult. I'd seen douche nozzles. They didn't seem offensive. I ignored my rambling brain and whispered, "What did the file say? How long?"

He knew what I meant. I knew he would. He sighed, "Does it matter?"

I nodded, "Yeah, it does."

He looked down, "The whole time. He played you and her hardcore, apparently. He was found out and told to break things off with you both or he would be dishonorably discharged for fraternization. He told the commander you were pregnant."

I gasped, "My father was the commander then!"

"The file says it was recommended he do the right thing. I am assuming that was your father's recommendation." His voice was cold and hollow. It made the news easier to take somehow. I remembered the look in my father's eyes, when we told him we were pregnant and getting married.

"So he married me and screwed her for a decade, and our whole marriage was a lie? A lie my own dad knew about? What the hell?"

He sighed, "Yeah."

I closed my eyes and nodded. I got up from the bed, but he grabbed my hand when I walked past.

"You need sleep." He pulled me back toward the bed, ignoring the fact I was pulling back.

I pointed towards the door. "I need to get the papers and video. I left it all downstairs."

He shook his head, "No. I told you that you don't follow orders. I already got rid of it all. I took a huge risk coming here. I told you to burn it, not leave it next to the chunky monkey you were eating right from the container. That was a disturbing sight."

I bit my lip and fought the chuckle that slipped out, "You're a dick."

He pulled me onto the bed, "I know. I get that a lot. So do you want me to just tell it all to you? That was my idea from the beginning, but the commander thought you would want to be alone when you heard the sordid story."

I pulled away from him and crawled into the covers. When I was comfy, he looked down at the floor and started talking quietly, "When you were in, did you ever work on a file pertaining to a man named Gustavo Servario?"

The light bulb came on. I smacked my forehead, "That was him in the pictures. Damn… Servario filled out his khakis. Yeah, I remember him well. He was a young, cocky little shit. His mom was Italian and his dad was an Italian-Serbian arms dealer who owned a shipping company as a front. They were sort of a small-fry operation."

He looked back, "Wow, that came back fast."

I laughed bitterly, "Bad things stay with me."

He narrowed his eyes, "I'll remember that. Anyway, the small-fry operation lasted a little while, but when his old man died, he took over. Everything changed then."

I nodded, "Yeah, I worked his files then. It was 9/11 and he was a gunrunner, so we kept a close eye on him. We knew then, he would outgrow his dad. He was smart and savage."

Coop shrugged, "Well, after that he went underground. Then we heard he was not only running arms, but he was also dipping into prostitution and drugs. We could handle those things, stop him here and there, make it look like we were putting in an effort. The orders were to let him run it, and if he slipped up, and got carried away, to slap his wrists."

I shook my head at how much it hadn't changed. We didn't want to stop them and end the wars; we wanted the appearance of trying. Funding was dependent upon supply and demand. No demand, no supply.

He shrugged and continued talking, "We kept an eye on him until three years ago. Then, things changed again. He got harder to trace and then he would pop up somewhere. It was like he was putting himself in our way, trying to be noticed."

"Diversion," I said softly.

He looked back at me: our eyes met in the dark, "Exactly." I noticed the way the light hit his lips when he pursed them, "He was toying with us. We sent James in, not as a spy obviously, but as a rogue informant. Trying to create misinformation amongst his people. We wanted to see how his line of command went and how he reacted to the lies we created. We wanted to know, who we could get to. We think it was then, that James went rogue for real."

"Not to sound disinterested, but when the hell do I come into the picture?"

He chuckled, "The video you saw, we were watching him, and we caught that transmissions between him and Melanie Ashcroft. It was dumb luck..."

I cut him off, "Bullshit. You knew he was cheating, and you kept close to blackmail him if you had to. You were building a file against him."

His lips curled, "In the yoga pants, it's easy to forget you used to play this game. We had more than enough to charge him and ruin his life, but then we caught wind of him and Servario talking about the Burrow. Then again with Melanie; you heard it there on that video. It was taken only a couple weeks before he died. We don't know what the Burrow is, and we don't know where it is. We think Servario believed that James had it or had access to it, through you..."

I cut him off again, "Why would he kill James, if he believed him to have it? Who does that? Who kills the man with the answers?"

He sighed again, "We think it was you he was after. Kill James and get control of your whole life. Then he could make you his pawn and make you give him the Burrow. All I know is, we didn't kill James, and the only actual proof we have of you being mentioned, is that video. I said it wasn't enough to bring you back in. I honestly think, he might have suspected us watching him and made the video to lead us off the tracks, or to bring you in. But higher-ups feel like you have the answer, and they're willing to gamble with you."

I sat up fast, ignoring everything he had said, "What? Wait... If he died in the line of duty, I'm not paying for the whole funeral." I felt outraged. I didn't even want to go to the damned thing anymore. I was angry on a whole other level of angry. I covered my eyes and massaged my temples.

He started to laugh, "Did you hear the rest of what I said?"

I shook my head, "I've never heard him or anyone mention the whole Burrow thing. I think it might be some bullshit he was doing, 'cause he knew you were on to him. Where the hell is Melanie? I was told she was on mission. Why haven't you all brought her in? James is probably still alive and with her. Burned-out bodies in cars tend to be someone we found along the way to replace us, when we fake our deaths. Typical cover-up."

"I know that."

Of course he did. I wouldn't be surprised, if they never suspected James dead at all. But they had no problem letting my kids think it.

I looked up at him, feeling the years of abilities and skills finding their way back to me. Granted they had to crawl through layers of bake sales and fuckerwear parties. I made a duckface and processed the fact, I should have bought a dildo at that last one I went to; it had been almost half a year since I'd been laid.

I mentally slapped myself. I was losing my mind.

I started to giggle.

I gathered myself and wiped my face of the tears I hadn't realized I was crying, "What a night."

The awkward silence was broken by his voice, but it was softer than before, "More like two months. I'm sorry this is all happening to you."

I nodded, "Me too. I feel bad for Melanie. Her heart must be broken. Will you be bringing her in? You never answered me."

He cleared his throat, "If it was really him in the car, then she was in there with him. It was a bomb."

I was frozen again; she had been one of my best friends in the whole world. I wouldn't let her be dead in my mind. It was easy to suspect her of faking her death with James, after seeing the video. If she had actually died, I wasn't sure I would recover from it. I muttered emptily, "What evidence do you all have, that it was actually them in the car? I'm assuming the bullshit I was fed from the two men who notified me of his death wasn't real?"

He crossed his arms, "The notification wasn't staged, but what we told you wasn't true."

I pointed at him, "I mean it—I'm not paying for that bastard's funeral."

He chuckled, "I'll tell the commander. The car bomb was real though. We have her rings and some dental. Him—we have the wedding band you were given back. The bomb was a type that uses chemicals to damage and erode the remains."

I frowned, "And that doesn't say set-up to you?"

He shook his head, "We had eyes on them. They were in the car. This isn't Mission Impossible, Evie."

I let the words all sink in and shook my head, "I don't know why, but her possible death hurts more than his."

"Bros before hos."

I frowned as tears streamed down my cheeks, "What?"

He looked confused, "You know that old saying 'bros before hos'? She was your bro and James was like your ho."

I laughed, "Oh my God, you are so twenty. That's not an old saying. I was a teenager when Snoop Dog made that up. Jesus."

He chuckled and stood up, "I know who Snoop Dog is. Jeesh, I told you I'm twenty-eight. I just mean she was bigger in your heart, even if it didn't feel like it, 'cause she was your friend, not your lover. She was never blinded by love; she just wanted to be your friend. Are you going to be okay?"

I nodded and wiped my face again. It was a lie, I didn't think I would ever be okay. He walked to the bedroom door, it was then that it dawned on me how weird the whole thing was. He was standing in my dark bedroom, staring back at me. I didn't know him and I didn't like to cry in front of people I did know. I cleared my throat, "So, I guess we meet with Servario tomorrow then?"

He nodded, "We think so. Our intel on his movements is bad. We don't have much to go on. He's been playing us for a while. That lawyer was our first real break. We traced your deeds and paperwork back to him, through about a dozen other lawyers and a bunch of fake companies. The video of James mentioning you to Melanie, and the one of him and Servario, and the paperwork we have from the lawyer, are all the things connecting you to all this. Upstairs feels like it's enough to bring you back in."

I shook my head, "I can't believe, they would sell me down the river for so little. What the fuck is this Burrow?"

He shrugged, "No clue, but Servario froze everything so he could control you and make you need him. He did all that for a reason. The thing can't be that little, if the government and a huge arms dealer both want it. He needs you for something."

I bit my lip and thought for a second, "I don't like going in blind."

He nodded again, "I know. We made sure the phone you got was one we could control, if you press 9-1-1, we can get to you. Servario may call, he may show up, we don't actually know."

"Useful!" I rolled my eyes, "I love that I'm being risked out like this. Do I know about him and James and about The Burrow?"

He shook his head, "No. Play dumb for now."

My stomach clenched, "That won't be hard. Will I be in danger? Should I get a gun?"

He laughed, "No. When was the last time you fired a gun?"

I shrugged, "I don't know, a long time ago. Will you be there?"

He smirked, "I've been there all along."

I nodded and tried ignore the super-creepy feeling I got from the comment, "Okay.... Just turn my cell phone and house phones back on...okay? I need to be able to reach my kids if I'm out and they need to be able to call out, if there's an emergency."

He nodded and grinned, "Night, Evie." He left and closed the door. I didn't go to sleep. I waited for him to leave, or at least gave him long enough to be gone. Then I got up and started to debug my house. It helped me process the fact, I would never get to be me again.

Chapter Four

Goodbyes aren't nearly as bad, when you hate the deceased

To say I was pissed would be a HUGE understatement. It would be like saying Bostonians enjoyed the odd game of baseball or hockey.

James' service was lovely, but I couldn't cry—not even for my two, desperately-sad children. His parents hugged and kissed me, all the while telling me how much he loved his children and me. If I had to listen to his mother go on about the flower arrangements, or how the army was being so good to us, for one more minute, I figured I would kill someone. The more time I spent celebrating my husband's life, the more forward I was looking to meeting the infamous Mr. Servario and getting the shitshow James had left me, over with.

I wanted to be sick. I wanted to spoil the sweet, knight-in-shining-armor-bullshit appearance, James had managed to maintain. He was a real gem of a husband, all the while, fucking my best friend and the PTA bitches. I only knew he'd fucked two in the group of them, but there were several floating about the funeral, all crying. They smiled and pretended to be sad for my kids. It was a bit disgusting.

Every time I glanced at Mitch, I felt a sickening fury. His birth was a lie. Our marriage was a mistake. I was the girl James had accidentally gotten knocked up. The girl James wouldn't have picked, had he had the choice. James, who was more than likely still alive and hiding out with his mistress, my best friend. Meanwhile, I would be going into a deep cover op and risking my life to keep his kids safe. I could have chewed my nails and spit bullets.

I glanced around the room, looking for the one man who would not fit into the party. The one man who was now in my life, because of my asshole husband who had apparently, burned to death in a car. God help him, if I ever found him alive and well.

What I saw around the room, broke my heart further. Jules was clung onto my mom; her sweet blue eyes were filled with tears, real tears. Crocodile tears, as James always called them. They seemed so big compared to her tiny face.

Next to her sat Mitch, looking stunned. I could tell he felt lost, like he might flee any second.

It all made me sick. My babies were crushed, James' parents were devastated, and my mother was saddened by the loss, of yet another husband, in the family.

I excused myself from the people I was standing next to, who I wasn't listening to anyway, and walked to the ladies' room.

My breath was getting caught in my chest again. I leaned on the sink and took huge deep inhales. Looking up at my reflection, made me grimace. I was worried about the girl in the mirror. Her dark hair was greasy, at least it looked shiny in the tight bun. Her green eyes were flat and dull. No sparkle, no life lived in there. Her lips were cracked and she had a cold sore on the corner of her mouth. Her eyebrows had weeks of plucking to be done and her olive skin was blotchy. She was gaunt and sort of gray in the places that weren't reddened. It was not the face of a woman who was going to win the confidence of an arms dealer. Those guys always hung with the blonde girls who had perfect bikini bodies and stylish sunglasses.

I looked at my tired-looking body and sighed. No wonder James was fucking Mel. I would have fucked her too. There was no scar from having his kids marring her stomach and her tits didn't sag slightly from breastfeeding. She was fit and looked the way she always had. I was different though, my body was different. I imagined he liked the changes because they were associated with his children.

A sob tore from my lips as my momma-bear brain switched on. I wouldn't let myself feel shame for the way I had changed. I had born children to that bastard. Well, now they were my kids—screw him. They were all mine. He could rot in Hell or Prague or Holland or wherever the hell he was, with the best friend I apparently never had.

My anger died when I caught a glimpse of the pain on my face.

I didn't want them in Hell. I wanted them there with me. Even if it meant they were together and I was alone. It was better than really being alone, like I was. My nerves started to pick up, as the fears and stress started to become real. I wanted to do what all widows did, crawl into my bed and wait for a year to pass, before I had to function again.

I left the sink and opened the door to the bathroom, but the back of a black suit was barring the way.

"Excuse me," I muttered.

He slipped a card over his shoulder without looking back at me or turning at all. My stomach dropped. I took the card and looked at it.

"6 p.m. Presidential suite."

The card was for the Hilton downtown, in the financial district.

I frowned and looked up. The man was holding a fifty-dollar bill over his shoulder. I took it. "For the valet," he muttered and walked away from me.

He disappeared into the crowd of people wearing black.

I looked down at the fifty and the card. I wished Coop were with me. That was a bad sign. He was right, I was in over my head.

I slipped the cash and the card in my clutch and wiped my eyes, before walking back out into the wake.

My mom came up to me, smiling weakly, "I'm taking these guys home."

I swallowed and looked around the room. "I think they need some time away. You up for a road trip?"

Mom frowned, "What? Honey. We can't run away from our problems."

I shook my head. "It isn't ours, but we may need to run anyway. We'll talk about this at home." I had so many things to tell her. Things that weren't going to be easy. I had found forty-eight bugging devices and cameras in the house and garage. I figured Coop would be there with a team reinstalling them all.

My nerves were shot and when I looked at the picture of James at the memorial table, I felt worse. Worse because I wished he were there to solve this for me.

A hand reached out for mine, "I'm so sorry, Evie."

I looked up to see our neighbor from across the way, Jeff. I smiled and let him embrace me. He held me tight, "If you need anything—anything at all, just call."

I pulled back and nodded, "Thanks, Jeff." His wife Megan walked up and smiled compassionately.

"Honey, I am so sorry. James was the best." She looked distraught as she covered her face and started to cry again, "I...just...am so sorry."

I noticed the way Jeff's face tightened. He looked at me and smiled weakly, "She's been really broken up about it."

I nodded, "Of course. I better circulate." I turned and walked away. I didn't circulate. I ran for the exit. I was going to be sick if I saw one more, teary-eyed woman. I was either becoming that jealous psycho widow/ex-wife, or I was actually accurate in my assumption he was also fucking our neighbor.

The End of Me

I drove home in a near coma. I was so out of it by the time I got in the front door, I couldn't see straight. I slipped up the stairs and flopped on my bed. His scent wafted up into the air from his pillow. I grabbed it and threw it across the room.

"Easy tiger."

I jumped seeing Coop standing where I threw the pillow.

"What are you doing here?" I asked looking around.

He put a finger to his lips. Jules came running into the room and jumped on the bed. She curled into me and cried. Mitch wasn't far behind her. He wrapped himself around us and joined in on the crying.

It broke everything inside of me. Their suffering wasn't a random accident. It was the recklessness of a philandering father. A man I would let die, even if it meant I was in danger. No matter what, they would always believe the lies. I was selling my soul to the devil to ensure it.

I held my children to me and forgot we had an audience, until my mom came in. She stood in the doorway and smiled, "Fresh cookies on the rack downstairs cooling."

I kissed Mitch on the cheek and smiled, "Go on." He wiped his face and shoved his ball cap down, then he stalked past his grandma like a tough guy. Jules was asleep. I nudged her, "Cookies."

She didn't stir. I lifted her off the bed and carried her to her room.

When I came back in, I climbed on the bed and smiled at my mom, "Thanks for making those."

She shook her head, "No. No thank-you needed. This is what family does, when one of theirs is hurting."

I nodded, "You always were a good mom. You're an even better grandma."

She laughed and sat on the bed. I glanced around, looking for Coop but he wasn't there.

"That's the payment for suffering through having kids. You get grandkids," she beamed.

I rolled my eyes, "Me and sis were easy."

She folded her arms around her and grinned, "I never said you weren't. But you were kids. Kids are kids."

I put a hand on hers and saw the resemblance. We had the same hands. I had hers. I squeezed, "I need you to leave town."

She shook her head, "No, the kids need stability."

I pressed my lips together and took a deep breath, "They need to survive something I'm about to tell you, that you may never speak of to anyone. I am telling you, not only so you are prepared to run and raise them on your own, but so you understand what I'm doing."

She squeezed my hand back, "Evie honey, you're scaring me."

I looked into her green eyes and nodded, "You should be scared. James did some bad things. He betrayed the country. He sold secrets. He was a rogue agent."

She shook her head, but I could see the truths making their way into her mind. Her eyes showed the doubts she was having and the uncertainty of her headshake.

I whispered, "A bad man owns everything of mine. My home, my van, my car, my bank accounts, everything has been transferred into the ownership of this bad man. I have nothing. CI has basically told me, I will help or I will fry for the things James did. I have to help fix James' mistake. It's the only way to get the danger out of our lives and get what's rightfully ours back."

Her face changed and I didn't know the look she was giving me. She looked around oddly, and whispered so silently, I barely caught her word, "Evie, we can run. We can take the kids. I have a little nest egg your father put aside, for just a moment like this one. I know a place." She looked frightened, as silent tears slipped down her pale cheeks,

I shook my head and cut her off, "No. They'll find me. They'll hurt the kids or you. They know all about all of us. There is no way."

Ideas flew through her mind; I could see them rolling by like clouds in the sky. She twitched and shook her head, "We can go to the FBI."

I laughed, "James hasn't broken a law they govern. As far as they're concerned, he's dead. CI is going to take the three of you and go pick up Sissy, and take you somewhere. Somewhere safe. I won't help them if they don't do this. I want you safe until this is over." My voice cracked, "You keep my babies safe."

She pulled her hand away, "God damned him. What was he thinking?"

I shook my head, "He was leaving me for Mel. It never was me he wanted. He got me pregnant. I just never knew. Dad told him to do the right thing."

Her hands flew to her eyes, "You know?"

I gave her a look, "What?"

She sniffled and shook her head, "You know that for certain?"

I nodded.

She sobbed and shook her dark head. I crawled to her and wrapped my arms around her.

"You can't do this to them. You can't abandon them."

I pulled her back and smiled, "I'm not. I'm giving them the only person I trust in the whole world to keep them safe." I looked to the side of the room and spoke softly, "You can come out, Coop."

He stepped from the walk-in closet with a savage look on his face, until my mom lifted hers. Instantly, the clouds from his face were gone and he smiled at her. It wasn't his cocky smile either. It was sweet. I could see just how handsome he was with it.

"Who are you?" she asked him. She sounded terrified.

His eyes darted at me, "Everything she said was true. James was a bad man and has put the country in danger. My name is William Cooper. I'm in the section of the government where Evie and your late husband used to work. We need her to come back to work and help us."

Mom looked at me and shook her head, "Will she be in danger?"

I bit my lip and looked down. I didn't want her to see the face I was making, she could read my face too easily.

Coop smiled and shook his head, "No. I'm very good at my job, ma'am. I will keep your daughter completely safe." He offered her his hand, "You have my word."

I rolled my eyes. He was nine years old for God's sake; what word did he have to give? Mom ate it up though. She smiled and eventually got up off the bed.

I looked at Coop and nodded but spoke to my mother, "Can you go tell the kids they get to go on a fun trip and I'll make arrangements here with him."

She looked at us both and then walked from the room. She wasn't happy and I didn't blame her. I would kill Jules myself, if she ever said something like that to me.

She closed the door and instantly Coop lashed at me. He grabbed my arms, "What are you doing?" He shook me. I jerked free and shoved him back, "You aren't keeping them here as fucking bait. So you can play ball with me or I walk. I will go to jail for whatever the hell James did, just to see them safe."

He paced across the carpet for a minute and then picked up his phone. He dialed and held it to his ear.

He shot me a dirty look as he spoke "I need an evac and I need it now."

He hated whatever they said to him next; the look he gave me was absolute fury, "You tell anyone I've called you and that weekend I may or may not have footage, goes live." He ran his hands over his short, dark-blond hair and then looked back at me, pointing as they talked in his ear. He mouthed the words, "You are a pain in my ass."

I rolled my eyes and crossed my arms.

He continued, "No, she wants the family evac'd. She wants them out now… tonight. No. She wants them in a safe house… out of country. I'm thinking Canada, or even Alaska. Find a fishing lodge, or something the kids can have fun at, and they can blend. Something where we can post people and make them look like part of the resort. I want this to be handled by Martin's team." He paced, still holding his hand on the top of his head.

My frantic eyes searched him for signs of body language. In the tiny space between his t-shirt and jeans I could see his stomach. I wasn't certain if the tattoo on his side, which dipped into his pants, suited him or not. It was sexy and fun looking, whereas he seemed like an asshole most of the time. His face was a storm of repressed fury. He reminded me of my dad a bit.

He snapped a finger in front of my face when he caught me looking him over, and continued to speak into the phone quietly, "I want the jet ready and directions to be disclosed in the air like with the MacLean case. The pilots will be at the resort with them the entire time. No leaks this time. Make sure it's some place we own, sheriffs and whatnot as employees. Don't even mess with me, Mickey. I got your wife on speed dial. Yeah, fuck you too. See ya, man."

I frowned and mouthed, "This time."

He shook his head at me and snarled. I glared back.

"Done." He tapped the off and pointed at me, "Don't fuck with me. I run this show; I tell you how it goes. No more stunts."

I swallowed and looked away, seeing the anger on his face I decided then that he didn't suit the tattoo. Cute and flirty Coop was not consistent enough to suit the sexy tat.

He leaned into my face and shouted, "I mean it, Evie!" His nostrils flared when he was angry.

I flinched at his rage. He softened when he saw my face, "What time did the card say?"

I felt a strong desire to kick him in the face. I hadn't been yelled at like that, since I was in basic training. I looked down at the floor and took a breath.

He dropped to his knees in front of me, "I shouldn't have yelled," he brushed it off.

I scowled at him, "You're single aren't you?"

He chuckled, but it wasn't friendly, it was sort of bitter. "You're not really my type. I get the whole cougar thing is huge, but I'm not into it. I like it when I'm on top and all you forty-types always want to steer."

My hand flew at him, he caught it and gave me an outraged look, "What was that for?"

I yanked my hand from him, "I'm not a cougar! I'm not forty! I wasn't hitting on you, you moron, I was mocking you!" I got off the bed and walked out of the room looking back at him with daggers.

The End of Me

"Little bastard," I muttered and stomped down the stairs.

Chapter Five

From Ma'am to Madam

Kissing my kids goodbye wasn't painful, it was too much pain to only measure with human emotions and words.

A thousand times I wanted to jump into the van in the garage.

A thousand times I wanted to hold them to me and beg the men getting into the van with them to take me too.

A thousand times a bad thought filled my mind, and all I saw were horrid images of my vulnerable babies.

Mom kissed me and shook her head, "Be strong, safe and fast." She kissed the tip of my nose. My eyes watered. It was what she always said to my dad when he left. My mom was a military wife. She knew, at any given time, my dad's work could make her life painful. She knew it, all too well. She loved it when he got too high to go on mission anymore.

I looked into the van and crossed my arms. Thankfully, my kids were confused enough that they didn't ask too many questions. I had already explained that it was a military thing for the men to ride with them, as an honor to their fallen father. They did it for every fallen family.

I took both their hands in mine and spoke softly, "Daddy had it in his will that we were all to take a vacation, if he ever died. He didn't want us to be sad or heartbroken. He wanted us to be happy and remember him. We are going to take that vacation, like he made in his last dying wish.

The End of Me

Grandma is going to go ahead with you and I'm going to stay behind and deal with the rest of his stuff. I love you both."

Mitch shook his head, "I don't want to go."

I gave him my look for 'I don't give a rat's ass'. "Mitch, this is your father's dying wish. We have no choice but to respect it."

He cocked an eyebrow at me, making me snap, "Behave for Grandma or I burn the electronics."

Mom climbed into the driver's seat of the minivan. A man got into the passenger side and laid the seat back. My kids were put in the middle seats with men on either side on the floor and two men lying in the back. How they had all made it into the house from the backyard, was disturbing. Had my neighbors really not noticed the military combing through the backyards in broad daylight?

I glanced over at Coop, ruffling the hair on Mitch's head and joking with him. I wanted to tell him to stop, but it was sweet to see Mitch laughing and trying to be a man in front of him.

I stepped away from the van and blew them kisses as the doors closed. Coop closed the last of the minivan doors and walked to me.

He wrapped himself around me, helping me inside of the house and closing the door. I pressed my face to the cold metal and cried against it. He didn't try to comfort me, thankfully.

I dropped to my knees and sobbed, "T-t-t-they only finished their father's memorial hours ago. I've m-m-made a mistake," I wailed.

I curled up at the door, keeping my fingers on the cold metal of it.

I heard him close to me and opened one puffy eye to see him carrying things from my kitchen.

"What are you doing?" My tone was edgy.

"Get up, Evie," he answered back with a tone of his own.

I turned to tell him to kiss my old, saggy ass, but I was stopped by what I saw. I started to laugh.

"You are so twenty-years old. You can say twenty-eight, but I know," I whispered as I sat up, shaking my head and licking my wrist. I snorted as I gave it to him. He shook the salt on it and handed me the shot. He did the same on his wrist and held his shot out, "To your mom and kids arriving safe and staying that way."

I muttered, "Cheers."

He clanked our shot classes together and gave me a mischievous look.

"Stop trying to be nice to me. I have seen the real you," I snarled and licked the salt the same time as him. I shot back the tequila and grabbed a lemon from the plate. I sucked the juice as he did. He reached over and wrapped his empty hand around mine, holding the empty shot glass, "I am nice."

I gulped.

The lonely corner we sat in, with our shots and lemons, seemed darker suddenly, matching the gloomy day outside. He took my glass from my fingers and poured us each another shot, and passed me the glass back. I licked my wrist and held it out for him to pour more salt on.

He held his drink up again, "To James, may he rest in peace." His eyes twinkled. I grinned and nodded, "And Mel. May they be at rest together, happily."

He half smirked, lifting only his upper lip on only the right side. He licked his lips and I tried not to notice how plump they were. Or how he had the subtlest cleft in his chin. Or the way his pulse beat rhythmically in his thick neck. It was like neck porn. I licked my wrist and sucked back the drink. I grabbed the lemon and sucked, all while watching the neck porn.

I needed a nap and to be away from him. He was jailbait and he called me a cougar, and I was an emotional wreck who was about to make a poor choice out of grief. I jumped up and shook my head from the two shots.

"Thanks," I walked past him and up the stairs.

"No prob," he muttered.

I curled up in my bed and slept, until he woke me with a shout from the bottom of the stairs.

I jumped up and pulled on a casual outfit. I didn't even look at myself. When I met him at the door, he gave me a disapproving once over.

"What?"

He cocked an eyebrow, "Is that really what you want to wear?"

I growled, "I'm a grieving widow, ass."

He put his hands up in the air, "Alright fine; let's sort this out then. I'm your cabby. Meet you out front in two." He nodded all snarly again and vanished. I looked at the foyer and crossed my arms around myself.

How had it all happened? How had it gone so wrong? How could James die, or even worse, fake his own death and abandon us?

I waited the two minutes and walked out the front door.

He sat in the same cab as the night before. I climbed in and looked down.

He spoke as he backed up, not looking at me, "He's going to talk to you and ask you questions, and you are going to have to seem like a devastated widow who knows shit all." He drove like a maniac and dropped me off at the lobby without saying much, "Be safe. I'm nearby, okay?"

"No last advice?" I gulped.

He shook his head, "Say yes to everything."

I scowled at him and closed the door. What was the everything?

"Good evening, ma'am," the bellhop said and opened the door. I looked up and walked across the lobby, wondering how many hotels I would be entering if this continued. They would start thinking I was a nearly middle-aged hooker, if I kept coming back and visiting hotel rooms. I glanced at myself in the mirror I passed and felt a little better. At least I didn't look nearly middle aged or like any hooker I'd ever seen. Whose fantasy was to have their mom show up in their hotel? Maybe I could nag them to pick up their clothes and wash their faces.

The bellboy was a young man with an infectious smile. He nodded at me as the elevator opened, "What floor?"

I smiled back, ignoring the fire in my stomach and stepped inside, "The presidential suite please."

He gave me the up-down and smirk, "Yes, Ma'am." I could have pulled off my sports bra and choked his little ass.

I sighed, partly because everyone had been calling me Ma'am lately, and partly because, I knew I would never get my sports bra off fast enough. The thing was a death trap.

The elevator stopped on the top floor.

As I stepped off, he said, "Have a nice night, ma'am," and pressed a button. I glanced back at the shit-eating grin on his face and raised an eyebrow.

Had he had a mocking tone?

Was he laughing at the fact the guy opening the door was getting a mom hooker? He was probably used to seeing three girls in miniskirts with red lips and syphilis entering the presidential suite.

I looked at the single, white door in the hall. The suite must have been nearly the entire floor. I pushed down my fears and walked to the door. The fact I'd already done this routine was making it less scary, like I had wasted the real fear on the practice run when I met Coop. I didn't feel as scared as I should have been.

My hands didn't shake. My stomach burned but never cramped.

I placed my fist up to knock, but the door opened.

"You're late." The man from the photos with James scowled at me. He looked so much better in person.

I winced, while trying to smile, "Sorry. The taxi was late."

"I gave you valet money for a reason."

I stammered, "Uhm...I was too tired to drive."

He watched me for a second, before letting me in. His short, dark hair was thick and styled nicely. He looked my age but his face was actually tanned, so his skin was aged, but only slightly more. His hazel eyes had a greenish tint to them, but were mostly brown. I could imagine them getting quite dark if he were angry. He was tall, much taller than me in all my five-foot-four glory. He had to be at least six foot three.

He smiled and made slight dimples in his cheeks, "Please, come in. My name is Gustavo Servario." His smile was hypnotic and calming. This... this was the man threatening my life and children?? I was having a terrible time believing it possible or seeing him as threatening. My nerves were barely registering or just refused to participate on account of the handsome man.

I could feel awkward nervousness making attempts to take over. He was sophisticated and smooth and handsome, beyond what I had expected. I had only ever seen surveillance of him. Up close, he made me breathe irregularly. I regretted my choice of yoga pants, a three-quarter sleeve sweater and sneakers.

I entered the suite, nearly jumping when he placed his hand on the small of my back. He chuckled, "You'll need to get used to that feel, my dear."

My stomach dropped, the charming dimply smile couldn't even rescue me from the panic of my nerves showing up all at once.

I would need to get used to that touch? He was planning on touching me? What did that mean?

He guided me into the living room and put a hand out, "Sit."

I gripped my clutch and sat in one of the fancy cream and yellow chairs. The room was lovely.

He picked up two champagne flutes and brought one to me. Were we celebrating my husband's fake death or his taking over of my life and forcing me to hide my children?

I took the delicate stemware in my suddenly-shaking hand and forced my nerves down.

"What do you know of your husband's dealings with me?" he asked as he sat.

I frowned, "Nothing." I noticed everything about him. I couldn't help it. He was big—over two hundred pounds, but at the same time, graceful. His greenish-grey slacks fit him perfectly. He filled them out as if they were made to be his. His cream-colored dress shirt was open, like he had just taken his tie off and was about to relax for the evening. He was thick and fit for our age. The closer men got to forty, the less likely they were able to tie their own shoes. But not him, he was strong. It made the feelings of fear and panic worse. There would be no escaping him. He could snap my neck in a heartbeat. The flute looked ridiculous in his huge hands.

Every observation I made of him, linked itself to a dirty thought. I'd been reading too many naughty books. But I had to give it to him, he had aged nicely, more than nicely. I couldn't shake the bratty boy he had been, when I was watching him at twenty-three.

He sighed and watched me checking him out. I blushed as he smiled, "You seem afraid of me, Ms. Evans."

I tried to nod, but it was more like a twitch. I steadied my hands and brought the flute to my lips. The champagne was perfection.

"Is it alright?" he asked.

I nodded, "It is. Thank you." The awkwardness of it all was bizarre. I was living like it didn't matter my children were being flown into hiding. Guilt trickled down my throat with the next nervous sip.

He licked his lips and smiled softly, "I'm sorry if I seem distracted, you're a very beautiful woman."

I wanted to giggle nervously but I forced a frown, "You murdered my husband." The words came out, before I could stop them. He was making me uncomfortable, and acting like a grieving widow was harder than it looked.

He laughed, "Did I?" He all but confirmed my suspicions with his statement, and his amused sparkly eyes.

I shook my head, "I don't know. Didn't you?"

His eyes narrowed as he brought the drink to his lips and sipped. He shook his head and chuckled, like he was laughing at something I didn't know. Like there were jokes in the air that I couldn't see, well at least he didn't know I saw them.

My hands were shaking harder. I gripped the flute firm enough that I figured it would shatter. I lifted it and drank the champagne in one long gulp.

His eyes widened.

He stood and walked to the bar in the far corner. He grabbed the bottle from the ice bucket and brought it to me. He took my hand in his and lifted the flute with my hand. The warm strength of his grip, felt like it was burning mine.

"Your hands are cold. You need to calm down. Stress is very hard on women. It ages you." He poured the glass but paused before letting go of my hand. He ran his fingers up my empty ring finger, "Over the marriage so quickly?"

I shook my head, "I get dry skin." It wasn't a lie but my voice broke slightly under his scrutinizing stare. It felt like a hot lamp.

His eyes flashed, "You know about his infidelity, don't you?" He sat down.

Jesus, did everyone know?

Was I honestly the last person to know?

Taking a breath, I spoke softly, "I know. I found out the other day. A friend was in town and felt like I deserved to know after all these years." I was panicking. If he had been watching me, he would know it was lies.

He filled his own glass and put the bottle back. He sat again, watching me.

I sipped the champagne.

"Do you know anything else?" His eyes were like lie detectors.

I focused on the fact, I was terrified of him and shook my head.

"You seemed edgy." His eyes narrowed.

"I am. You're scaring the shit out of me. I don't even know if James was ever my husband, for real. He was fucking everything he could get on top of, except me. Which now I'm sort of grateful. I don't know you and we're having a very private conversation. Not to mention, you killed James and Mel, and sent a lawyer to my house to tell me you've taken everything from me." My voice wavered. The champagne was just doing all the talking.

He put a hand out, "Don't cry. He isn't worth a single tear." When he said the word tear, I caught the slight accent he hid. He continued quickly, "James was a bad man. He doesn't deserve a single tear from your beautiful eyes. You deserve someone who would cherish you and respect you, and make you more important than everything in the world." He paused and drank. Like he was stopping himself from the awkward moment. We were both just saying random things.

I pulled at my sweater and looked around, was it getting hotter?

He whispered, "You deserve a love like no other person has ever had."

It was the nicest thing anyone had ever said to me. An arms dealer had given me the best compliment, I had ever had. Just great.

"Thank you," I said quietly. I was getting confused as to why I was there. I hoped it was the champagne, tequila, and general lack of food that was making me dizzy, and not the fact he was beautiful and I was desperately emotional.

He shook his head, "No, it was the truth. You're a special woman. You deserve a special man."

His words were making me uncomfortable. I glanced over at the bottle we were drinking from, to see how much was missing, and realized there was an empty bottle next to it. He got drunk before meeting me and was hitting on me.

That was special. I would bet he was even using his best lines on me.

I wondered if all the spies had experiences like that, or if I was just that lucky? The word spy made my palms sweat.

"Getting back to the reasons you are anxious. I haven't taken anything from you, Ms. Evans." He sipped the flute.

I cocked an eyebrow, "Call me Evie please, and yes, you have. You have everything of mine frozen."

He pointed at me with the hand holding the drink, "Ah, but that's not the same thing, is it? You have something of mine and I'm going to have everything of yours, until I get it back." The way he said everything, and lifted one corner of his mouth, made me cringe inwardly.

My chest rose and fell faster, as I processed all his words and the comfort with which he spoke them. Could he force me to give him everything? Coop had told me to say yes to it all. Surely, he didn't mean everything.

He put a hand out and waved me off, "We can negotiate what everything is later. For now, I want to give you what I like to refer to as my test run."

I swallowed the champagne in my mouth. It felt as if it curdled in my throat.

He grinned leaning forward and slid a white envelope across the table to me, "I will let you peruse this, whilst I attend to something in the other room." He said whilst like a foreigner and left the room.

I gulped back my drink and placed the flute down. The white envelope felt weird when I picked it up, like Mission Impossible combined with True Lies. I watched too much TV, while glorifying my 'good old days' in CI.

I opened it and looked inside—a room key for the Bellagio and a picture of a man with a chubby face and huge lips. He was in his sixties maybe and greasy looking. He was wearing a white suit in the picture.

"Ew," I whispered and examined the white suit. Beyond Don Johnson, no one ever rocked that bad boy.

There was nothing else in the envelope. I tapped my fingers against it and processed the whole thing.

It could be a hit...please God, no.

It could be a trace, please God, yes.

It could be stealing something, please God, let it be the trace.

I frowned and looked back at the room, he had walked into. I stood up, placing the envelope down and walked to the other room where the lights were off and the curtains drawn.

"Mr. Servario?" I spoke softly. My mommy/spy/widow senses told me to run. When I turned to, it was too late. He had been behind the door and closed it as I turned around.

In the dim lights coming from the alarm clock, I could see the serious look on his face.

"I understand you were once in Intelligence," he spoke softly, taking a step towards me.

I swallowed and took one back, "I barely finished training," I lied.

He smiled, "Let's not lie to each other, Ms. Evans."

My fingers balled into fists as I whispered, "I told you, call me Evie," and took another step back.

He reached for my hand, "I think you were good at your job. You were good at it, and your quitting to be a mother was a tragedy."

Ouch. Maybe, he too would throw up the maternity leave quotation marks and my week would be complete.

My legs backed into something. I hadn't looked around the room. I didn't know where I was—rookie mistake.

He stepped too close to me, pressing our chests together, and towered over me. "I need you to do something for me, Evie," he whispered my name. It sounded deliciously frightening on his lips. He bent this face close to mine. So close, I could smell the champagne coming off his breath, as he whispered again, "I need you to kill the man in that picture."

My stomach dropped.

I shook my head, "I've never had to kill anyone. That wasn't my job."

He was so close, we were nearly kissing. He ran his finger down my cheek and whispered again, "But you will kill him." He didn't have to threaten me, that was implied.

I parted my lips to speak again, but he delicately brushed his thumb across my lower lip. "It's non-negotiable. It's that or we have no deal." He closed the tiny distance between our faces and replaced his thumb with his mouth. He sucked my bottom lip gently, before kissing me once. My breath left my mouth in spurts, as he pulled away.

I closed my eyes and let the millions of emotions flood me, until air rushed between us and he stepped back. "The flight to Las Vegas leaves in two hours." He turned and left the room. "You will be outfitted on the plane."

I followed him back into the light, completely stunned by the fact he had made me want the kiss. I was losing my mind. I needed to switch back to red wine, no wonder the women I knew all drank it. Champagne and tequila were making me a giant ho.

He walked to the front door and opened it but stood in the way, with his back to me. "If you pass this, I will give you back your life."

I frowned, "So I do that and I'm free?" I was confused. I thought he too wanted the Burrow thing. I was clearly in over my head, like Coop had said.

He glanced back at me wickedly, "No. I will own you, I won't need those other things."

I shook my head, "You've preyed upon my circumstances. You already do own me." The sickening truth of it all was killing me inside. He owned me. He kissed me. I had wanted it. The way he had uttered the threat with such confidence was disturbing, and yet, I had wanted it.

He smiled, but it was bitter and harsh, "Then I guess we won't have any issues." He stepped out of the doorway and let me pass. As I walked by him, he grabbed my arm and held me to the side of him. The heat of his body was intense and yet inviting. I wanted that kind of warmth to cover me. I hated myself for the thought, as it passed through my brain.

His breath was irregular, like he wanted to say something or do something, but he didn't. He left it as another awkward moment between us... us perfect strangers. Perfect strangers who acted like old lovers, but without reason.

He released me and stepped back inside. I noticed, as I walked to the elevator, the men standing in the long hallway. Had they been there when I arrived? My skills needed honing.

I was obviously out of my league.

I pressed the elevator button and waited.

The door behind me opened again. Panic filled me when I heard him cross the hallway towards me. I didn't look back, I just waited for whatever thing, he was going to do next. He grabbed my arm, spinning me around. He passed me the white envelope but continued to grip my arm for a moment. His eyes sparkled with something, trouble and temptation maybe.

He smirked and let me go. He walked back to the room and closed the door, as the elevator arrived.

"Ma'am."

I turned to see the bellhop. I blushed and stepped inside.

I pressed my back against the wall of the elevator, and waited for him to call me ma'am once more. I would clip him in the ear with the envelope.

I struggled to breathe until the elevator stopped on the main floor. I walked across the lobby and tried not to feel like a whore, or have a panic attack.

Coop was sitting outside in the valet parking with the cab. I climbed in and noticed it wasn't him, as I closed the door. It was a lady. I had gotten in the wrong cab.

She was young, not quite thirty, and maybe a little bit butch. She grinned back at me, "Hey, where to?" and winked.

I shook my head, "What? Uhm, Jericho drive in Weston."

I didn't know what to think or do. I didn't have the money to pay for the cab. I would have to get the Visa from the other envelope and pay with that.

She drove for a block and then pulled into a car wash. "Mind if I wash the car quick? Hit a bird."

I shook my head, "No, of course not."

She winked again, "Supa." It was super, but she said it like a true Bostonian. Was she a real cabbie? I was about to relax, when she held up a piece of paper as we got into the car wash. I read the writing and pulled out the white envelope and passed it to her.

She fished through it and then held up a small, round battery-looking object. She opened the window a bit and tossed it out into the water. She paused a second and then fired the white envelope out the window.

"Hey!" I said.

She laughed, "The first one was the decoy. There was one actually pasted into the envelope seams. They're getting sneakier."

I smiled, "Oh well, they've come a long way in the last few years, I guess."

She rolled her dark-brown eyes, "I'm Luce."

"Evie."

She nodded, "I know. I knew your husband."

I scoffed, "Yeah, apparently everyone did."

"Yeah I didn't know him like that," she laughed and handed me back the picture and the room key.

I folded the picture and keycard and put them in my purse.

In between the water and soap cycle, the car door opened. Coop jumped in and slammed the door. He shook his head and pulled off the wet coat he was wearing.

"That was fun." he smirked at me.

"What are you doing? You should have told me, I was getting a different cabbie. Did you hide in the carwash all this time?" I asked looking around the car wash.

"No. Can't always get the same driver. Duh." He leaned forward and slapped Luce on the arm, "You get the bugs out?"

She stared back at him with a deadly stare. Her body looked thicker than mine, how an agent should look. I bet she could bench press me. I looked at my feeble arms and remembered how they used to look. I used to be beefier. Yoga was relaxing, but I wasn't building any bulk in those classes.

Coop turned and smirked, "How was it?"

I frowned, "I can't do it. I'm going to have to run for it."

He frowned back, "What? Did he hurt you?"

I laughed, and tried not to think about the thing he did do to me. I shook my head, "No. He was a perfect gentleman," I lied.

Luce looked back and smirked, "He's hot, like what-the-hell hot. I'd let him hurt me for an hour or two. Shit, I might hurt him."

I continued laughing and tried to cover my blush, "Yeah, uhm—wow. When did arms dealers stop looking like Boris Yeltsin or Bin Laden? I actually remember when George Bush Junior was the hot guy in amongst the dictators and presidents."

She laughed with me, but Coop frowned, "He's a murderer."

I nodded, "I got the impression he didn't think Mel and James were dead. Of course, there is also the fact, he asked me to murder a fat guy in a cliché, gangster white suit."

Luce winced, "No one looks hot in a white suit. Not since Miami Vice."

I pointed at her, "True story."

We were instant friends. I liked it.

Coop looked confused. I liked that too.

The wash ended, forcing Coop to slink back in the seat. He ducked down quickly when Luce started the car and drove out.

"I can't kill that man," I muttered, not wanting Luce to hear I was all bark and no bite.

He nodded, "I know, and yet, you have to." His eyes twinkled. The steely blue was gone and in its stead was a sarcastic brightness.

I felt my eye twitch with nerves, "You're getting off on this, aren't you?"

He nodded and snickered, it was a real snicker like a kid would do. "I am. You are well known as a former female counter Intel agent. It's fun to see you freak out and not know what the hell to do."

Luce turned back as she drove out of the city, "It's true. I am honored to be working with you. It's good to have you back."

I shook my head, "No. Not back. I'm not working again."

She gave me a look in the rearview, "You sure about that."

I sighed, defeated, "No."

Coop put his hand on mine and squeezed, "I've got this. Trust me okay?"

Looking into his eyes, I could see it was back. The flash of light and funny was gone. His eyes were almost gray, they were so icy.

I did trust him. I didn't know why, but I did. Maybe because, he was mean enough to be capable.

When Luce dropped me off, Coop whispered, "See you in five."

I gulped and got out, "Thanks for the ride."

She nodded, "No worries. See you soon. Vegas baby!!"

I closed the door and walked up to the house. My house, that for the first time, I was scared of. I didn't know what would be waiting in the house for me. A small part of me wished it were my kids and my mom waiting for me. I would have even taken James, greeting me at the front door. He was the devil, I knew.

Instead, it was dimly lit from the setting sun and frightening. My home felt as fake as everything else. My life was a mess and the road to fixing it seemed outlandish, even to an ex-Intel agent.

I was standing in the middle of the foyer, terrified to enter the rest of the house and be alone in it, when Coop came through the kitchen. He walked across the rooms, making no noise.

Seeing his silhouette in the shadows of the house, made me feel better—less alone in the world. He whispered, "You need to get ready."

I whispered back, "I know." But I didn't know why we were whispering. I had debugged everything, hadn't I?

Chapter Six

The Mile-High Club

I scrubbed, shaved, used a loofah on everything, and then got out the tools for the plucking and primping. I didn't know the last time I'd done it and I didn't want to admit, why I was doing it. Instead, I told myself it was like shedding the skin of the old me. The me that bought all of James' lines.

I frowned when I thought about the fact, I was again thinking not-holy thoughts about the arms dealer who had made me want him.

I needed to focus on the mean cougar comment from the little shit downstairs. That was a libido killer if anything was.

I wiped the mirror dry and looked at my naked reflection. I looked good…pretty good. Okay, not nineteen good or however old Coop really was. Between him and James, I was feeling fairly hideous. James had me doubting my self-esteem and Coop had me doubting my wiles. Servario on the other hand, was making me feel pretty and sexy. In fact, he made me think things I only thought about when I was alone with a one-handed read.

I leaned into the mirror and whispered, "Your kids and your mother need you. This isn't about revenge sex. You have more self-respect than to let a man have you and not love you. Try to remember that."

My libido had gone a long time without any loving and was prepared to wrestle over the matter. It made comments fly through my brain like, 'sex is not love' and 'sometimes a little loving can help you get past things or clear your head'.

I was already justifying dry humping a criminal and possibly enjoying every second of it. His thick arms and sexy lips made me think there was no 'possibly'—I was going to enjoy it. I was going to savor it, like it would be the last time. Of course with him, there was a huge chance it might be the last time. Not to mention, I clearly wasn't great at it, James had fucked everything that moved for a reason.

I grinned at myself like a Cheshire cat, "Who better than to learn dirty shit from, than a bad man who I would end up killing anyway?"

I was letting my vagina do all the talking. I turned on the cold water and splashed it on my face and then pointed at my dripping face in the mirror, "Stop."

I distracted myself with the routine I used to do when getting ready, before marriage and yoga pants.

I put on body cream and deodorant and then styled my hair and straightened it. I ran my finger through the long, dark silk, it almost felt as good as it had when I was young.

I put on makeup and stepped back, looking down at my wedding ring and grimaced. I must have put it on subconsciously, again. I had been doing it for weeks. I pulled it off and put it in the drawer to prevent that same mistake. I would save it and give it to Jules when she got older, as long as she never found out the truth about her father. If she did, she might not want the damned thing.

I felt the need for a dirty, big cry poking around inside of me. I could probably save that for after I murdered the fat guy; I was going to need something then anyway.

I looked at myself appraisingly, I could do it. I could kill the fat man to save my kids. He was probably a bad man anyway. Nothing mattered but my kids' safety. The whole point was that we would get through this, no matter what I had to do.

The End of Me

I left the bathroom naked and crossed to my closet, where I picked out some matching panties and bra. I slipped on a knee-length skirt and a pale pink blouse. I finished with ballet flats and walked out. I looked at myself in the mirror and nodded. I looked pretty but innocent. I had gotten the outfit at Target and hadn't yet been able to wear it. It was a sensible choice; the flats would guarantee I could run and the blouse was baggy, in case I needed to bring a gun and have it tucked in my back.

Yay, all the old thoughts and all the old actions were fitting back nicely in my brain.

"You look pretty."

I jumped, "Stop doing that."

Coop grinned from the bed and watched me.

I scowled, "And get off my bed."

He laughed, "I came to tell you it was time to go and you streak across the room naked—and looking good by the way. I might take back that cougar comment, if I thought it might do me any good."

My face flushed, "You can't take back cougar. That's permanent damage." I turned and walked out of the room, forcing myself to chant cougar cougar cougar. I didn't need to add young, hot agent to my list of things that triggered my instability and raging hormones. The adrenaline was getting to me. It was how James and I had hooked up in the first place. I had a thing for the thrill and the sex afterward.

I made it to the bottom stair before he was there. He grabbed my hand and spun me, "I'm sorry. I didn't know that you didn't know you were a cougar."

I gasped and dragged my hand away from him, "Cougars are forty. Forty and up."

He raised his eyebrows and then nodded, "Okay."

I felt the disgust creep across my face.

"You're beautiful. You deserved so much better than you got in life." He sounded sincere. Of course he also sounded like I had one foot in the grave, no doubt because I was thirty-six. I was nearly retirement age, apparently. My eyes wandered the house briefly, terrified someone was watching us.

"How long have you been watching me?" I asked, starting to feel a bit weird.

He shrugged, "A while. We weren't watching you though. We were watching him."

"Did you watch my kids in the bathroom and shit?"

He looked horrified, "What? That's disgusting. What's wrong with you? No. No one watched the kids at all. Bathrooms and bedrooms had listening devices only. We aren't perverts."

I put my hands on my hips, "I want whatever shit is still here, out of this house. No more bugs and cameras." I knew I had found most of them, but I didn't want to chance that I might have missed some.

He closed his eyes and sighed, "You are so aggravating. I'm not even having this conversation." He turned and walked away.

I glanced at the clock and took a breath. "It's time to go," I said.

He came back in, "Do you know who the fat man is? He's a brother to an arms dealer in Havana. Dangerous family."

I shoot him a look, "You went thorough my purse?"

He shrugged, "You didn't give it to me and I needed to see it, and you were in the shower. You took forever in there."

I shoved him but he grabbed my hands and dragged me into the broom closet beside him. In the dark he cupped my cheeks, pressing his face against mine. His lips were softer than I had imagined they would be. His hands left my cheeks and grabbed at me, pulling me into him. I didn't fight it. It was the best kiss I'd ever had. I let him wrap around me, cupping my ass. Our lips glided against each other, from the gloss that lubed our kiss.

He sucked my lip in and nibbled it. I moaned into the kiss, as it got deeper. His tongue slipped against mine, caressing it. I sucked it, rubbing my body against his. My hands clawed at his chest like a real cougar would. I stopped kissing and listened to my screaming brain. One half was chanting cougar and the other half was already taking my blouse off.

I stepped back and pressed my back against the door. I felt around in the dark for the knob. I caught my breath, "Are you insane? You've insulted me like eight different ways since we met."

"You need to be prepared for something like this." He took a step closer, "Evie, we need to talk about the things that might happen," he whispered.

I shook my head, "Oh...uhm...no." I opened the door and turned running up the stairs.

"Evie, wait." He ran after me, but I slammed the bedroom door, locking it and running to bathroom. I closed the door and locked it. He was in the bedroom and banging on the bathroom door, by the time I turned the bathroom lock.

"We need to talk, not here," he spoke softly into the crack between the frame and door. Clearly all the listening devices were not gone. That wasn't even counting the ones Servario might have in the house.

I looked at my smeared makeup and sighed. I glanced back at the door vibrating from his pounding on it and shook my head, "No. That was wrong on a whole variety of levels. Firstly, I'm apparently a million years older than you. Secondly, you called me a cougar. Thirdly, my husband might have died two months ago, or he might have just run off with his mistress. Either way, he has abandoned me. Lastly, his funeral was today, as was the first meeting with a man who is blackmailing me to murder someone." My hands were waving about like a maniac. I wiped my face clean and started reapplying the makeup.

"Evie, we need to talk about things for the mission." He sounded sweet. I wanted to open the door.

I looked at the blush covering my entire face, and the clock that said quarter past nine, and sighed, "I don't want to talk about this. I'm emotional and this is wrong. I need to get Vegas over with." I knew I was rebounding on him from the rejection of my entire marriage being a lie and my being a moronic idiot, who was attracted to an arms dealer. Coop was the safer bet of the two men. And I was not even touching on the fact, I was about to become a spy and a murderer, or that my family was being flown to safety.

I ran the brush through my hair again and looked at the finished product. I was respectable again.

I readjusted my boobs, 'cause they were not nineteen anymore either. At thirty-six, sometimes they got a little excited about what we were doing, and ended up out of my shirt. I was pretty sure they tried to jump in Coops face at one point. I touched the door and tried to swallow some of the humiliation I was feeling.

I opened the door and jumped back. He was standing in the doorway with his hands on either side of the doorframe, trapping me in the bathroom.

"We have half an hour before I leave and it's for sure a thirty minute drive," I said into his chest. I didn't look up into his eyes.

He loomed over me, not budging. "Can we talk?"

I shook my head and tried really hard to stare at his t-shirt.

He tilted my chin and I burst into laughter.

He frowned, "What?"

I turned back and grabbed a tissue. I wiped the smears of makeup off his skin. His eyes were cold again and his voice a whisper, "We need to talk about that kiss, but not here."

I laughed, "It was just a kiss. I think you've kissed a lot of girls, Coop. You're pretty good at it."

He smirked and arched his eyebrows. His eyes were suddenly sexy and not cold at all. I rolled mine and pressed on his thick chest.

"You called me a cougar," I muttered.

"Grudge holder," he mumbled, mocking me.

I ignored him and walked out to the garage and got into the car, starting it as he jumped in the passenger side and laid the seat back.

"What are you doing?" I asked, as I backed out of the garage.

"Making sure you arrive safely." he grinned.

I sighed and backed out. I looked at the clock and glared, "Great, now I'm going to be late."

"Drive fast."

I grumbled under my breath and punched the gas pedal. I knew how to drive. I learned on a racetrack like everyone else. I just hadn't done it in a long time.

"So are you scared?" he asked.

I shot him a confused look, "What is your deal? Are you bipolar? You were a dick to me and then you're kissing me, and now you're being sweet—why?"

He laughed, "I'm not bipolar. I'm just trying to mess with you. Get you back on your toes. The kiss wasn't just me seeing you naked and wanting to kiss you. It was also a way to catch you off guard. You need to remember that training, wherever any of this goes. If fat man kisses you, he's going to be pissed if you freeze up like that. You're no doubt going in as a hooker."

I felt the horror in the truth and the fact I liked the kiss.

He continued, "You gotta be casual. You're going to have to convince him you're something special. You're a bit old for a hooker. Most guys who want hookers are leaning more toward that barely-legal thing."

I shot him a glare.

He put his hands up, "What? It's the truth."

"You're an asshole. I don't look thirty-six, and even if I did, that's not old." My palms started to sweat. I shuddered and looked around, anywhere but at him. I was ready to strangle him, but I was doing forty over the speed limit. I needed to focus.

He laughed, "I'm not an asshole."

I snorted.

"Okay, I am an asshole, but I am really trying to make you better at this. You've been hibernating for a long time. I seriously have a bad feeling about this whole thing." His voice changed when he spoke again, "You're sexy for thirty-six and I don't think that's old. I was messing with you. Trying to get you feisty. Trying to get your blood boiling. I'm not sure you're going to be able to do this, Evie."

I scowled, "Well head-gaming teenager, I don't get feisty with the old hot and cold, for one. I get shut down and less confident. Not to mention, I am a pretend widow, this is new to me. I've been with the same person for a long time. I'm not playing this game with you. I'm here to save my kids and the last time I checked, you need me. I am fine running with my kids."

I felt something and looked down. His hand was hovering above my thigh. "Liar." He chuckled.

I shook my head, "Coop, I'm not kidding around. I'm not interested in playing games with you."

He laughed and trailed his fingers up my leg, lifting my skirt, "What if the old fat guy touches your thigh like this."

Tingles covered my leg. I nervously laughed and pressed the pedal to the floor. The car shot ahead.

He chuckled but didn't take away his hand. Instead, he grabbed a handful of my inner thigh. I jerked.

"Wrong response, Evie."

I bit my lip and forced myself to relax again.

My chest was rising and falling rapidly.

His fingers were scorching against my thigh. The way he grabbed was rough and not expected, after how lightly he traced his fingers.

"How do you kill him?"

I was lost. My brain wouldn't turn on. All the blood in my body was sitting in my tingling and pulsating underwear.

"Evie, how do you kill him?" he asked again and let one of his fingers brush against my panties. I almost took the car off the road. I swerved and shouted simultaneously, "I DON'T KNOW! I DON'T KNOW! STOP! JUST STOP!"

He ran his finger across my panties once more and then pulled his hand away. "You just blew the whole mission."

I almost told him it wasn't the only thing I almost blew. Fuck.

I was panting and feeling like an idiot, when I pulled the car over to the side of the road and parked. I turned and face him. He sat up and scowled, "We need to get there." I could hear the mocking tone.

I was trying to get my breathing and heartbeat under control. I wanted to kill him. He was toying with me.

I felt burning tears creeping into my eyes; there was a ton of rejection inside of me that had been brewing. I hadn't let it out yet. I hadn't let myself feel the fury and the shame of my husband never actually wanting me. The playful head games of the boy in front of me were what was going to break me. Not the ten-year marriage. Not the friendship I thought I had with Mel. No, it would be a boy rubbing my underwear.

I refused for it to be the straw that broke the camel's back. I took a deep breath and pulled the car back on the road.

"I will kill him, how the fuck I am told to. I will do whatever the fuck Servario asks me to do. You will keep your hands to yourself. I am not a teenage sorority girl. I am not playing your games." I looked at him severely, like his mother would and shouted, "DO YOU UNDERSTAND ME, COOP?"

He licked his lips and nodded, "You're hot when you're pissed. This is a good look for you. Try to maintain this the whole time, okay?"

My nostrils flared as I looked back at the road. I was going to have to kill him when I finished with the fat man. That was a given.

I parked in the parking lot and grabbed my small purse. I had brought nothing else.

I was about to close the door when he smiled at me and spoke, "The code for evac is floor 17, room 723. Dial 9-1-1 and tell that to Jack and I will meet you out front of the hotel, and we run for it. See you in Vegas."

I snarled and slammed the door.

The parking lot was dark. I couldn't help but wonder, how alone I really was. I entered the airport and immediately started to look around. Would they come for me? Would they give me plane tickets? They had frozen my accounts so buying tickets would be hard, unless I used the Visa from the envelope. I had that in my clutch but if I used it, how would it look? I grumbled and looked around. My paychecks from the government hadn't exactly kicked in yet. I knew, well enough, how missions worked. I never paid for anything with my own money or my own credit. We only ever used untraceable currency, cash. Of course the problem with not being a real agent anymore, was that I didn't have any cash.

A woman in a beige dress suit walked up to me. She had sandy-colored hair and bright-red lips. She looked about my age, if not older. She was tall and thin with very high heels. I wondered if her back hurt in them.

"Evie, it's so wonderful to see you." she beamed.

I frowned and then smiled back, "Of course it is. How are you?"

She embraced me and slipped something in my pocket.

"Say hello to James and the kids for me," she muttered and walked off. Her words stung but she smelled nice, like expensive French perfume. I tried to focus on that more than anything.

"I will," I called after her. I slipped over to the woman's washroom, not checking my pocket until I was in a stall, with the door closed.

The thing in my pocket was a ticket and ID and a piece of paper with a gate number. I crumpled the paper and flushed it.

I walked to the sink and gave myself a once over. I didn't look convincing as a hooker. I was definitely more mom than prostitute.

Leaving the bathroom, I noticed Coop. He was across the way, watching me from a payphone stall for a hotel.

I scanned by him and walked on. I passed through the security and walked through the domestic gates, until I got to the door I was meant to go through.

"Let me get that for you," a man's voice spoke suddenly.

I turned to see Servario's guard from the hallway in the hotel.

"Thank you," I muttered and walked down the hall with him.

"You seemed a bit lost," he said, still keeping his voice low.

"I was."

"The plane is just ahead." He pointed and walked a bit faster than I did. He was meaty, they always were. It was such a cliché. Dark hair, olive skin, beefy bodies. They never just got a skinny, pasty guy named Steve to do their dirty work. It was always the one guy I would pick out of a crowd as a possible mercenary.

"What's your name?" I asked, mostly because I wanted to see if he really was a mercenary.

He glanced back at me, flashing me dark eyes and thick lashes. He even had a scar on his left cheek, "Steve."

I laughed.

He frowned, "What?"

I shook my head, "Nothing. Where you from, Steve?"

He grumbled, "Wisconsin. Where you from, Evie?"

I laughed and pulled the ticket and ID out, "Today I am from Seattle. Are you ex-military?" I asked, certain that had to be it. He reached over and grabbed the fake ticket and ID from my hand.

He shook his head, "No. I worked as an English teacher in Taiwan before I got this job."

My jaw dropped, "You did not. You're from somewhere like Belarus and you are named Serge, and you worked as a mercenary. Stop the lying."

He laughed, "I don't know what that means. I met Servario in Macau. I lost a ton of money to him at the poker table. He offered me a job, instead of killing me. I was on the wrestling team and shit, so I took the job. Better money than teaching little brats English."

I pointed, "What about the scar on your cheek? Bullet graze from saving Servario's life in Monaco?"

He gave me a horrified look, "No, dog attack when I was eight. Thanks for bringing it up."

It was unbelievable. Steve, the teacher from Wisconsin who was scarred from a childhood horror? Wow.

I sighed, "Does your mom know what you do?"

He looked at me funny, "What do I do? I travel and keep Servario safe. He had me trained with VIP Special Forces in France. I haven't actually had to do anything."

He was chatty for a gorilla. I kind of liked him.

"Do you knit too?" I mocked.

He gave me a sideways glance, "Just 'cause I haven't had to do shit, doesn't mean I won't. Are you going to be trouble, Evie?"

I smiled, "Oh yeah, Steve. Tons."

He grinned, "You do sort of look like my eighth-grade teacher, Mrs. Sanderson. All sweet and kind. You probably have fresh-baked cookies at home."

I scowled, "I do but, please don't call me old, Steve. I'm having a rough week with that one. I've counted at least twenty ma'am's in one week."

He sighed, "I'd say you're just having a rough couple months. But don't worry 'cause Mrs. Sanderson was hot and she was young."

"God bless you." I laughed as he opened the door at the end of the long corridor and held it for me. I walked past him and looked at the jet in front of us. "Wow." It was beautiful. Long and white and sleek.

A lady in a uniform stood at the bottom of the stairs, smiling at me like a normal attendant. I knew she probably wasn't normal.

I walked to her smiling.

"Welcome aboard." She was pretty—fake, but pretty.

"Thanks," I said and climbed up the stairs. The jet made it real. Steve climbed aboard after me and pointed to the back, "Go get comfy."

I looked around, wanting to whistle. The jet had its own pods in a row in the back and a few rows of seats. It was the opposite of a normal plane. I walked to a pod and sat. I fastened my seatbelt and folded the bed back.

There was a laptop desk in the front of the pod and a flat screen. It was all very fancy.

I curled into the duvet that was there and laid my head on the pillow. I was beat, there was no doubt, but I wasn't sure if I would be able sleep.

I closed my eyes but the sounds around me made me nervous. I opened them to see Servario sitting across from me grinning.

I sat up quickly, "Oh. I didn't know you were here."

He frowned, "It's my plane."

I nodded, "I know. I just don't get why you would give me the piece of paper and the room key, if you were going to be on the plane."

He shrugged, "I needed you to get acquainted with the idea. I know you've never killed anyone before."

I sighed and lay back on the bed, "Did you custom build this rig? Why are the good seats at the back?"

He didn't look up from his laptop, "Best chances of survival are in the back of the plane. The rich always die when it crashes."

I hated talking about crashing, right before flying.

"Where are your kids, Evie?" he spoke without looking at me.

I shook my head, "I don't know. I told my mom to drive and not come back, until I told her it was safe."

He sighed, "That was smart. How will you reach them since her cell phone is still at the house, and the kids don't have anything plugged into the Internet?"

I hated that he had checked that. I hated that he knew my kids existed at all. "I gave her a pay-as-you-go cell phone. I am the only one with the number. I'll call when it's safe." The lies came fast.

He glanced at me with a grin on his lips, "You think it will be safe one day?"

I shook my head, "I don't know. I won't have them live a half life here with me."

He nodded, "You're a very good mother."

I hated that he was nice to me. He nodded at the flight attendant. She came right over and smiled at me, "I'm Roxy. Can I get you a drink?" Of course she was a Roxy, foxy Roxy.

"Red wine?" I asked.

She batted her long lashes and listed the wines, "Cab, merlot, pinot, blends, countries, we have it all. You have a favorite?"

I open my mouth but Servario spoke before I could, "She likes something called Apothic. You'll find some back there. I'll have a glass of the same."

My cheeks flushed, "You drink Apothic?" I ignored the fact he knew what I drank.

He shrugged, "I drink whatever. I'm not picky when it comes to red wine. I like most. Vodka and tequila though, very picky."

I sat my bed back up into a seat and snuggled into it. She delivered our glasses of wine and smiled when she told us about dinner. "We are starting with French onion soup, then having a side of lyonnaise, and for the main we are having steak béarnaise with sweet potato straws, and finishing with chocolate mousse for dessert."

He nodded, as if she told us which sandwiches were available from the vending machine, "Sounds good."

"Soup before takeoff?" she asked.

He gave her a thumbs up without looking at her or thanking her for the wine.

I smiled at her, "Thank you. For everything."

She smiled before she walked away.

I could smell the food as soon as she was gone. The soup wafted through the jet.

I sipped the wine and sighed. It was divine. It needed a little more air, but it was still the nectar of the gods.

"Have you eaten much lately?" he asked still looking at his computer.

I sipped, "No. Mostly alcohol and coffee. I had something yesterday, I don't recall what it was."

He looked at me and shook his head, "You're skinny and need to build back your muscles. You were in much better shape when I saw you working last."

I scowled and sipped the wine, "You watched me then? You knew I was CI?"

He didn't look at me but I saw his lip lift into a half grin. He ignored my question when he spoke, "It's an easier life as a house wife; I suppose that was why you quit."

My jaw dropped but I saw the grin grow across his face. "Not even funny."

He looked at me and laughed honestly, flashing his dimples, "It seems like wretched work. You could have kept your job. You were good at it. We worried about you and your abilities, the entire time you worked. Everyone knew, one day you would be a great spy like your father. For what I was giving your husband, you could easily have afforded a nanny and a maid."

I scoffed and forced myself not to think about my dad or how great I might have been, "It wasn't that great of money."

He cocked an eyebrow and looked back at the computer. He typed for a moment and then turned the screen to me, "This is your husband's payroll bank account with me."

When I saw the seventh number in the balance column, I pressed my eyes shut tight for a moment. When I opened them again, I looked harder at the number. "What the fuck is that?" I whispered. My voice wouldn't work.

"Watch your language," he said and turned the screen back to him, "That is the account, I paid your husband with. You understand what payroll is right?"

I felt sick. Sick with rage and betrayal. I was coupon clipping and scrimping and saving like a madwoman to stay at home with my kids, and still have them in all their activities and sports.

He looked up, "You can get angry about it later. Right now, the soup is here."

He reached over and flipped down my tray for me. I was frozen. When she placed the bowl in front of me, my body reacted to the smell and sight. I nestled in the chair better to focus my energy around the soup and not the vibrating anger threatening me. The soup smelled divine. The crouton top was covered in crusty cheese.

I cracked the top and dug my spoon in. The onions were cooked to perfection. They instantly broke up, instead of staying long and stringy. The first sip was unbelievable. "She's an amazing chef." I muttered softly.

He chuckled, "She is that. It's why I keep her around."

I rolled my eyes and took another bite, "Yeah, has nothing to do with her tight ass, or perfect face, or fabulous body."

He glanced at me sideways, "I told you to watch your mouth. I understand you're angry, but you can't direct it at me. I didn't do it."

He was right, being rude about Roxy was petty.

But no matter how hard I pushed it all away, I couldn't get past the money. "You know he made me feel like shit for not going back to work. He told me we were going to struggle until I did find a regular wife job, like bank teller. He made me feel like every week was another hard sacrifice for him. Like my house keeping, cooking, baking, and parenting was just a hobby. Sometimes, I drove them to twelve different sports and activities in a week, between them both. I was a chauffeur and slave to all three of them. He made me quit my yearly membership to hot yoga. I had to buy the punch cards and not go all the time."

I dropped the spoon and covered my eyes, "I am an idiot. I fell for it all. I swore they were just friends. You know, at our wedding they were dancing and she was crying. I thought she was so happy for us. Then later, when I couldn't find them, either of them, James said his brother was drunk off his ass and he needed him to help him to bed. He said Mel had left; she was being designated driver for people. He tried to make me feel bad for not saying goodbye to her. Arggg!" I shook my head, fighting the tears and losing the battle.

When I looked at him, he looked horrified.

I picked up my spoon and started eating again. "Well, I'm done being sorry he died. I'm done being the widow of the great fucking James Evans. I hate my name." I started to laugh like a madwoman, "I hate my name. I was Evie Anderson, before I got married. Evie Evans sounds stupid. My name is Evangeline Erica Evans. Three E's. I liked being an Anderson. I liked being in the military. I liked my life, just the way it was. I didn't want a baby with an asshole either. He wasn't the only one, who got something he didn't plan for. But you know the difference? The difference is, that when it happened I was all in. I didn't just show up, I was there for it all. My son will never know he wasn't planned and wanted by both of us. Even if James is alive."

I closed my eyes again and took deep breaths. I had spent half an hour on my makeup and he wasn't ruining that too.

I opened my glassy eyes and pointed my spoon at the poor, helpless drug and arms dealer in front of me, "I am going to kill that fat man and I am going to finish this shit. Then I am taking some of that money, and going on the vacation we haven't been able to afford the last ten years, because I wasn't working." I cackled like I was crazed and started eating my soup again.

I muttered crazily about the sacrifices he made to keep us in the custom of life we were used to. The sports and the activities that cut so deeply into our funding. Now I was on a jet with a bad man, eating the most delicious soup I had ever eaten, and lying to clean up his mess. His mess that got him fake killed, so I could be a single parent.

I pointed my crazy spoon again, "You freeze that account, Servario. You make it so he can't get a dime. That is going to my kids."

I would be a rich, single parent who would never have to worry about money again, or stress about the fact, she didn't have enough to pay all the bills. A single parent with no husband to cheat and shame her to everyone in the world. A single mother who got to have all the say. No more arguing about our differing parenting.

I sipped my wine and processed it. I nodded, "This is actually quite good. We will kill the fat man and I will move on."

"You're a very scary little thing," he said, as Roxy came back and took our soup bowls.

"We are going to start taxiing now," she spoke softly and filled our glasses.

"Thank you," I said again. She gave me a quizzical look.

I glanced at him, "You never thank her, that's really rude. And I'm not scary. I'm a regular woman."

He raised his eyebrows, "I think not. And I thank her with a very large paycheck. Trust me, she is compensated."

I drank back the wine and watched him, "You don't look the way I imagined you would," I said softly.

He gave me a funny look, "What do you remember about me?"

I shook my head to stop from panicking, it was a tactic I had used before, "I meant as a man who orders people to kill others and does bad things." The wine was getting to me.

He studied my face as I answered. Seeming satisfied, he nonchalantly spoke, "How did you think someone like me would look?"

"Like the fat man in the white suit, or Bin Laden, or Rush Limbaugh."

He grimaced, "The white suit went out with the mullet and Bin Laden wore his beard far too long. If I do a beard it's always groomed and stylish."

I shook my head, "I have never seen you with a beard. You were so baby-faced as a boy."

He was up and out of the chair far faster than I would have imagined him able to move. He undid my seatbelt and dragged me to the back of the plane. He opened a door and dragged me in, slamming the door shut, "What do you remember of me from before?"

I stuttered, "I-I-I re-re-remember you from be-be-before, as a k-k-kid. M-m-maybe twenty-five."

He looked into my eyes with scrutinizing severity. He towered over me. I didn't dare look around the small space. I stayed with him, let him lock my gaze.

"You remember me from before?" he sounded confused.

"When I worked—before the kids, I followed you for a time. They always knew you would outgrow your arms dealing, when you took over the company from your father. I knew who you were when we met. I had watched you for a couple years." He was killing my wine buzz.

He licked his lips and lessened his vice-grip hold on me. My skin burned where he touched it. He looked at the welt on my wrist as he let go. He took a deep breath and chuckled. His face was a mixture of relief and confusion. I was a mess. I trembled and tried to back up, but I was against the counter in the bathroom. Why had he pulled me down there? Why had he not roughed me up in front of Steve?

"What did I say about lying to me?" he asked softly.

My stomach dropped, "I swear—I never lied. You never asked if I remembered you."

His hands trailed up my back, pulling me into him. He cradled me against him. I didn't know what to make of it. He was insane, that much was clear.

He released me and reached for the door, but the jet took off. He was thrown against the wall behind him, with me pressed into his chest.

He smirked at the helpless state of me. His hands roamed my back, eventually cupping my ass and lifting me up into his lips. I pressed on his chest, fighting the whole way but he won out, with the plane pushing me into him and the considerable difference in our strength.

His mouth owned mine. His hands lifted my skirt, grabbing handfuls of ass cheek, as his tongue slid into my mouth. I felt him harden against my belly. He ground himself against me, rubbing me into him.

He swung us around and sat on the toilet. My legs draped over his lap, as his mouth roamed my neck. He kissed and sucked, nibbling at my tender skin. His huge hands rotated my pelvis against his, forcing a lap dance out of me.

His soft lips nipped at my shoulder as he dragged my blouse to the side.

I shook my head, "I can't do this."

He looked up from the buttons on my blouse and shook his head, "I didn't ask you for your opinion. I told you I own everything, Evie. Right now that includes your pussy."

I gasped as a feverish heat claimed my entire face. He sucked the air from me with his kiss. It was passionate and demanding.

He stood up with me in his arms, and placed me on the counter, with the pressure of the plane pushing him into me. He dropped to his knees and lifted my skirt. He pulled my panties to the side and licked hard. I cried out, gripping his head. He pulled at my clit in short, fast sucks and then licked the length of me, sticking his tongue inside.

I bucked forward but he held me in place. He started the sucking spurts again and I lost the battle. I let go of his head and leaned back into the wall. I let him lick and tongue-fuck me. Every inch of me was on fire, when I felt his finger at the entrance of my pussy. I cried out a second time as he thrust his thick finger inside. I was well lubed from the near orgasmic state I was in. His finger moved with his tongue flicks, sending me over the edge. My body clenched down on him, just as he slid a second finger in. He pumped me with his fingers bringing me to climax.

I made a sound I'd never heard leave my lips, as even my ass clenched. I felt it in my toes, but before I could even finish it, he was standing between my thighs and sliding his cock head up and down the length of me. He pushed inside, finishing my orgasm with his cock pumping hard.

He leaned over me; he was all consuming, as he growled down onto me, "Tell me who owns your pussy, Evie."

I was flabbergasted and dizzy. He ripped open my shirt and tore off my bra. He grabbed behind me, arching my back and flicked his tongue across my nipple, before wrapping his lips around it and sucking hard.

The strange sound escaped my lips again. He pulled me down and bucked harder. I placed my feet on the wall behind him, so he could get deeper. His balls slapped against me, spanking my ass.

"Do I own your pussy?"

I nodded, catching a glimpse of his devilish smile through his lashes, as he looked up from my breast.

"Do I own you?"

I nodded again, "You own me."

He gripped my hips, jerking me into the wall again. I felt something I had never felt before, a second orgasm. I dug my hands into his hair and dragged his face up to mine. Hungrily, I sucked his lips into mine. I could taste myself on his lips. He kept his pace, feeling my body tightening.

"You want that orgasm?" he broke our kiss and murmured in my ear, as he nipped at my lobe.

I nodded my sweaty face against his.

"What do you say?"

"P-p-please," I panted.

He gathered me up in his arms and spun me again. My back slammed against the wall. I wrapped my legs around him, gripping his huge shoulders. His hands dug into my ass. He fucked me against the wall, harder than I had ever been.

He bounced me on his cock, spreading his legs to make a plateau for me to rest against. I clawed at his skin, trying desperately to keep at the angle I was at. I came, biting down on his shoulder. He grunted and moaned into my nape. I felt him pulsate and fill me. He jerked his orgasm into the wall and me. His legs twitched. "God damned," he whispered.

I nodded, "I think God had a hand in that."

He laughed, but I was serious. There was no way, one man could make me feel like that. Nothing on the planet, had ever made me feel like that. It was a release like I had never had.

It was better than crying and letting my steam off. I might never cry again, if he could keep that up. I slapped myself mentally, and reminded my filthy brain that I had just let a criminal screw me. I started to giggle when he kissed me softly and helped me stand on my own, pulling his cock from me.

"What's funny?"

I shook my head and looked down at my underwear on the floor, torn off. I didn't even recall that moment.

"What?"

"We just joined the mile-high club." I felt the blush, still on my face, redden. Inside however, I was freaking out and screaming.

What had I just done?

He brushed off my mile-high comment, "Oh that."

I bit my lip and knew he had joined the club, long before I ever came along. He was probably the chair of the arms-dealer sector. I tried to straighten my clothes, but I noticed the rip in my skirt and lack of buttons on my blouse. I grabbed the destroyed ends of my very expensive, lace bra and gave him a hostile look. He did his pants up and left the bathroom. He returned seconds later, passing a robe through. "Just come eat in the robe." He closed the door again.

I scowled, "I'm not eating dinner in a robe," I shouted through the door but he was gone. I picked up my clothes and started to clean up.

Looking into the mirror, I could swear I didn't know the girl looking back at me. If I looked too hard I would see me, and then I would have to let in some of the shame I was repressing for having fun, while my kids and mother were on the run.

Chapter Seven

New you means new shoes

"I wish we could put you in something classic. You would make a beautiful widow."

I frowned, "He told you my husband was dead?"

She shook her head, "I overheard him talking about it. Anyway, this is going to look amazing on you."

She passed me a charcoal leather mini skirt and I felt like Julia Roberts in Pretty Woman, only the movie was going backwards.

I looked at the label and coughed, "Silvia Eisele? Is this for real? It must have cost a thousand dollars for this skirt?"

She smirked, "I know, right. He always has the nicest shit."

I scowled, "Does he bring a lot of women on board?"

She shook her head, "No," her eyes were wide, "I think you're the first. He doesn't bring anyone but Steve—well and me. I live on this damned thing, I swear. Well, and the yacht too. That's where the ladies come and then they cum. You should hear the dirty shit that's said in those hallowed halls." She winked at me. Was she oblivious to the fact, he had just shredded my clothing off in the restroom? Did she think I went in there like Superwoman, but realized after, I had shredded my clothes that my costume was at home?

She did up a zipper and nattered on, "The women's clothes are for me. We stop everywhere, so I have clothes for my off time."

The End of Me

I laughed, "Rough."

She gave me a serious look, "I am probably going to get cancer from this bloody plane. You know how much radiation flight attendants are exposed to?"

I flinched, "No."

She rolled her eyes, "A lot."

I looked around the back room for a shower, "There isn't a shower in here is there?" I wanted him off my skin. I wanted him out of me.

She laughed, "This isn't an RV."

I sighed, "I smell."

She laughed and pointed to the clothes set out, "Just dress. He wants us back out there in like a minute." Her bright, glossy eyes narrowed, "We don't make him angry, ever."

I nodded. I had sort of assumed that, with the profession he had undertaken. He was a bad man.

A bad man my vagina crazy loved.

And I was back to the Pretty Woman analogy.

I hiked up the skirt and pulled on the black-lace underwear that shaped around my ass perfectly. I checked the tag and nodded, French, of course. They were probably hundred-dollar underwear.

Did James buy these for Mel? Did they laugh at me, when they pretended to be at work, but were really spending crazy amounts of money, and living it up with his millions? Did she have millions too? Was I the only idiot who missed the affair, that was suddenly so obvious from every angle I looked at it now?

I sighed and pulled on the charcoal-leather-pushup bandeau that matched the skirt. I attached the clasp and looked at myself. I looked sexy, my stomach was flat, my legs were long and toned from the running, and my boobs looked hot in the bra. I felt dirty though. It was a bra bought with drugs, guns, and blood money. I looked at myself and remembered what my dad always told me, "When running an Intel op, you have to remember that you aren't the person you were when you woke up. You're the person you need to be. You're whatever your country needs you to be, and that is the hard part of the job, Evie. Can you be what they need and not who you want?"

I would nod and he would say, "Because I can tell you, those two or three or four people will never be the same, as the person you want to be. This job can rot you from the inside. You gotta let it hurt for a second and then you gotta turn it off."

In my green eyes, I saw his.

I saw the pride he had when I graduated top honors. I saw the way he introduced me. I saw the way he accidentally groomed me for the job when he was raising me.

I let it hurt for a second and then I turned it off.

I looked down at the Christian Louboutin ankle-boot pumps and smiled. My back was going to kill me, but I was going to look sexy as hell while in that pain. I styled my hair with mousse, making it look euro trash. I could be receiving a CMA award with that hair. I glued the false lashes on and back-lined them. I fluttered my eyes and balanced it with mascara and steel-gray shadow. I dabbed the Russian Red MAC lipstick across my mouth and slid the gloss on after. Seeing myself like that, I was stunned. I hadn't looked like that in a long time. My brain, the dirty, cheap, fighting, bitch she was, made a snide-asshole comment about that being the reason James had strayed. But I knew, he had been straying from the start and no low self-esteem, was going to convince me otherwise.

I slipped on the boots, getting my balance before attempting anything else. Then I pulled on the leather halter-top and called to Roxy, who had gone in the other room.

The curtain pulled back, but the hands that touched my back were not hers. I looked up suddenly in the mirror. He smirked, "You look like trouble." He zipped me up and then slid his arms around me.

I smiled and tried not to get any Russian Red on my teeth.

His hands grabbed my hips, pulling me back into his groin, "I like your ass at this height." He rubbed himself against me again. Was he hard already? My body had a response for that, I may or may not have agreed, but the response was there.

He moved my huge hair to one side and nestled himself in my neck, "Odd, I just had you and now I want you again. Maybe it's because I can smell sex on you still."

I blushed, "I was hoping to take a shower." I didn't want to have that conversation in front of a mirror, while he dry humped me and made me watch.

He shook his head and never even tried to fight the shit-eating grin that crossed his delicious lips, "You smell as you should for the job you're about to do."

I shuddered when he spoke into my nape and left a single kiss.

"Isn't it going to be too late for a hooker to show up at a room?"

He chuckled and kissed me softly, "No. We gain several hours back and he has the order in for one in the morning. We land just in time."

I shook my head, "But that's four in the morning to my body. I'll be dead on my feet."

He licked my neck, "You'll be on your back, I imagine."

The fire inside of me tried to lash out at him; I had loads of smart-ass comebacks. I fought them all.

He winked, "Your daddy trained you well, Evie," and spanked my ass as he walked back out of the room.

My lower lip trembled. I smeared the gloss on one more layer thick, and walked after him. I sat in my perfectly-made up chair. It was like I had never been there. "Roxy must have OCD."

He laughed, "She does. Best qualities in a cook and assistant."

I sat and crossed my legs. I loosened up and grabbed my wine. It was the only remnant of my meal. I drank the glass back in a gulp.

"So I really have to wear this?" I looked down and shook my head.

He laughed, "We won't ever negotiate on your clothing, ever."

I rolled my eyes, "Yeah, whatever. I'm a yoga pants sort of girl. Me and you will be hitting us some Lulu, at some point. You think my ass looks good in this skirt—you should see it in Lululemon yoga pants."

He looked confused, "You are truly an odd woman."

I sighed, "No, you're just used to being around twenty-year-olds. They lack the I-don't-give-a-shit attitude that hits when you reach your mid-thirties."

"Maybe I could get past that, because everything else has been quite entertaining."

I scoffed, "Wait until I get a hot flash and scream at you, because you have a sweater on that's making me hot. I had a hysterectomy when I was thirty, put me directly into menopause. How hot is that?"

"Quite hot if you run about ripping your clothes off, when you get one of those flash things?"

I laughed, "No. I basically turn red and sweaty and yell a lot. Hot yoga keeps them at bay. Yoga and saunas. I basically need to sweat a lot to stop them."

"I can make you sweat," he muttered and leaned over closer to me, running his finger down my bare arm, "Do you realize how odd it is that you believe I had your husband and his lover murdered, and yet, you let me make you cum with my mouth and cock?"

He was goading me.

I smiled, "He wasn't really ever my husband, though was he—not really. And I don't think he or his lover are dead. Besides, the sex was nice."

He arched an eyebrow, "Both times? I think it was a lot more than nice." He adjusted himself and looked up at Steve, "Go sit up front and tell Roxy we don't need her till we land."

Steve got up and walked to the front of the jet. He closed a door, leaving us back there alone.

I looked at him and sneered, "You've got to be kidding me; what are seventeen?"

He shook his head, "Stand up and shut your mouth, unless I tell you to open it."

My heart started to race. I stood up. He admired me and nodded, "Turn around."

I glanced at his huge erection and turned around slowly.

"Take your panties down, slowly and bend from the waist, no knees."

I was his plaything.

I winced and trailed my sweaty hands up my thighs, dragging my skirt with them. I looked to the right at the single door stopping everyone from seeing what I was about to do. They were probably taping it. I swallowed my fear and the onion soup threatening to come back up. I looped my fingers in the panties and pulled them down slowly. I bent forward, grateful I had done all my ablutions before I got on the plane. I dragged them right down to the boots, bending all the way. I was about to step out of them when he spoke, "Don't move."

I felt the heat from his fingers lingering over my ass cheek. He traced across and down. I lurched forward when he slid his finger inside of my slightly-swollen pussy.

His other hand came across my ass cheeks hard, "I said don't move."

I held my core tight as he pumped his finger in and out like he was bent on torturing me. It was too slow and soft, but still I was mouth breathing into my own knees.

I started to relax, until I heard him rustling and then felt his body behind mine. His finger pumped hard, making me gasp, before his cock replaced it. He shoved in hard. I cried out, it was too loud for an airplane door to conceal.

He thrust in a circular motion, all the while holding me bent forward. I thanked God I had gotten addicted to hot yoga. My spine was flexible and able to take the assault.

"God, you feel good," he muttered, taking long, rhythmic strides.

He shortened his pumps, like he was using me, enjoying me.

My brain tried to register the fact, he was using me and I liked it.

"I am never letting you go. You are mine, forever. Sweet fucking God," he cried out when it felt as if he had reached something of a peak, and then started pumping again. "You. Get. So. Wet. For. Me. Evie."

He jackhammered me almost, with the angle I was at. His thrusts slapped his balls against me, spanking all the way to my clit. I gripped the seat next to me, moaning into it just as he came. He slowed his thrusts and then stopped suddenly.

The End of Me

"You are the hottest piece of ass, I have fucked in a long time."

Blood was rushing to my head. I needed to sit up, but he held me down.

I felt him touching where his cock was plugging my hole. He dragged the moisture of his semen up to my ass. My eyes bugged when he touched the wrong hole.

"That's never been touched has it?" he asked, just dipping his finger in the very entrance of my asshole.

I shook my head.

"Hmm, we'll have to remedy that in the near future," he slipped the finger in farther. I had dozens of bad thoughts.

"Relax. I'm not going any farther, I don't have the right tools for the job and this is not the position to do it in anyway," his voice was soft... satisfied.

He pulled out his finger and his cock at the same time. He slipped past me and walked to the back of the plane. I leaned on the seat in front of me and tried to catch the sobbing tears in my throat. I hated that he got off and I didn't.

Wait, that was the thing that was burning me the most?

My brain forced the thought of the ass-sex comment to the forefront.

I needed to make that bigger than not having an orgasm.

Anal was a huge no for me.

I would kill him, before I let him put his cock in my ass. I had always been a "Me First" sort of girl in that area. I told James, if I could do it to him with a dildo, then he was welcome to do it to me afterward. Needless to say, we never had the conversation much.

I grabbed a linen napkin, a bottle of water, and kicked off my underwear. I picked them up and walked to the back of the jet for a second sponge bath, and a possible mental breakdown. I wondered if you were allowed to smoke on private planes? Or if Roxy had any for when we landed.

I was sitting with my legs pulled in, near fetal position, when Roxy came back with a glass of wine.

I took it, avoiding her eyes.

"He's an asshole sometimes. He's a perve and a total bigot. He doesn't see you as anything but a means to an end. He sleeps with everyone." She spoke so quietly I could barely make out the words.

I glanced up and her, smiling weakly, "I got that message loud and clear. I've known him for a whole day and here we are."

She looked scared, "If you get the chance... run." She left it at that. I nodded and we spoke things with our eyes.

She softened instantly and pointed, "You need to take a seat though. We're in Vegas."

I shuddered again and left the chair in the small change room, to follow her back to my seat.

He glanced up at me and smirked, "So, I want you to do two things for me."

Swallowing my pride, I sat and tried not to notice the constant throb in my hundred dollar panties.

"Kill him fast, otherwise he's going to be expecting something," his voice was calm.

I shot him a look. He laughed, "You know why he's got you coming? The hotel told me he has a standing order, new girl every night."

Coop's words flashed in my mind, "He won't be expecting someone younger?" I asked.

He looked me over, "He won't be disappointed when you show up looking like that." He leaned over to me, "He doesn't touch what's mine, so I expect your training better be as sharp as it was. You will pay if he touches anything."

I gulped. He was taking the whole caveman, 'you are mine' thing too far. It was much further than I expected, even from someone like him. I assumed it was a heat of the moment sort of thing. He would get over it when he saw me watch a chick flick with snot running down my face, and Ben and Jerry keeping me company.

He reached over and ran his hand up my thigh, "I have a suite in the Bellagio. You will meet me there afterward."

I frowned, "Alright look, the sex was nice. It was fun. I feel young and adventurous again. Thank you for that. I'm feeling more alive than I have in years. I owe you for that. I feel like I might have compensated you already for it, but we can argue over that later. But you must need to rest at some point. I personally have been married for the last decade. That means sex once a month, and only really on a day where I drank too much wine and read something hot and naughty. Usually a Saturday or a Sunday. To be honest, we haven't actually had sex in seven months. Looking back, I'm not sure how I missed that as a bad sign for the five months he wasn't pretending to be dead. But I can't be having sex every hour on the hour. I'll need an ice pack for my hoohoo."

He cocked an eyebrow, "I don't know what you're talking about. I don't know what a hoohoo is. Focus. You will come back to the room and I will clean you myself."

Was he goading me again? He had to be kidding. Even David Duchovny didn't have that much sex in one day. I was going to get a rash if this continued, or at the very least, a bladder infection. Clearly, he hadn't been reading much Cosmo.

He ignored my protests, "The second thing I need you to do is, take this and write on the mirror in the hotel room." He handed me a tube of lipstick. It was Russian Red. He was setting me up. Why the hell was he setting me up?

I took it and nodded, "What should I write?" My stomach was in my throat. It was panicking and plotting an escape, instead of a murder.

He smirked and tried to dazzle me with his hazel eyes and handsome face, "Whatever you like."

The room would be bugged, the hotel would be bugged, he would be watching my every move. If he had the manager telling him what the fat man was doing about hooker supplies, he was watching the surveillance cameras.

I remembered the phone I had in my clutch, the one that if I dialed 9-1-1, I would get the young man. That would get me Coop. I shoved the lipstick in my clutch and snapped it shut. "How do you want it done?" I asked.

He shrugged, "Make it interesting. Surprise me." His smiled turned devilish, "Thus far, I have to say, I've been very pleasantly surprised by you."

I hated myself in that moment—the me I wanted to be, not the me my country needed me to be.

All I could think was, that the Burrow had better be something so fucking important the president himself would thank me for finding it, and taking a finger in the ass.

Chapter Eight

What happens in Vegas... Shit

I dialed 9-1-1 from the stall of the ladies' washroom.

The young man was there instantly.

"My, you look spiffy. Where are you going, the CMA awards?"

My hands shook, as I nearly cried with joy, "Bellagio. Bathrooms by the slot machines on the east wall." My old ways were slowly coming back. I could tell directions again and notice things.

"Coop said he'll be there in a second. Hold tight."

I shook my head, "I don't have seconds. They're watching the doors, halls, and floors."

He winked, "We've got this." And the call ended.

He was a cheeky little shit. CMA awards, really?

I heard the door to the bathroom open. I held my breath as footsteps made their way across the shiny floor. I stepped up onto the toilet and waited.

Dark-brown dress shoes stopped outside the door. My heart was almost leaping from my throat, "Do we have a secret knock or just whatever?" His voice was my saving grace. I reached for the lock and turned it. He swung open the door and smiled. His eyes were serious. "You okay?"

I felt the tears coming. I shook my head. I wanted to tell him everything and nothing. I wanted to touch my filthy disgusting face to his soft beautiful face, but I didn't. I looked down, ashamed.

"Did he hurt you?" his voice was deep and scary.

I parted my gooey lips but nothing came out.

Had he hurt me?

I supposed he had, but he had also made me cum like no man ever had. I closed my lips and shook my head.

Coop's huge hand cupped my chin and lifted my face, "We all do things we're ashamed of for the job. I worked as a gigolo for three months in Sweden, once." He fought a grin, "It was rough."

Someone else whispered harshly, "Speak for yourself. I woulda nailed his ass in every crevice of that airplane and never felt a moment of shame. Did you get some for me?"

I laughed when I leaned forward to see Luce. She winked at me.

I sighed and whispered back, "The plane ride isn't the issue; I have to kill the fat man, and write with the lipstick I'm wearing, on a mirror. He's setting me up."

Coop processed, "Then what?"

I gulped, "Back to his room upstairs."

His lip twitched as he took it all in. He looked crazed, "His room?"

I nodded, "Hopefully for some sleep."

He spoke after a minute, "We'll deal with that later. For now, we need the hit to go smooth and look like an accident. The room is gonna be recorded, you know that right?"

I nodded.

"You have to make it look like an accident—smother him while having sex?" Luce gave me a weak smile.

I scowled, "I've been getting molested the whole way from Boston and could have come up with better plans, than whatever you two have right now. What the fuck were you doing on the plane?"

Luce grinned, "I watched a couple movies."

My face dropped. She laughed, "It was a joke. We have a plan. Just need to sort through the couple variables you've added."

I glanced up at Coop, he was still wearing his processing face. He slipped his hand into his pocket and dialed his phone.

"Jack, I need two of those potassium chloride pills." He put a hand up to his head and closed his eyes, "There's a table with flowers on it in the hall outside his room. Put the two pills next to the planter, she can wobble in the shoes she's in and pick them up. Write him a prescript for it all and make it look like he's filled it dozens of times, in the last few years. He's fat. He's probably already on it all." He hung up the phone and smirked at me, "Write something kinky on the mirror, before you kill him."

I nodded. We were still planning the death of a man. He must have seen the look in my eyes. He grabbed my arms, "I wish I could do it for you."

I nodded and let it be enough. It was going to have to be. I walked past him and Luce.

"You look sexy as shit, by the way," he muttered.

I looked back and raised my eyebrows, "So far it's been really fun being the sexy plaything of the arms dealer, who never really killed my fuck-up husband."

His lips curled into a bigger smile, "Don't piss me off, Evie. It's a bad idea."

I rolled my eyes and walked out of the bathroom.

I tried to look calm but if the cameras saw me, they would see I was on edge. I made my way to the elevators in the hotel. The shoes were ridiculously comfortable. I had no idea. Two grand for shoes actually paid off.

I stepped into the elevator and inspected myself. I looked like a high-class whore, no doubt. My only saving grace was so did every other girl in Vegas. I blended perfectly. I coifed my hair and walked out of the elevator when I got to the floor. I looked at the wall to see which way the room was. I spotted the table with the flowers and took a deep breath. I could do this. I could be the person they needed. I wobbled and placed my hands on the table. I scooped the pills up and dropped my clutch. I bent to pick it up, flashing my ass for the cameras. Hopefully that's what they saw. I popped the pills in the clutch as I lifted it. It was fluid, like I had done it a million times. I reached into the clutch again and grabbed the keycard. I swiped the right door and put it back in my purse.

I took a breath and stepped in.

The fat man was listening to Frank Sinatra, as if he couldn't be more cliché with his white suit.

He looked up and grinned at me, shaking his jowls. His face was sweaty, even though he wasn't actually doing anything. He was sweating from existing, like that took work.

He looked me up and down, "You're hot. I'm gonna have to get the name of your company." He smiled like he was being sexy as he undid his dress shirt.

I almost gagged. Instead, I grinned like I was about to backcomb my hair and tell him about saving whales and orphans. In my best Miss America country accent, I smiled and twirled my long, dark hair, "Why, thank you."

I always had a thing for accents. Whenever I read aloud, it was with a British accent.

I reached into my clutch and chatted like it was small talk, "I heard you like it kinda rough, so I was thinking maybe we could do a little spanking first."

He chuckled, "Oh my God. You're a gift from God. I gotta remember to thank Vince tomorrow. The last girl complained." My stomach dropped at those words. At least it would make killing him easier. I was only guessing about the spanking.

I smirked and nodded, "Yeah, Vince said to say hi. I think that was his name." I tilted my head and made a confused face as I pulled my lipstick out, "My name is Wanda. It's short for Wanda Lynn."

I wrote my new name on the mirror in the foyer, like I was one of those waiters in the restaurants with the paper tablecloths and the upside-down writing.

"Wanda huh, I like that name." He shot back his drink. The sound of the ice made me want some too, but I didn't need that clouding my brain, not yet. I would need it later, when I wanted to drink away the memory of his naked body anywhere near mine. He poured more and walked towards me.

I stuck the lipstick in the clutch and walked to him as I fished the two pills out. I held them in my fingers and dragged my hands up his sweaty fat chest, pinching the pills between two fingers.

I giggled, "You wanna spank me first or me spank you?" As the words left my lips, I contemplated just taking the poison myself and ending it there.

He laughed and grabbed my breast in my thousand-dollar halter-top. "I think I'll spank you first."

I tilted my head and smiled sweetly, "Okay." I looked around, "Where do you want me?"

He pursed his lips, "Bed, ass in the air."

"Skirt on or off?" I dragged my empty fingers along the waistband of my skirt.

He nodded, "Skirt on and pulled up."

I blushed and walked to the bed. I looked at him, as sexy as I could and lifted the skirt slightly, letting my ass cheeks peek out the bottom. He smiled like he got a new toy, or let's be honest, a sundae. He licked his lips and I decided it was a sundae for sure.

I bent over the bed and placed my hands on the bed, still gripping the pills.

He walked over and rubbed his hands over my nearly bare cheeks. The French underwear rode a fair amount. He rubbed in a circular motion and then gave me a hard smack. I made a sexy face and moaned.

"You like that, huh?"

I nodded, "I do."

He smacked again and then rubbed more. His fingers were brushing my underwear. I wanted to bury my face and cry, but I smiled. I gave him my sexy bedroom face. He smacked again. The vibration was actually not bad, considering I had never been spanked before. Not that the feel could take away from the fact, I was being spanked by a three hundred pound sweating beast. He rubbed my cheeks, "You work out, Wanda"

I nodded, "I do. I run sometimes."

He gripped my ass and nodded, I could see the filthy thoughts burning through his mind. He spanked once more and then pulled my underwear to the side. I stood up fast and planted a kiss on his squishy lips. I could smell cigar and paint chips, I swear it.

"Lie back," I whispered into his lips. He lay back on the bed. I crawled towards him and unzipped his pants. I coughed. It was part fake and part smell. He smelled like sweat, old booze, and smoke.

"I need a drink."

He pointed, almost panting. I got up and pranced over to the table. I took his drink he had before and drank a sip.

"You want the rest?" I asked.

He nodded.

I took it in my hand and slipped the pills in, as I walked to the bucket of ice. I clinked in one more and stirred it with my finger.

He licked his lips again. The capsules were fast dissolving I guessed, because they were gone by the time I got to the bed.

He shot it back and reached for me, but I grabbed the glass and pulled away, "I still have a tickle."

He chuckled, "I'm gonna tickle you."

I laughed, "You are a bad man."

He nodded, "I am."

I narrowed my eyes, "You want me to punish you for a minute?"

He nodded. I poured the scotch into the glass and carried it to him. I drank a sip and passed him the rest. He gulped it back and scrambled off the bed.

I pulled his belt off and wrapped it around his wrists behind his back and bent him over the bed.

"Pull it out, stroke it," he muttered into the bedding.

I gulped and used my mom voice, "I'm in charge. I'll pull it out, when I'm ready. You've been a bad boy." I ripped his pants down and spanked his flabby ass cheek. He moaned into the bed. I spanked again, harder. He moaned into the bed and then he started to twitch. He jerked like he was having a heart attack. I stepped back and put my hands to my mouth. I cried out for help, "Help me."

I look around the room. No one was there to help me. How good was it looking on the camera? I turned and ran for the door. I screamed, "HELP ME!"

A man was walking down the hallway. He looked up at me.

"Help, please!" I shouted and turned, running back into the room. The man followed. When we got inside, fat man was dead on the floor. His pants were down and his hands were bound behind his back.

The man untied the fat man's wrists and pushed him on his back.

"Call 9-1-1!" he said frantically.

I was having a proper panic attack. I grabbed the phone next to the bed and dialed 9-1-1. The phone made a noise and a person answered, "Front desk?"

I shook my head, "I need 9-1-1. My...uhm...boyfriend. He's had an attack. We were playing around and he got sick. Hurry. Please hurry." I covered my eyes and hung up the phone.

I grabbed the fat man's hand and sobbed fake cries. I didn't have any tears. I should have had some, but apparently, I couldn't cry when I was being the person they needed me to be.

My panic attack was authentic by the time the ambulance arrived. I was hugging myself and pacing.

The man from the hallway, who had come to help, wrapped an arm around me as they attached the fat man to the stretcher.

"Had you been dating long?" he asked.

I shook my head, "We just started."

He squeezed, "You wanna come back to my room and I'll get you a drink?"

I glanced up at him and smiled, not that it mattered. His eyes were focused on my chest.

"No thanks. I just want to go home."

The man in a dress shirt and slacks eyed me up. I had already given him my statement. "It's a heart attack they figure, so you're free to go." I nodded and hugged my arms around myself. I picked up my purse and the glass I drank from. I poured one more shot of scotch and drank it back. I carried it from the room.

The dark-red Wanda, with a heart, on the mirror made me sick, as I made my way to the elevator.

I didn't know the room he was staying in, but I sort assumed it would be the presidential suite. I also sort of assumed, that he would expect me to find him.

I stepped in past the bellhop. I hadn't recalled there being one before.

"Presidential suite, please," I muttered like I was stricken with trauma.

He tapped the cell phone in his belt, like it was to the beat of a cheesy Celine Dion song. I looked over at him and smiled when I saw it was Luce. She honestly looked like a guy, in a bellhop's uniform.

I glanced at the screen of the cell phone and read the sideways message, making a smirk cross my lips. I hugged myself tighter, as she started to get a head bob to the music. She dropped her hat on the floor. I bent to pick it up, palming the powder she dropped in the tiny packet. She smiled when I passed the hat to her.

I stepped off the elevator, ignoring her completely, and made my way to the door. I knocked, holding my clutch and the packet in the same hand.

Servario answered and smiled bitterly, "That was a show and a half." He stepped back to let me in and shook his head, "I should have guessed you would find a way to ensure that it was a legit kill."

I shook my head, "I don't know what you mean. It was horrible, the way he had a massive heart attack like that."

I entered the room, opening my clutch and passing him the lipstick back and slipping the packet in.

"This is yours," I said softly.

His eyes were burning, "You disappointed me in so many ways."

I felt fear creeping up inside of me, when I glanced at his twitching hands. I had learned to take a hit in training but I really didn't want to take one.

He grabbed me and ran his hand up into my hair. He pulled back slightly, tilting my head and exposing my throat, "You let him touch you," he whispered into my cheek and tugged hard on my hair. I sucked a breath in, trying not to wince.

He smiled pleasantly, "I told you, this is mine." He reached down and brushed his fingers along the center of my underwear.

I shook my head slightly, "He didn't touch that."

His eyes flashed, "You let him have an experience with you, that I have not."

My ass started to hurt, just imagining the things he was going to do to it. I needed the powdered belladonna packet in my purse. I needed him to pass out. He towered over me, almost putting me on my tiptoes in the six-inch heels. My fingers dug into his thick chest.

"I really want a shower," I said softly. It was true. I did.

He looked me over, "You're lucky. You have another job to do in a couple days. I need you rested."

I felt the relief creeping through me, trying not to be obvious. He released me and scowled, "Go wash his hands off of you," he muttered and turned away.

I staggered, feeling the breakdown coming on as I walked into the bathroom, slipping the belladonna from my purse. When I got into the massive bathroom, I leaned against the counter, slipping the teensy packet under the tissue box. I took one of the tissues and pretended to blow my nose, as I pulled off my heels. I flung my purse in the opposite direction of the belladonna and started to pull clothes off. My back and feet weren't killing me, as I assumed they would be.

When I stepped down, my feet spread back out. They hadn't hurt when I was wearing the heels, but being barefoot was nice.

I struggled with the zipper on the halter and the clasps of the bra. My fingers were weak.

I killed a man.

My first kill; he was dead and I was alive. I killed him to survive. I was no better than Servario, or Coop, or my father.

I dropped my clothes to the floor and stepped into the ridiculous shower. The whole room was ostentatious, but the shower was like Extreme Home Makeover.

Six showerheads lined the wall with double-rain showerheads above and steam jets. I turned it all on, as hot as I could take, and tried to let it wash off some of the bad things I let them put on, and in me. I squeezed disturbing amounts of body wash into my hand and started to scrub. I used my nails, raking them over every inch of me. I washed a second time before starting on my hair. I scrubbed until there was nothing left but false lashes, floating on the floor for the drains.

Under the hot water and hiding in the steam, I let it out. The tears mixed with the rain from above and my back slid down the tiled wall.

I slumped and rocked and let it hurt for the minute I could give.

The problem with only having a minute to succumb to the greatest pain you've ever been in, is it hits like a truck.

I was curled in a ball and rocking back and forth when he stepped in with me. He lifted me into the air and cradled me against him.

"Not so tough, now are you?" he asked.

I sniffed and sobbed and let him hold me, "I've never killed anyone before."

He kissed the top of my head, "If I wasn't so angry with you for the way you played me, I would say it was the best hit, I have ever seen."

I didn't take the pride he was trying to pass me. I ignored it all. I finished crying and looked up at him.

He set me down, "You okay?"

I frowned and wiped my face, "Do you care, if I'm not?"

His eyes were greenish under the light, set off by his tanned face. He shook his head, "I don't want to."

I swallowed my hate and nodded, "I sort of assumed that."

His eyes narrowed, "You are the most dangerous kind of woman in the world."

I snorted and shook my head. I stepped under the water again, covering my breasts.

His words turned to a whisper, "You make me want to be worthy of you.

That's a dangerous effect to have, on a man like me."

I kept my eyes closed and tried to block out the fact, that again he had said the nicest thing ever spoken to me.

"I don't want you to be anything but mine," he said and stepped closer, taking the water from me.

I looked up into his eyes. They had darkened like a storm had rolled in, and he looked like the most dangerous man in the whole world. The difference between us being, that HE was one of the most dangerous people in the world and I was a yoga-addicted widow.

His arms wrapped around me, pulling me in. He bent and kissed the top of my head, "I don't want to have to kill you to make this feeling go away, Evie."

His words made me instantly sick. I was at my threshold for disturbing shit.

"Don't make me love you," he muttered, "Because it will end badly for us both." He finished washing and left the shower.

The trembling housewife was back instantly. I held myself and tried to come up with a plan.

When I left the shower, my clutch was emptied onto the counter. I had assumed he would go through it, but I sort of expected him to put it back like he hadn't. My clothes were gone and in their stead was a sexy, silk nightgown. I sighed and stepped into the body dryer on the wall. I lifted my arms and pressed the on button.

I ran my hands through my hair, maximizing the hot air's effects. I needed to be a bitch. I needed to nag him and whine, and make him see the real me. I had the ability to drive my husband into the arms of every woman we knew. I was badass at not being loved.

The hot air spared something inside of me. Something that made me want to finish it. The death of the fat man was a disturbing guilt that ate at my insides, but the survivalist in me was ready to let that one death slide. She was ready to finish this and get her family back. I liked my survivalist's instincts.

I slipped on the fuzzy robe on the back of the door and tossed the silk on the wet floor. I dragged it with my foot and left it there, on the floor. If I had learned anything in a decade, it was that men hated wet women's clothing on the floor of the bathroom. Which was odd, since they always seemed to leave everything of theirs on the floor of the bedroom. Either way, it was us women who picked it all up.

I left the bathroom and the belladonna. I didn't need it. I had a decade of experience, I hadn't even harnessed yet.

"Is there anything to eat?" I asked, almost rudely, when I left the bathroom.

He was on the phone. He looked unimpressed with my fuzzy white robe and huge blown out hair.

"Babe…" I clapped my hands at him, "Food?" I said again and mimed eating.

He looked horrified and shook his head.

I rolled my eyes and walked to the mini bar that wasn't so mini. There were stacks of chocolate bars and different types of packaged foods. All the expensive stuff, no Hostess or Nestle. I grabbed a jar of caviar, some crackers, a chocolate bar, and a soda. I purposely left the really good toasts that the caviar was no doubt for. The cheaper crackers would taste better. They always did.

I ate the chocolate first in huge bites. I was starved. If European men hated anything, it was the way Americans ate. I stuffed my face, like I was at Bob's Big Bar, and opened the can of soda. I drank it back and burped a little. Soda always made me gassy. I covered my mouth and wiped with a napkin. I left the unfinished chocolate and dirty napkin on the small table and walked with the soda and remainder of my meal to the huge couch. I sat on it cross-legged and turned on the TV. Designing Women was on. I smiled and sat back.

I crunched loudly and left crumbs. The caviar and soda was interesting but I ate, moaning and enjoying.

He scowled at me, so I returned the look. If he didn't want to love me, I would just treat him the way I treated my husband.

A major flaw in the plan of course, was the fact Servario was ridiculously scary, and considerably hotter, than my husband.

I looked back at the show and forced the crackers down. I started to feel sick. Too much liquor and not enough food was starting to catch up. I put the food on the coffee table and finished my soda. He was about to see something that would turn him off forever.

I had been bulimic for years as a dancer, when I was a young girl. Our dance teacher taught us we could be hungry or just throw our food up, but we were forbidden to gain weight. I was a foodie so I had chosen to throw up, rather than starve.

I quit when I was eighteen; my dentist told me he knew what I was doing. It was affecting my enamel. He threatened to tell the commander (aka my father), if I didn't quit. I quit doing it, enlisted, and was scarfing back enough carbs to kill someone, when I went through basic. I couldn't keep weight on then. I stopped being bulimic then and never looked back. Well, I tried not to. Sometimes when I felt a loss of control in my life, I would succumb to a binge and purge. James had thought I was lactose intolerant. It was a sad secret no one ever knew about, except Dr. Miglio and the other dancers.

The sad memories brought back flashes of seeing the other dancers later. We were mid-twenties and all of us were still damaged from the effects of Mrs. Smithers. The effects of constantly seeking approval and hurting our bodies, to be what she wanted.

One girl was still on mass doses of laxatives and ephedrine. Another was anorexic. My favorite, Becca, was three-hundred pounds. If you traced each of our timelines back, you would see the corresponding moment we ended being the person we were supposed to be, and became who she wanted us to be. When the pressure was too much, we snapped and quit but our bad habits stayed with us.

I had quit dancing before the rest of them, but I still had an ulcer and a lot of cavities. I still had triggers that made me sick—fast food, milkshakes, cheesy pasta, and chocolate eaten while drinking soda.

I burped again and placed the soda on the table. I took a deep breath and closed my eyes and started my visualizations.

I was swimming in a cool lake, the water was lapping against me, rocking me. The chilly breeze swept across my face. I could see the rocky shore and hear the laughter of the other kids swimming.

It was the only memory that made the nausea go away.

I burped again and shot up from the chair. I leapt the coffee table and skidded across the silk nightgown on the still-wet tiles. I landed with my face in the toilet, thank God. Everything left in a series of heaves. My body was still the professional purger it had been all those years before.

The sickness left as quickly as it had come. I flushed and waited for the feelings to completely pass.

"You are disgusting. That was a horrif...are you alright?"

I cursed myself silently when he started out annoyed and turned to sympathetic, upon seeing me kneeling over the toilet.

I flushed again and waved him away, but he didn't leave like James would have. He crawled up behind me, kneeling in the water and silk. He held my hair and rubbed my back and speaking in a soft tone, "When

I was seventeen, my father took me for a ride in the car. He told me that he was going to make me a man."

I cringed, imagining where the story could go. I knew a lot of bad things about his father.

He continued softly, "I imagined he was taking me to one of the premier brothels in the area. Of course, I was already a man, but I was willing to humor him. Instead, he drove us to his factory. He owned a company that packaged goods. He parked and we walked into the factory. I was disappointed, I could have gone for a whore. I'd only been with teenage girls at that point."

I started to become afraid but his voice was rhythmic and soft. It flowed with the motion of his massaging. His accent seemed thicker.

"We got inside and I saw all his workers were lined up. There were other men there. I rarely went to the factory but I knew who they were. Father clapped his hands and shouted for a man named Roberto to come forward. The poor man shook when he walked but tried to look proud. I was so naïve. I had no idea what my father wanted."

I knew exactly what he wanted. I was biting my lip and waiting for it.

"He handed me a gun and told me that I was to shoot Roberto. I asked him why? He backhanded me in front of the men. His ring cut my cheek slightly. I was scared and confused, I guess. I stood up and took the gun from my father and pulled the trigger. The gun never fired. It was empty. My father laughed and took the gun from me. He backhanded me again and told me that a real man chose for himself, what he did and didn't do. He told me to take what I wanted in the world and let no man be the ruler of my choices. He said even if I got slapped around by the world, I still needed to make my own choices."

The story was sad but I was grateful what I assumed was going to happen, never did.

"Then he raised the gun and shot Roberto. He knew the chamber I fired was empty and the next was not. Roberto died in front of me, bleeding to death and gasping for air. My face stung and I hated my father. He laughed and patted me on the back, then took me to see the real family packaging business. Business was what made me a man. It was never firing the gun. He knew I had that in me, all along."

I was lost. His story contradicted the back massage, and the fact he was sharing it with me, made me want to run away. I didn't want to get close to him, not emotionally.

He sighed, "It was the first time I saw someone die. Very sad day indeed."

I closed the lid and grabbed some toilet paper to wipe my face. I focused on the silver handle of the toilet and the sensation of the paper wiping my face. I didn't want inside of his world. I didn't want to know what he had been through.

He pressed his face against the back of the robe and kissed me once before standing, "So you see, I understand the feelings you have over killing him. It gets easier I'm afraid." He left the bathroom. I felt considerably worse. Not about killing the fat man, but about the fact I would have to kill him. Servario would have to die, if I was going to get away. He was fucking insane, like his father. And his stories were creepy.

I washed my face and brushed my teeth with the one toothbrush on the counter, I assumed was for me. I rinsed with mouthwash and left feeling the hopelessness of the situation. I slipped the belladonna in my robe pocket.

He was waiting on the couch. I walked past him, towards the bed in the smaller bedroom of the two I had noticed. I curled into the sheets and closed my eyes. Every inch of me hurt. The weird bathroom-plane sex had more than likely left marks on my back. The second time made me uncomfortably sore between my legs, and the death of the fat man, and the loss of my children's safety made my heart heavy.

"Is there a reason you're sleeping in here? There is a huge bed in the master quarters," he asked. I opened my heavy eyelids to his silhouette in the doorway.

I sighed and rolled over, "Sleepy."

"Fine." I heard him close the door but he was still in the room. I cringed as he unzipped. I tucked my arm under the pillow and turned my mind off. I refused to let his warm body next to mine be anything beyond a reminder of my predicament, which there was nothing I could do about. I was his, for the time being.

The next morning he was on the far side of the bed, as far as he could get from me. I shivered and rolled towards him.

I could let him be a body pillow. He was roasting with intense body heat. I wrapped my freezing feet around his calf making him jump.

"What are you doing?" he shouted.

I shivered, "It's cold in here."

He gave me an odd look and then put his arm out for me. He wrapped around me, when I laid on it.

Instantly, his hand took mine and placed it on his huge erection. I sighed, "No," and pulled it back.

"What?"

I shook my head, "I need to eat. I'm starved."

He pulled my hand back and began stroking himself with my palm.

I gave him an unimpressed look, earning me a grin. I hadn't been expecting it. I snorted, "You're cheerful in the morning."

His eyes were filled with green flecks, "You are having a strange effect on me, Evie."

"Ditto," I said and wrapped my hand around his rigid, morning wood and squeezed.

Chapter Nine

A silver locket in my pocket

I rolled over and cuddled into him, pulling the covers up and smothering him with my body. I felt his body go rigid; even in his sleep he disliked intimacy.

It made me smile inside. He wasn't comfortable with anything but fucking and working, and of course, talking about things that made me uncomfortable.

I still didn't understand why he had chosen to sleep in the small bed with me for the past few nights. I thought about that more than my own escape or why he had tried to set me up, for killing the fat man.

We had grown closer and closer, my cabin fever lessening with every moment. Three days of the spa-like bathroom, any meal I craved, and ridiculous amounts of sex had changed me.

I felt like something inside of me was waking up. Like the hibernation of marriage was finally starting to end and the fun, sassy girl I had once been, was emerging from her cave. It had to be the result of multiple orgasms a day.

Of course I had tried to fight it. I drugged the shit out of him with the belladonna. Apparently, his reaction to it wasn't the intended one. He got relaxed and wanted slow, intense sex. I had come to the conclusion, he was a magician with his tongue. I blushed just watching him sleeping, forcing myself not to want to like him, let alone desire him, as much as I did.

He stirred and woke, giving me a look, "You're like a cat. Do you have to touch me while you sleep? I'm sweating from it."

I nodded, "You're warm and Steve has the damned air conditioning on so high, I can see my breath in here."

He rolled his eyes and sat up, sort of pushing me off of him.

I liked watching him squirm.

He pulled his computer up onto his lap, "Is breakfast here?"

I shook my head, "I don't know. I haven't left the room."

He cocked an eyebrow, "Well, you can't spoon me all night long like a girlfriend and then not act like one in the morning. Go see."

I shook my head, "This is my first vacation in forever, fake or not—I intend on enjoying it. You go get me breakfast. You want to fuck me as much as you possibly can, then you'll have to start acting like a boyfriend. I want spooning and breakfast in bed. Later, you may read to me," I chuckled.

He growled and I rolled on top of him some more.

"I'm trying to type," he said, not bothering to hide the annoyance in his tone.

I nestled in closer and moaned.

I was getting good at ignoring the sad fact, I had a life that was in chaos outside of the hotel room. Denial was an easier emotion than guilt, or fear, or anything I didn't want to deal with.

I disregarded the fact his body had been doing bad things to mine since we met, and embraced that I had yet to not enjoy one of them.

Well, that wasn't entirely true.

The day before, he had demanded a blowjob. I had tried telling him I was shit at them, and besides that, we were in the shower. All those jets and showerheads had nearly drowned me, when he grabbed my hair and pushed my face down farther on him.

He didn't appreciate it when I shoved him back and shouted that I was a wife, not a deep-throating porn star. Thankfully, it had earned me a hard fuck on my hands and knees instead. I struggled and worked at pretending I didn't like it.

I plucked at the dark hairs on his arms, "So what's the job?" I asked.

He spoke distractedly, "Firstly, you're going to stop plucking at me like I am a chicken and get me some damned breakfast. Secondly, I am going to fuck you, when I am done sending this email, and then we are going to take a shower. Thirdly, you will then go and kill a man named Derringer and you will do it messy. Fourthly, we will then be taking the jet back to Boston."

I looked up at him, fully blocking out the demand I kill someone else, and shook my head. "We can't have sex in the morning. We can have it on the jet back to Boston. I don't do mornings."

He gave me a look and sighed, pinching the bridge of his nose and closing his eyes, "My God, you have a lot of rules. Why can't we have morning sex?"

I licked my lips nervously and then just said it, "I can't have it until I've had coffee and a full bathroom experience. Otherwise, I won't go all day and I'll have a bloated belly."

His hand dropped, "Did you just tell me you can't have sex, because you need some coffee and raisin bran to complete the morning… first?"

I nodded.

He bit his lip and processed, "That's sickening. You have to learn about appropriate sharing and not appropriate sharing."

I climbed off the bed, pulled on the sweats I had made Steve go buy for me, and tied my hair into a messy ponytail. I stretched and yawned, "You're keeping me here against my will. I am a thirty-six-year-old woman. You can't expect me to be a giggly, twenty-year-old who keeps secret the fact she poops and passes gas."

He grimaced and continued to type on the laptop, "Good God, you aren't going to start passing gas in front of me, are you?"

I laughed, "No. My mother would beat me if I did that."

He looked wounded, "You know you're not here against your will. You may leave, if you want."

I stopped the act of disgustingly-lazy housewife and frowned, "What?"

He nodded, "You can leave anytime. You know the deal we have."

I walked out of the room to where my clutch was on the table in the foyer. If I stayed, I would have to kill the Derringer man, messily. I needed out. I needed to take my chances and run.

He called out of the room, "Take with you what you brought. None of the things I've bought for you."

I looked over at the door and sighed. I pulled off my t-shirt and slipped the sweatpants down my legs. I kicked them to the side. A noise behind me of choking, got my attention. I looked back and blushed, "Sorry, Steve."

He waved me off and gulped back some coffee to wash down whatever he was choking on.

"Thanks for the fun!" I shouted and bolted for the door. I held my wobbly bits and ran past the guards, flinging open the door to the stairs. I had a clutch and a hair elastic and my own hands for coverage. I sprinted down a flight and opened the door to the next floor. I closed it and tiptoed down the next flight. Just in case they were following me,

The End of Me

they would think I'd left. I slowly opened the door on the lower floor and knocked on the first door I found.

An elderly lady answered and jumped back.

I blushed, covering my pubis and breasts, "My robe got stuck in my door. My kids are laughing and won't open it."

She started to snicker and opened the door for me, "Little brats!"

I stepped inside and closed it, still covering myself. She passed me the robe from her door. I pulled it on and shook my head, "Little brats is right."

She laughed, "Oh my. I bet they'll have sore bottoms."

I nodded, "Sure will. Do you mind if I call the front desk from your phone?"

She shook her head and laughed, "Lord no. Use the one in the bathroom."

I slipped in and dialed 9-1-1 on the phone I pulled from my clutch.

The FaceTime screen came up. "Where are you?" The young man spoke while sipping something looking like Starbucks. I put my fingers to my lips.

I winked, "My kids locked me out of the room, floor 17, room 1723."

He nodded and was gone. The code was what we had agreed on, when I left the car in the parking lot of the Boston airport. It meant I was in severe shit and needed an evac immediately. It meant there would be a car waiting at the front door. I would have to find a way to make it there, without being spotted and taken back to the room, or worse.

I slipped the phone back in and thanked her. She chuckled again and walked me out. I ran along the hall to the other set of stairs. I opened them and sprinted down. My bare feet were nearly silent at first, but the flights started to get unbearable. I opened up a door on the tenth floor and ran across the hall. I pressed the elevator button, but ran for the stairs on the other side. I opened the door and ran down the next two fights. I opened the door to the eighth floor and ran for the elevator button. I pressed it and waited. It came almost immediately. When it opened, a young couple of plastic-looking people gave me a confused look. I wrapped the robe tighter and jumped in. I pressed the main floor button, and the second and third floor buttons. I gave them a weak look, "My kid got away on me. Made a run for it while I was in the shower. He's playing in the stairwell around the second floor."

They both smiled and nodded.

I hated how fast my lying had come back. I was a master. Although I had to admit, it was much easier to lie when you had kids. There was so much more to lie about at thirty-six than there was at twenty-four.

When we landed on the third floor, I jumped out and ran for the same exit I had been in. I pulled the door and ran down the last two flights. I kept going the last flight to the parkade and dialed 9-1-1 on the phone.

"Parking garage, top floor!" I shouted and opened the steel door at the bottom of the stairs, as I pressed the button off on the phone. I ran across the parkade in the robe. My feet were officially killing me, but the thundering heartbeat and sickening feeling in my stomach were pushing me forward.

The slapping sound of my bare feet filled the garage, as I looked for the car that would be coming for me. A white car with black windows squealed around the corner. Relief and excitement filled me instantly, as I saw his face.

"Evie!" I looked back at the stairwell door as I ran for the car. Servario was huffing at the big door. He shook his head, "What are you doing?"

I turned and walked backwards for the car, blocking the view of Coop. "You said I was free."

He laughed and shook his head, "Yeah, but I also said you had to leave naked. I didn't think you would." He let go of the door and walked toward me. His pants were done up and belted, but his shirt was ruffled. He had thrown on his clothes in a panic.

I shook my head, "Guess you don't know me very well."

I continued to take steps backwards. I heard the car door open. I prayed he wasn't stupid enough to get out and anger Servario. Seeing a young attractive man picking me up might make him slightly angry. Or psychotic. I wasn't sure which it was.

"You can't leave. I own you." he smirked and I could see the look in his eyes. He knew he didn't. I had won the game of 'Who framed Evie Evans'. He had nothing on me but my finances.

I shook my head, "You don't. I know where my kids and mom are and you have nothing on me for the heart attack he had. Keep the money."

His smile turned dangerous; I was poking the bear who liked to do the poking. "I didn't mean that kind of own. You knew that though. You're mine. You know that."

I shook my head, "I do know you don't want to love me, or that'll end badly for us both." I stopped when I felt the metal of the car stab me in the back.

He looked like I had killed his dog, "Don't leave."

I grabbed the door and jumped in and he broke into a sprint. He punched the back of the car as Coop sped away. He blew through the gate to pay and skidded along the street, cutting off a wall of traffic. I screamed as trucks were coming for my door. He hit the gas, jerking me back and laughed. "Evie, what did you do to that mean terrorist?" He joked, "He looks crushed."

I felt sick. I had the strangest arms dealer hangover as we drove off.

I looked over at Coop and smiled, "Thanks for coming."

He shook his head, "I'm gonna get my ass chewed for it, but whatever. You okay?"

I nodded, "Yup." I would be, after years of intensive therapy and the possible misuse of red wine and vodka.

"He wanted me to kill a man named Derringer today."

Coop frowned, "He's an agent?"

I shrugged, "Glad I ran then."

Coop nodded and looked like he was processing.

We drove to a safe house in Summerlin, just outside Vegas.

"I don't want to go to a safe house, but Luce and Jack are there. We're going to be on the run after all this, if they don't like that you ran away from Servario."

I looked at him, "I had to. He wanted me to kill again and he… he was…" How did I explain what he was?

"Want to talk about it?" Coop asked. I looked at him and noticed his knuckles were cut and bruised. I reached over and ran my fingertips across them, "What's that?"

He smirked and gave me a look, "So no then?"

I shook my head.

He lifted his hand and straightened it, "That is a bar brawl, at a biker bar last night."

I frowned, "Why?"

He shook his head slowly and kept his eyes on the road, "Just needed to blow off some steam."

I smirked back, "Teenage girls can rile you up like that. When you get older and date women, it gets easier, I promise."

His jaw clenched and he turned and gave me a stoic look, "It was a woman that caused this."

"If you say so." I rolled my eyes.

He opened the garage and drove in slowly. He closed it before we got out.

"Did he hurt you?" he asked.

I shook my head, "No more than I hurt him."

He winced, "Did you…? Forget it. I don't wanna know." He made a weird face and climbed out of the car. He stormed inside, leaving me feeling conflicted. I wasn't really sure what it was that we were about to discuss. Was he going to get angry because I said yes to everything, like he and my libido asked me to?

I walked inside to see Luce smiling at me. She crossed her arms and tilted her head, "Leaves the Bellagio in a robe? You are going down in history, my friend." She put her knuckles out for me. I patted them again, awkwardly. She laughed at me, "You are a crazy woman."

I laughed, "A crazy woman who could go for a shower and some clothes, and maybe some oatmeal, or a protein shake. Are any of those things possible? Maybe some therapy?" I asked.

She nodded and pointed at the kitchen to my right, "Fully stocked, except for the therapist. Jack, you remember Evie?"

I looked into the kitchen to see the young man who was always on the phone. I smiled, but he gave me a look and nodded, "Good afternoon, Mrs. Evans." He walked past me. I looked back at Luce. She shook her head and walked into the kitchen with me. She leaned against the counter as I rifled the cupboards for food, real food.

"He's BFF's with Coop. He's pissy 'cause Coop went scary psycho yesterday and got drunk and started a fight in a biker bar."

I noticed the tinge of blue under her eye and winced, "Because of me being on a mission?" I whispered back.

She nodded, "We were all upset. We figured you would be in and out of the hotel. We didn't get told you were staying there until the day after the fat man. After the first two days Coop went a little snaky."

I sighed, "Join the club."

She folded her arms, "We wanted to evac you two days ago but upstairs wouldn't hear of it. Coop made the call and they said we were not to interfere. They were letting it ride. You were not to leave under any circumstances. Coop's gonna make the call and tell them we had no choice."

I felt the horrified look creep across my face, "They risked me out like that? I don't even work for them."

She nodded, "Coop was pissed. He went off; almost lost the mission to someone who could remain detached. You being there had no bearing on the mission."

I leaned on the counter, "They left me in there on purpose? They made me stay there for three days? It had no bearing on the mission? I don't even understand why they made me do any of it. Servario doesn't trust me, and he sure as shit doesn't have anything on me. What was the fucking point?" My voice rose above a whisper.

She nodded, "Precisely." She leaned in and barely spoke when she whispered, "He thinks they're working with Servario. He thinks you were Servario's demand all along."

My stomach dropped. My voice dropped low, "I just got whored out by the fucking military to the arms dealer, who is being blamed for my husband's fake death?"

She nodded against my face, "Oh good, at least you know that no one thinks James is dead. We think he's still working with Servario. Or maybe even CI. We're starting to think, the shit has been piled on us. Like the mission was a fake too. Something to appease Servario."

My skin tingled and my brain worked overtime. Had my husband just agreed to let a criminal have his way with me? Had he let that same criminal take everything away from our family? His children's food and money? I felt like I was going to burst out of my skin and go in every direction at once. I looked at her and nodded, "You got running clothes here?"

She nodded at the ceiling. I tugged at the robe and ran from the kitchen. I took the stairs several at a time. My feet screamed but I didn't care.

I burst through the bedroom to find Coop standing in the middle of the room with his shirt off.

I stopped and noticed the cut of his abs and the thickness of his chest. His arms were veined and bulky. He was strapping and brawny without a shirt on, but still cut nicely enough that he didn't look huge and beefy in clothes. I noticed the single round blue and orange tattoo on his right hipbone. It was the one I had caught a glimpse of before.

His eyes met mine with cold blue fury. He walked past me and out of the door, leaving me upstairs with the smell of his deodorant and the scent that was just him.

I walked to the duffels of clothes and found things I could make into running clothes.

I strapped on Luce's runners, which were a half-size too big and headed for the front door.

I slipped out the front door and burst like a shot. It was how I ran, fast and furious.

My feet slapped the cement in horrid amounts of pain, but I pushed it.

I heard the sound of someone else running. I looked back, seeing Coop. He was gaining on me. His legs were thick and strong. Good for the short spurt. Mine were long and lean. I could carry a distance, he couldn't. I knew that just by looking at him. I sprinted ahead and let my stride widen.

He caught up almost instantly.

His face was red and angry.

I shook my head, "You won't last with me, Coop." I gasped for air. I loved it.

He huffed along, "I think I'll surprise you."

I shook my head, "I'm older. I've got better stamina that's been built up over time. I've been running for a long time."

He grinned, "I got your stamina, baby." He licked his lips, "I think I could outlast you easy."

I laughed and shook my head, "You're a perve."

He nodded, "I want to hear it. I need to hear about it."

I felt my chest tighten. I stopped running and wheezed. I put a hand up, "You don't want to know."

He paced around me with his hands on his hips, "I need it. I need to know."

I shook my head, "I don't want to talk about it."

He grabbed my arms and pulled me to him, "You're different than you were before. I wanna know why."

I frowned, "I'm not different."

He nodded, "I watched you. I saw it. The mundane, bored, fucking housewife to that prick, James. God damned, Evie. How are you so smart and so clueless at the same time? James never loved you. I saw that the first time I watched you all."

I huffed for air and watched his angry eyes fighting the things he wanted to say. "I saw it right away. You were so lonely and sweet. You did everything for everyone else. When was it ever going to be your turn? They were sucking the life out of you. All three of them just took and took and took. Like leeches."

I pulled my arms from him, letting rage fill me, "It's called being a parent dumbass. You make your kids first." Momma bear was starting to surface. I put my finger in his face, "YOU wanna know so bad, for your fucked-up little game? Fine. He fucked me. He fucked me on the plane and he fucked me in the hotel. It was fabulous, if you have to know. Happy?"

"No."

I scowled, "You were watching me and my family? That's fucking creepy."

I turned back to the house but he grabbed my hands and held me tight, "I HAD TO WATCH! IT WAS MY JOB! IT BECAME MY WHOLE LIFE TO WATCH YOURS SUCK! TO WATCH YOU BE SO PERFECT AND SO AMAZING AND GET NOTHING BUT THOSE LITTLE MOMENTS ALONE OR ONE FUCKING NICE WORD FROM YOUR KIDS!"

I slapped him, hard. His eyes lit up. He grabbed my hands, "You feel better?"

I started to laugh/cry, "NO! GODDAMMIT!" I ripped my arms from his and turned and walked back to the house.

How the fuck did a frat boy see so many things that I had missed? "Don't talk about my kids like that!" I muttered.

An instant pain ripped into my ankle, as I lost my balance and went down on the grass next to me. The fury ended with that.

"Fuck! I wore those stupid, six-inch heels without an issue and now I've twisted my ankle in runners."

He plopped on the grass next to me but never said anything for a few minutes, as I rubbed my ankle.

"You're different. I can see it." he finally spoke.

I nodded, "You were right. I was lost in it. I let them get bigger than me, all of them. I'm an extremist. I do everything one hundred percent. It's why I quit CI. I knew I could never be a mom and an agent. I need to be the best." I lay back on the lawn of the strange house I was in front of, and looked up at the desert sky, "Is it ever this blue, back home?" I asked, not wanting to discuss it anymore.

"Not in Boston. But then again my home is Hawaii, so it has its moments there."

I turned my face, "You're from Hawaii?"

He nodded and turned his face to me.

I sniffed again, "Is the symbol on your hip Hawaiian?"

He shook his head. I saw him shut it off when he spoke the words, "My little brother drew it for me when he was eight."

I let him have the last word. There were too many things in the sentence he wanted to stay hidden. Instead, I asked the obvious, "So you think James is alive?"

He nodded, "Some shit has happened in the last couple days that makes no sense."

I flinched, "You think they traded me for something?"

He nodded, "I have no idea what. I knew something was up when they let you ride on the plane with him. That's a huge risk for an agent. But then to make you kill the fat man, who by the way, had done time for bad things with a fourteen year old girl in Havana and gotten away with it."

I smiled, "Thank you."

He nodded, "Then for them to make you stay in the hotel with Servario? Why? For what? To kill Derringer, a lame agent who means nothing to anyone? No, none of this is adding up."

My brow knit together, "That doesn't make sense."

He nodded, "I know. I mean what's so special about you?"

I laughed as he backpedaled quickly, "I mean… well, you now. He's like a rich arms dealer and you're… a regular…"

"You mean a cougar?" I gave him my most offended look and shoved him.

He laughed and pointed, "Admit it."

I crossed my arms under my flattened chest and nodded. "You're right. He can buy any girl he wants. Why me—and did James trade me to Servario? If that's the case, I won't recover from that one. I'm not a prostitute."

He rolled over and faced me, "What about what James was working on?"

I shrugged, "You know as well as I do, he never told me shit."

He narrowed his eyes, "We are missing a piece of the puzzle and I know you're the key."

I looked back at the house we were in front of and then back at him, "We need to get off these people's grass. I would be flipping out, if I were them."

He laughed and stood offering me a hand, "How's the foot?"

I sighed, "Sucky."

He bent down, "Get on."

I frowned, "What?"

"Get on. Piggy-back ride."

I shook my head but he backed into me. I wrapped my arms around his thick neck. He lifted me like I was nothing and carried me.

"Feels like a camel ride."

He chuckled, "Focus. So what kind of gigs did you have as an agent?"

I closed my eyes and remembered, "We mostly worked September 11th back then. It was fresh. That was our major goal. Servario was a gunrunner; we focused hard on anyone who was involved in weapons."

"Did you uncover anything you shouldn't have?"

I laughed, "I was fresh off the farm. I ran coffees and got into the field for basic shit. I never was a big player, ever."

He tapped his fingers against my calves, "Weird. You don't recall seeing anything and thinking, this is weird or anything like that?"

I shook my head and wrapped my legs and arms tighter.

"You like having me between your thighs?" he asked sarcastically.

I grinned, "I do, actually."

He looked back, "Yeah?"

I nodded, "It's nice. I can tell all my older-lady cougar friends that I rode on you."

He looked back, "If you want, I can give you something to tell them about."

I rolled my eyes, "I don't do the whole notch on the belt thing, Coop. Wasn't my thing fifteen years ago and it's not my thing now. I am not the person I was in the hotel. That doesn't happen to me, ever. You may have been a gigolo in Sweden, not me. I ran coffees and Intel."

He crossed the street to the safe house and walked up the driveway. He opened the door and carried me in.

"You can put me down." I slapped his shoulder.

He squatted and let me climb down. I limped to the single couch in the room.

Luce gave me a nod, "You hurt yourself?"

"Twisted ankle."

She carried in my purse and dropped it in my lap. "This thing has been vibrating so much, I almost stuck it down my pants."

Coop grimaced and pressed an ice pack on my ankle. I winced from the cold and opened the stupid clutch. I pulled out the phone and sighed, "Twelve missed calls."

Something silver caught my eye. I frowned; I'd forgotten I had put it in there. I reached in and clutched it in my fingers. It always made me feel stronger.

"What's that?" Luce asked.

I opened my palm and ran my thumb across the engraving, "Locket from my dad for graduation."

"What's it say?" she smiled sweetly, making her face light instead of intense.

I smiled back, "It's his grad date and mine. We both graduated from Fort

Huachuca, twenty-five years apart."

"Yeah? Cool. Your old man was well known. He ran some crazy ops, back in the day. The cold war had to be awesome." She sat on the folding chair across from me.

"Yup. He worked a lot during the cold war." My level of pride for the man was immeasurable.

Coop leaned his head in, "You wanna take a shower with me?"

I frowned and was about to throw my shoe at him, but he winked and scratched his head.

I shrugged, "Sure." The house must have been full of bugs. I slipped the locket around my neck.

He came and picked me up in his arms, "You can't walk to the shower with that bum foot." he grinned.

Luce laughed, "You wouldn't rather my help with the shower, Evie?"

I cocked an eyebrow, "Pretty sure I would rather it, but I have a really disturbing desire to see what he's packing."

Luce laughed, "You know it's one of two things, Evie, and neither is a good thing."

I laughed.

Coop winced, "You guys say we're dirty."

"Payback. We owe you for the centuries of oppression and abuse." I laughed.

He climbed the stairs, "Do not even get me started on the things you owe me."

He stepped into the bathroom and closed the door. He started the shower and turned on the fan.

I didn't know what was happening, but he pulled his shirt off and I smiled like an idiot. He lifted mine off and then dropped his jogging pants but kept his briefs on.

I slid my pants down and stepped out of the runners and socks gingerly. My ankle was pretty swollen. At least it wasn't a sprain. I stood in just my panties and bra and shivered slightly.

He lifted me up and carried me to the shower. Our skin against each other was hot and sweaty. He closed the door and whispered, "I was apart of something about your dad once. That locket reminded me of it."

My stomach sank, "I don't understand."

He swallowed, "I saw files once about a mole op your dad was heading up. The review of the op basically didn't happen, until after he had died. They were looking for something. They felt that he had kept vital information from his reports, purposely."

None of it was about James or me. It was about my dad. I was a pawn. Was that possible? I shook my head, "My dad was a hero. He never betrayed his country. He died for this country."

He shook his head, "I didn't say he was traitor. I said he kept things from the files purposely. He might have been keeping it safe from eyes and ears for a reason. I was new when it happened and, honestly, the locket is the only reason I remember it."

I whispered, "You have a photographic memory. I've seen it."

He nodded, "I do, and I remember it like it was yesterday, they had taken all your dad's things into custody, nothing was cleared for your mom to have from his office. I was new; we were to go through his things, cataloguing everything and boxing it up. Everything was considered to be suspicious and we were to run all documents through known codes."

I frowned, "He wasn't a mole. He was a good spy."

His eyes trailed down my throat to the locket. He reached up and grabbed it between his fingers, grazing the swell of my chest. "There was a receipt for a locket. The surveillance team had seen him buying it. We never found it though. A team was sent to your parents'. We searched everything, the safe, the cellar. There was nothing ever found. They were pissed about us not finding it. I remember that. I also remember, that James let them conduct a thorough search of your house and nothing was ever turned up there. It was way back in the day. I was brand new. We were interviewed separately afterward, about the things we found, and the ways they were handled." His eyes twinkled, "Weird way to handle a deceased man's effects. Especially when he's a national hero."

I hugged myself harder, "He gave the locket to me, the week he died. It was four years late. He had already given me tons of things for graduation, so it seemed strange he was giving me this too. But when I saw the dates, I was pretty excited. He never wanted me to enlist. Then, he never wanted me to go CI, even though my entire life had been spent preparing for it. The last straw was James. We had fought because he hated James. He never seemed happy for me, or the choices I made. I told him I didn't want to see him, it was after the wedding. He came and picked me up in a weird car I had never seen before, and we drove to a place by the water. We sat in the car in the rain and he gave it to me and told me he was sorry for saying the mean things. He was glad I was leaving, retiring when the baby came. He never wanted this life for me. I thought it was because, he thought I couldn't do it, which hurt. He had always protested when I made choices, but then he was proud of me when I completed them. This felt like he was glad I was leaving."

Coop's eyes burned down on mine for a moment. I couldn't help but pull back and stop the moment, we were obviously having. He wiped the water from his face, "He wanted you safe from it all."

I glanced up into his face and nodded, "I think so. I think he wanted me out of that life and away from James. At least if I wasn't at work, I wasn't the laughing stock of the office."

He looked conflicted about things, "We need to run those dates and see if it's some kind of code."

A terrible feeling bit into my stomach, "Are my kids safe?" I asked feeling the nerves filling me.

He nodded his head, "You remember the orders I gave?"

I nodded back, preparing myself for the worst.

"That was FBI. It wasn't CIA or military run. I have a friend in the FBI. No one will know where they are. I don't even know. I gave the orders because Martin's team specializes in mole operations. I wasn't sure what we were dealing with and I know he's the best. They make the snap decision in the air and the pilots are members of the team. When you wanted them hidden, I had a bad feeling you knew something."

I finally breathed, "Oh my God. Thank God. You're much better at this, than I've been giving you credit for." The move was smart. It was something my dad would have done. He never trusted anyone. I looked up at him, "Where are we gonna go?"

He whispered back, "Not a fucking clue. If we leave here and you don't go back to Servario, we won't have any help or resources. The people looking for answers in your dad's shit were my bosses, our bosses. They told me not to take you from Servario. I disobeyed a direct order. Until we have some answers, we need to be off grid. This shower is the only place they can't hear us if we whisper. Not to mention we probably have about an hour, before they arrive here and take us into custody."

I sighed and looked down at the locket, "It's just a necklace."

He forced a grin, "Nothing about your dad was ever simple. He was a genius. Let's not talk about this again, until we're out of here. They always have eyes on the house. We need to get out of here and regroup."

I looked up, getting a face full of water. I sputtered, "I know where we can go."

He nodded and stopped the water. We stood there in the dripping and silence, he clenched his jaw. I looked down and forced my thoughts away from his lips. I heard him open his mouth and interrupted whatever he was about to say, "Pass me a towel, please."

"Sure," he sounded weird. I didn't want to think about it. I didn't want any of it. I wanted to be a parent and a widow, even if it was fake, and forget the rest. I defiantly didn't want to think about the things I had done with Servario, or the fact I was still thinking about him. The memory of his face in parking garage tugged at me.

We dried off, not speaking. I hobbled, still soaked, to the bedroom and changed into the spare clothes.

Downstairs we met in the kitchen, "Who wants breakfast?" Coop asked.

Luce nodded and glanced at Jack, who nodded back at her.

"IHOP?" Luce asked.

I nodded, "Yeah, I love it there." It was a lie. I hated all chain restaurants.

I followed Luce to the dining room, which was filled with black cases. She opened them and started putting guns in her pants and boots. I followed suit. It felt weird to hold a piece again, it had been so long. I had only trained with them; I never was forced to work with one, ever.

The walk to the car was tense and awkward. If the eyes on the house were suspicious before, they would be increasingly so, after we left.

Chapter Ten

Hot-wire my heart

The car we stole, after we ditched the car we left in, was a beater. The vibration was annoying me. I looked at Luce next to me in the backseat and frowned, "We need a different car."

She laughed, "I know. We'll ditch this one and take another."

Coop looked back at me, "Where are we going? I got on the eighty like you asked."

I swallowed, "Salt Lake City."

He frowned, "What?"

I nodded and laughed, "My uncle Fitz lives there. He'll know what the heck is up with the locket."

He frowned, "Why is that? Why don't we have a record of a Fitz? I've never seen that name before. Is it short for something?"

I couldn't get the smile off my face, as I shook my head, "No, he's not exactly an uncle." I was excited to see him, nonetheless. It had been years.

"Your dad trusted him that much?" Jack looked back at me, giving me a sneer. It was weird on him. His face was usually pleasant, patronizing, but pleasant.

I shrugged, "It's a long story. I'll let Fitz tell it."

Coop shook his head, "Uh, no. We are not walking into a trap."

I laughed, "You aren't, trust me. He's not something I can explain. You just have to see it, to understand."

Coop scowled at me in the rearview. I rolled my eyes and watched out the window.

Coop's stare never left the rearview for longer than a few seconds. He was obsessed with whatever was behind us. He swerved off the highway onto an off ramp. I caught a blur of the word Lovelock. He drove like a savage, skidding around corners and through a neighborhood.

He pulled into the driveway of a random house and parked the car. We jumped out—well, they jumped out and I hobbled after them. We crept along to the house next door and then through the backyard of that house. We ran through the backs of four houses.

Coop moved quickly. My heart was in my throat. Had he seen something? They moved like they had been born working together. I felt like the only non-agent, limping along behind them. They ran to a huge fence, each did a pull up and hopped over. I stood there looking at the six-foot fence. There was no way I was going up and over. I grabbed the rough wood and instantly pulled my finger back. The sound of footsteps coming distracted me from the splinter, I was about to pick out. I ran to the back corner of the yard and dropped to my knees.

I grabbed handfuls of the weeds and dragged them out fast. My fingers cut and bled, but I ripped with savagery. I mussed my hair with my dirt-covered hands and then rubbed them across my face and clothes.

"What are you doing?" Coop hissed through the fence.

I threw dirt at the fence and hisses like a cat, "Psssst! Get outta here, pesky cat." I wiped my hair back from my face and smeared more dirt and blood across my face, "Darla, keep that cat in your own yard." I added a little Wisconsin flare to Darla, cat, and yard.

I turned and screamed when I saw the seven men in black clothes. I held my head at a funny angle and made a face, "You get outta my yard. We don't have any gang activity around here. I'm gonna call 9-1-1 if you don't go. I'm tired of you hooligans, thinking you can run this neighborhood." I stared at them with my mouth agape and the dirt covering my hands and face. I stuck my belly out as far as it would go and slouched.

One of the young men gave me a horrified look and put his hands in the air, "Sorry ma'am. You didn't happen to see some people run through here?"

I scrunched my face up and used my grandma's word for what, "Wha? Wha? No." My Wisconsin flare was getting stronger, "You get outta my yard."

He looked around and turned away, following the others around the house. My heart was pounding, but I turned back and started picking weeds again with shaking hands.

After a few minutes, I got up and walked around the side of the house to the garage. I opened the unlocked door and walked in closing it slowly and locking it. I leaned against the back of it and took in gulps of air.

They were military. The military was after us, we went off the reservation and they were looking for us. I didn't know what to think. What had I done? Why hadn't I just stayed with Servario, like they had wanted? I had risked my kids and mother.

"Are you insane?"

I jumped and looked up to see Coop in the far corner. I frowned, "How did you...?" I looked around the garage.

He looked angry, "That was stupid. Why didn't you jump?"

I huffed as I spoke, "Because my old, fat, lazy ass can't do a pull up, dick. My ankle is still sore and I don't jump fences. I have twenty-two percent body fat and almost no upper body strength."

He grimaced.

I pointed, "That is a respectable number for a woman my age."

He nodded, "Keep telling yourself that. The car is around the block. Meet us there in five." He walked across the garage towards me. I stepped out of the way for him to leave through the door.

I looked around the empty garage, "How the bloody hell, am I supposed to do that?" I muttered.

The old Honda Civic in the garage gave me an idea. I climbed in the driver's seat and pulled the wire box. I hot-wired the car and opened the garage door. I flipped the visor and looked at the dirt stains on my face.

I backed out and closed the garage again. I pointed at the men in black in the driveway next door and shouted, "Stay outta my yard!"

I drove away, grinning.

I didn't want the cocky feeling I was filled with to get me bad juju. Bad-agent juju always ended up with the cocky person getting caught. In my case, that would get me shipped back to Servario. The dirty part of my brain didn't entirely object to going back. Servario had ways of convincing you that you wanted to stay. I had a horrid inkling that I'd only run out of fear of my feelings for him.

I rounded the corner and stopped the car behind the minivan they had stolen. I could see Jack's dark head in the tinted window.

I jumped out and hopped into the back of the van.

Luce was laughing, "That was amazeballs, dude. Put it there." She held her knuckles out. Apparently amazeballs was a positive thing. Even Jack was snickering. I patted the top of her knuckles with my hand, earning me a crazy look.

I glared at them, "I hate you all."

Coop growled and drove the van like he was late for his kids' hockey practice. I mocked him behind his back with sneers. Luce smiled and nodded in his direction, "I thought he was going to have a stroke."

I rolled my eyes, "Yeah, well I woulda had a stroke, if I tried to jump that fence. My ankle is still sore and I'm out of shape."

Jack nudged me, "You look great to me. My mom is really out of shape."

My mouth dropped open, "I'm not old enough to be your mom, you little shit."

He blushed, contrasting his cheeks against his dark hair, "Sorry. You know what I mean."

I glared at him, "How old is your mother?"

He swallowed and looked at Luce for help, "Uhm... she's forty-three. She was twenty-one when she had me."

I pressed my lips together. My best mom friend was forty-five.

I snarled, "Whatever."

Luce looked back, "My mom's fifty if that makes you feel better."

I shook my head, "Screw you all."

She shrugged, "Did you hot-wire that car?"

I grinned at that, "I did."

Coop looked at me in the rearview, "Lucky it was an older model. They're easier."

I narrowed my gaze, "You're dead." He smiled his cocky, asshole grin, the one that made my blood boil.

I looked out the window as he drove, and Luce played a game on her iPhone.

"Can't they trace that one?" I asked.

She shook her head, "I buy my personal shit from a guy who makes sure it falls off a truck and lands in a tech guy's hands, and then gets sold under a table somewhere."

I snorted, "Nice and legal you mean?"

She looked up and winked, "It's the only way."

"Why are they coming after us for going off the reservation?" I asked.

Jack looked back, "We had no idea what we were getting into, with you and your husband. We honestly thought this was a weapon to destroy the world, as it always is, and someone betrayed the government like they always do."

My eyes narrowed, "Don't lump me with my husband. He isn't my husband. He's in on this on his own."

Jack's eyes glinted when he grinned back at me, "Regardless, we don't think that's the case anymore. We think your dad was in on some crazy shit and somehow you are being used to find whatever he hid, a long time ago."

I sighed, "What I want to know is why are they turning on us?"

He shook his head and turned back around, "No clue."

I bit my lips and prayed Uncle Fitz would know what was happening.

We arrived in Salt Lake six hours later. I was passed out when I felt the car stop.

The End of Me

I looked up as Coop parked and instantly felt my neck go out. I winced, rubbing the spot.

Luce too woke up and stretched. She yawned and smirked at me, "Crick in the neck?"

I nodded, "I am too old for this shit."

I sighed and got out of the car. I tried to stretch, but the pain in my neck was shooting down my spine. Coop walked over with his iPhone and held it out, "This is the map of the city. Where am I going?"

Jack got out and walked into the corner store we were parked at, with Luce following him.

"Grab me some chocolate and flavored water please!" I shouted at her.

She gave me a thumbs up and walked inside.

I looked down at the map, still rubbing my neck. Coop grabbed my arm and spun me around. He handed me the phone and started massaging.

"Let me. You look at the map," he mumbled.

I closed my eyes and let the warmth and strength of his fingers relax me. I moaned, "That feels amazing."

"Map."

"Shhhhhhhh. Just rub."

He chuckled, "Oh the things I could add to that comment."

I smiled, but kept my eyes closed.

"Your dad was a good man, right? The reports are true, right?" he asked after a couple minutes.

I nodded, "He was the best. He sacrificed everything for this country."

His breath tickled the back of my neck, when he let out a long sigh.

I opened my eyes and dragged the map so it zoomed in on a spot, "Corner of Edison and ninth, next to Randy's Record Shop."

He increased the pressure, digging into my neck. I closed my eyes again.

"You're so tense."

I scoffed, "Uh... yeah. Of course I am."

He laughed, "You gotta learn to roll with the punches a little better."

I pulled away and gave him a horrified look, "Excuse me? You bury your husband and the next day get molested on a plane by an arms dealer, and kill a fat guy who wants you to spank him and jerk him off, then tell me how YOU feel." I shook my head and climbed back into the van.

He clenched his jaw and gave me a steely look, "He isn't even really dead, and I said sorry about the plane. I had no idea."

I sneered, "Tell that to my kids. Oh wait, you can't. They're being protected by the witness-protection agency. Right." I slid the door shut and folded my arms. My neck ached still but he looked less than impressed, little shit.

Luce climbed in and passed me the small bag of snacks. I looked in and frowned, "This isn't flavored water."

She nodded, "I know, but you shouldn't eat all that artificial sweetener. It gave all the rats cancer, dude."

I wanted to snap at her, but I knew it was just that I was losing my mind. I took deep breaths and reminded myself, it was just flavored water.

I took the cap off the bottle of sparkling plain water and shuddered when I took the first sip. It was bitter and horrid. I gave her a look. Her eyes widened, "What?"

I snatched the orange juice out of her hand and passed her the water.

"I don't drink that crap, it's bitter." She reached for the juice.

"Then we compromise." I swatted at her and sighed taking the water back. I opened the van door and dumped some of the water out. I poured the juice into the bottle and passed her back the half empty bottle of juice.

She scowled, "You suck."

I nodded and sipped my flavored water.

Coop climbed in, stuffing a protein bar in his mouth. When Jack got in, we drove to the spot on the map. It was a flower shop, last time I had come by. I glanced out and frowned at the small sign.

"Lester's Art Hut?" Coop asked.

I nodded, "I guess. Maybe he sold it. Maybe they know where he went." I climbed out.

Coop did the same, "Wait. What if they're expecting you?"

I laughed and limped to the front door. I opened it and smiled. It was Fitz's place, for sure. It still looked like the set of the movie The Birdcage.

Coop stalked in behind me, stopping and pressing his body against mine. I don't think he even noticed me. His mouth was agape as he looked about, "Where the hell are we?"

It was decorated like it was a PRIDE float.

I looked back, wincing at my sore neck, "Uncle Fitz's."

He pointed, "It said Lester."

I shrugged, "This is Fitz."

He came around the corner in a pale pink bowling shirt and a beaming grin, "I knew that voice, the second my ears heard it."

His Jersey accent was replaced by a southern one. He was big on characters.

He spread his arms like wings and pulled me in when I stepped to him.

"Uncle Fitz," I whispered.

He kissed the top of my head, "I heard you are in some trouble, young lady."

I nodded into his silky, pale-pink shirt. Hugging him was like coming home.

"I'm in huge shit."

He chuckled, "Who is that sexy piece of military man-meat?"

I snorted, "Coop—Uncle Fitz, Uncle Fitz—Coop."

His hand left my back and I felt the motion of them shaking hands.

"Pleased to meet you, son."

I looked back at Coop and winced when my neck turned.

Fitz swung an arm around me and waved his hand at Coop, "Tell them others to come in too." He walked me to the back of the store and through a dark hallway, "You are in serious shit. Your dad never wanted you to find this."

I tried to look up but my neck was killing me, "What is it?"

He chuckled again, "Oh lordy, you are gonna be the death of me."

Chapter Eleven

Magic beans

The heat permeated through my flesh and into my muscles. I moaned as it vibrated softly and massaged my aching neck.

"Got that thing off of the Home Shopping Network. They sent it to me for free 'cause I spent over a thousand dollars on there last year. It's called the Magic Beanbag. You heat it in the microwave, and then plug the vibrator in and put the beanbag in the holders and voila, a heated massage." Fitz smiled and passed us each a margarita.

I drank the salty, lime drink and moaned, "I missed you." My voice had a slight vibration from the vibrator.

Coop watched him, still not mellowing out, "It's a bit early for marg's, isn't it?" he asked with a definite tone.

Luce scoffed, "It is never too early for a margarita, and after the week we've had, I think we should have two."

Fitz beamed, "I like you!"

She grinned, "Likewise. New favorite uncle, right here."

Jack smiled like he was listening to bible study or watching a documentary. He never seemed to engage much. It was like he was taking it all in.

Coop sighed and sat on the oversized, floral couch. It matched the room beautifully. I felt like I might actually be in Savannah, Georgia or somewhere South and warm.

Fitz's dark-brown eyes sparkled when he looked at me, "What do y'all know?"

I shook my head and leaned back into the massage, "Nothing."

He crossed his arms and sat in the fancy armchair, "Well, I knew this was coming. I knew James was onto something." He sighed and looked around, "You have to know, once this can of worms is opened there ain't no coming back."

I furrowed my brow, "Is this what killed my dad?"

He nodded, "You could say that." He looked uncomfortable, "I don't want this to ever come out. I don't want to be the reason you know jack shit."

Coop placed the full glass on the coffee table and leaned forward, "Who are you?"

Fitz's eyes darkened, which didn't seem possible. His old, tanned face darkened with them, "I was in with Lincoln, her daddy. We enlisted same year, joined CI same year, and I retired the year he was gone."

I could see the skepticism on Coop's face. It made me smile. Coop gave him a look, "How is that possible?"

Fitz brushed the comment off, with a truly-feminine hand wave, "My life before doesn't matter. I'm Fitz now, and I'm living the life I always wanted to." He stood and walked to the kitchen. He did what my mom did, and talked as he sliced and stirred, "Back then, Gays had no choice, but to be in the closet. But Linc knew, he knew day one. We were in basic together and he made a shitty comment at me. I could have slapped him silly, but I just laughed it off. We were friends instantly. He saved me tons of times. Covered for me, so I could meet up with," a slow smile crept across his face, "Friends. I was indebted to him the day I met him." He pointed his huge knife at me from across the room, "He made me godfather of this pain in the ass, the day she was born, her and Sissy." He winked, "I always imagined I was more of a fairy godmother though." Luce and I laughed, but Jack snorted some of his drink and Coop looked confused. He wanted the story.

"You're Lieutenant Daily," he whispered.

Fitz's eyes lit instantly. I could see his hand tighten on the grip of the blade. I put a hand in the air, "He has one of those memories, Fitz. Every detail of everything he has ever read or seen is in there."

Fitz's stormy look never left.

I looked at Coop glaring, "Keep your mouth shut and let him talk."

Coop gave me the look, I was getting used to, "You both have five minutes to have this all make some sense, before I drag your ass out of this place. This feels like a stall, like he's waiting for the backup."

Fitz started to laugh, "Oh honey, I am dead. Didn't you read that little chestnut in the files, Mister Memory Bank?"

Coop sighed, "I only saw a few comments about you, like the godfather thing. They didn't have anything about the fairy godmother though."

Fitz laughed, "You are an animal in the sheets, aren't you? I, myself, love control freaks."

I grinned at Coop's tightening jaw.

Fitz challenged him with his stare, but Coop didn't bite. Fitz finished cutting the fruit salad, "Anyway, how much do y'all know about the second world war?"

I rolled my eyes, "Can you stop with that accent? It's annoying."

He shook his head, "No. I choose my reality to be the gay version of Gone with the Wind." His eyes lit up, "I have some of the dresses; wanna put some on for the rest of the story?"

I giggled and shook my head. Jack swallowed nervously, Luce looked more scared than he was.

I winked at Fitz, "They don't get your sense of humor.""

Coop spoke through his teeth, "Second world war?"

Fitz pointed the knife at him, "Right. Anyway, did you all learn about how Hitler was taking the best of the best as far as scientists and intellects were concerned?"

I nodded, "Yeah. We've all seen Indiana Jones."

He shook his head, "I swear to God in Heaven, nine minutes is all I need with Harrison Ford in that outfit, with that whip." He fanned himself, "Whew!"

The others laughed, getting used to the show. Fitz was crazy.

He nattered as he peeled a massive watermelon and cut it into tiny pieces, behind the huge marble island in the kitchen. "Well, when the other countries, the Brits especially, found out Hitler was doing that, they went nuts. Thus formed the much more modern spy agencies we all work for. The scientists were lost as the war ended." I noticed the subtlest grin crossing his lips.

"What does this have to do with the Burrow?" Coop asked. I could tell he was beyond annoyed.

Fitz froze. He looked up, "You said you knew nothing."

I shook my head, "We know James was looking for the Burrow. Him and a guy named Gustavo Servario. That's it though. It feels like nothing."

Fitz looked at each of us, "You all are in over your heads."

My spine started to tingle; his Jersey accent was back.

He placed the knife down, "Have you spoken the word Burrow to anyone beyond you?"

I shook my head, "No, but we spoke about it at the bugged house. The government knows about the Burrow. They're the ones trying to get it." I was lost. I looked at Coop; he looked the way I did.

He slammed a hand down on the hard counter, "Of course they know about it! They made the fucking thing! They hid them! They made a unanimous decision and saved the world from ending, at the hands of idiotic idealists."

I glanced at Jack, "Guess you were right."

He nodded, "Yay."

Fitz closed his eyes and pinched his brow with his juice-covered hand, "We need to run now. They know you'll come here."

I frowned, "You're dead."

He shook his head, "Not where the Burrow is concerned."

My guts started to burn, "You said you knew James was going to find something out or be onto something. What the hell did you think we were here for?"

He shook his head, "I thought you found out about your mom."

"What?"

He looked at me, "She's one of us. Always has been. Close your damned mouths; you look like idiots. She was like the Mata Hari of our time. Magnificent spy."

I couldn't feel my legs and arms, "I don't understand."

He grinned, "She's retired. She used to be one of the head spies for MI6."

Betrayal and sickness rolled around inside of me, "She's English?"

"German and English. Her mother—your grandmother, was born in a concentration camp. Your great-grandparents both died there and your great aunt fled to England with your grandmother. She met an Englishman and married him and gave birth to your mother. It was obvious early on, your mother was far more intelligent than the boys in school. MI6 hired her in the sixties at eighteen. She climbed ranks faster than the men. She was the first female to reach those sorts of ranks. Brilliant, bloody deadly too. She can kill with her pinky finger." He spoke with such pride in his voice, but I nearly gagged.

"She has my kids!" I blurted.

He nodded, "Then they have never been safer."

I closed my eyes and tried to see it all. I shook my head, "None of it makes sense. She never left the house. She was always there. He was gone on mission, but she was there. She was baking and sewing and making ornaments. She let the lawyer into James' office, she let me go to the hotels, and she let the bad men get to James and me. How had it all happened before her eyes? She would have known if she was a spy, even a shitty one, much less, a brilliant one."

He sighed, "Then she did it for a reason. She has to be aware of what's happening."

I opened my eyes, "What kind of fucking operation is this?"

I could see sadness in Fitz's eyes, "She stopped when you were born. You and Sissy were everything to her. She wasn't supposed to be able to get pregnant. You were both a miracle. A set of twin girls for a lady who couldn't have a single baby. As you aged, she slowly got back into it. Small missions, tiny jobs, little things she could do while you were in school."

I shook my head, "Impossible."

The End of Me

He laughed, "Not for her. She was one of a kind. She could take you to the park, assassinate someone, and not even bat an eyelash, or have a hair out of place. She was a machine."

"What does that even mean? Did she do that?"

He shook his head, "Of course not. She never endangered you. She became a regular American mother. She doted on your father, but always maintained the aid to her country."

I ran my fingers through my hair and tried not to notice the grease, "What is the Burrow?" I didn't want to know anything else. I didn't have room for it.

I looked up to see Fitz shaking his head, "Something dangerous. Something that once you know about it, you can never come back from knowing. You leave the service the way I did." He looked sickened, "The way your father did."

Tears flooded my eyes.

He was alive.

He was another person who had pretended to be dead and left me.

I got up and walked to the hallway, "I need to lay down."

I walked to the spare room I had slept in before, and curled up in the sheets.

When I closed my eyes I saw it all. The obvious things that stuck out but seemed innocent with unknowing eyes. With jaded bitterness, I could see them for what they were.

The door opened, just as I was about to jump up and scream at Fitz some more.

Coop poked his head in, "You okay?"

I shook my head, "Fuck no."

He laughed and closed the door. He laid on the bed on his back, "Feeling stupid?"

I punched him in the arm, hurting my hand.

He snorted, "I'll take that as a yes." He turned, looking at me, "You hit like a girl."

I closed my eyes, "How could they? How could they lie and cheat Sissy and me? How could the very same shit happen to my kids? Do you see the irony in this? It's insane."

Coop was looking at me still, when I opened my eyes, "Almost like it was planned," he said.

I nodded, "I have no doubt, some of it was. Look at it all? It all fits so nicely when you stand back. Up close it's a jumbled mess, but from a distance you can see everything. You can easily just slip the puzzle pieces together."

He grabbed my hand, "Your kids are safe. She isn't going to hurt them. She isn't going to let them get hurt."

My eyes watered, "Why didn't she tell me the truth? Why didn't she let me in?"

He wiped a tear dripping down my cheek, "Did you tell your kids what you used to be?"

I scowled, "Of course not. They're only little."

He shrugged, "Did you ever plan on telling them about you being a spy? Do you plan on telling them about James' betrayal, or his still being alive, or what he really did for a living?"

I clenched my jaw.

He nodded, "You don't know why she never told you things, but you can see how easy it is to want to protect them."

I shook my head, "I was CI though. Why didn't she tell me then? Or when I was retired. We shared more things, than I ever knew."

"I don't know. You have to ask her."

I narrowed my eyes, "How do I reach her?"

He sighed, "No."

I climbed off the bed and left the room.

"What is the Burrow?" I shouted down the hall.

Fitz passed me a bowl of probably the most amazing-looking fruit salad I'd had ever seen. I sighed taking it and my seat.

He sat with a bowl of fruit too, "Well, I guess since the story of how the Burrow was created is the same as the story of how your mom became a spy, I can just head off from where I was before in the story. The newly-formed spy operatives joined forces and saved the weapons from the Germans. We didn't get them all, just the ones with the potential to destroy the world with their so-called brilliance." He ate a bite and chewed, but he seemed lost in it all, "We took them somewhere no one would ever find them. An asylum where they would be safe. At first the presidents and leaders were aware the Burrow existed but they didn't know where it was. Then the Korean War happened and they wanted the weapons. They wanted to win. The Master Key makes the call. He decides if the cause is worthy or not. He saw the request for aid from the Nations involved in the Korean War. He turned them down. It was then, that the first mission to try to find the Burrow was executed by our own governments. We had been brothers in arms and suddenly we were at war within our own ranks. The men working for the Burrow would die protecting it and the men working for the cause would die trying to find it."

I looked at Coop standing in the hallway. I could see he was as in the dark as I was.

Fitz spoke through the bite he was chewing, "Then came the Vietnam War. The CIA would stop at nothing to get those weapons. The Burrow had been moved in secret to protect it. It was no easy feat. Everyone was so angry when they couldn't find it, and then eventually more weapons started to disappear. Anytime a new one was created, it was taken. The Burrow grew as technology developed. It wasn't even during the Gulf War, Bosnia, Afghanistan and Iraq that we saw much threat against the Burrow. As technology grew, so did the Burrow's capabilities. Since 9/11, we have had the hardest time keeping the Burrow a secret." He sighed and ate another bite.

I took a bite and chewed, "What kind of weapons?"

Coop answered, "People."

Fitz looked back, "You are a sharp one."

Luce gave me a look, "People?"

I shrugged.

Jack inhaled sharply, "That actually makes sense."

I shook my head, "What does?"

Coop crossed his arms and leaned against the wall, "They're hiding the scientists and engineers, who pose a threat to society with their inventions and discoveries. Isn't that right, Fitz?"

Fitz nodded, "Yes, it is. You see, they always come from an innocent place. The intelligent mean well. The technology rarely has weaponry as the intention, but the governments, our own homeland security, CIA, MI6, and the UN always see it as potential. So we fake a death with a heart attack, or accident, or sometimes we just go with plain old missing persons. We take them and their work to the Burrow. We leave behind misinformation and lies. Nothing in this world is ever as it seems. You have to understand, everyone thinks the weapons will save them or give them the upper hand, but the council has to be able to see that winning won't save us in the big picture. Pollution, destruction of country's environments, destruction of land, deaths of innocents, upping the ante and winning, have to all be separated and looked at piece by piece."

I had only one question, "Where is the Burrow?"

He shook his head, "I don't know. Only the Master Key knows that."

Coop took his seat again, "Where is the Master Key?"

Fitz shook his head, "I would die before I would reveal that. He or she must find you, if they wish to be found at all."

"Was my father a Master Key?"

His eyes lit up, "He was so proud of you."

I shouted, "WAS HE, FITZ?"

He jumped slightly, "He was. The Master Key dies when it's his turn to retire. He always dies. There is no other way to protect his family, if it is discovered he was a Master Key. I have endangered you by telling you with these other people here. Your children will never be safe again. Are you happy you know?"

I fought a sob, "Fuck!" What other word was there?

I looked around the room for the magic beanbag, as my neck nearly seized.

Chapter Twelve

Love in all the wrong places

I stared up into the dark ceiling and knew.

There was one answer to the problem in my mind. I glanced over at Luce's rising and falling chest. She was either sleeping or very good at faking.

I reached for my clutch and slipped the phone from it. Coop had told me to leave it behind, but I hadn't. I didn't want to think about why. I looked at the screen and the number that had called seventeen times and pressed it. I pressed the message button and texted slowly, 'Come Find Me! I'm in SLC'

I pressed send and tried to keep my breathing even. What was he going to do to me, if I came back? Would he hurt me?

I slipped from the bed and tiptoed from the room and down the hall. I picked my shoes up, but as I rounded the corner I heard a whisper, "You won't get far you know. Mister serious, he likes you."

I turned to see a pair of dark eyes in the shadowed corner of the store.

I nodded, "He's like nine-years old. I need answers, Fitz. I'm done risking you. Tell them I went back to Boston. Tell them to forget they ever met you."

He smiled and I could see the glint of his teeth from the streetlights shining in the window, "I'll be out of here the minute they are, kid."

I shook my head, "I'm so sorry to have involved you."

He chuckled softly, "I knew it would come for me one day. I'm glad it was you. The Burrow can't stay hidden without a lot of work, and unfortunately, times are changing. It's getting increasingly harder to keep its secret."

I frowned, "What do you do with the doctors that don't want to stay hidden?"

His eyes narrowed as he stepped forward and hugged me, "Have a safe trip, kid. Go easy on the arms dealer." He ignored my question.

I pulled back, "How do you know it all?"

He kissed my cheek, "I still know people."

He slipped something like a business card in my hand, "If you get stuck, call this number. But don't call, unless you want to be gone forever."

I nodded, "Okay. Thanks, Uncle." I kissed his weathered face and opened the front door to the store. I walked down the cold sidewalk and turned up an alley. I pulled on my boots and tucked the card in my clutch.

The phone vibrated.

'Done with your uncle then?'

My heart hurt instantly. I went to the phone function and dialed in the code and then the number to the shop. Fitz answered, "You missing me already?"

"RUN, FITZ! DON'T WAIT! WAKE THEM AND RUN NOW!"

He hung up before I had a chance to explain. I started to run. I dialed the number that had called repeatedly.

"To what do I owe the pleasure of this midnight call?"

I sighed, "I need you to help me." I ran to a corner and stopped there. I pressed my back into the concrete wall and spoke softly, "I will do whatever you want, if you help me."

He sighed, "You know how to play hardball. Whatever I want?"

I bit my lip. I wanted to call him a pervert degenerate, but I didn't. I nodded, "Whatever you want. But you can't hurt anyone. Not my uncle, not the team helping me, and not my family."

A large black SUV pulled up the corner of the street. The window lowered. I gasped when I saw his face, "We can negotiate in the car."

I lowered the phone. How had he done it? No one should have known about Fitz. There was no way we were followed, unless one of us was a mole. And yet there in front of me was Servario, with a look that could skin a cat.

I looked both ways and walked across the road softly. I expected a bullet to strike me in the back, as he moved over and I climbed in.

The new car smell struck me. "Did you buy this today?"

His eyes had none of the green hints in them, that were there when he was happy. I closed the door and looked down, "Please don't hurt them," I whispered.

He tapped the glass in front of us and the SUV drove away. As we rounded the corner, I caught a glimpse of Coop running after us.

"Ironic, isn't it," he said and sipped from his glass, "Last time it was me running, desperate for you to stay with me, and it was young Cooper driving away with you in his car." He leaned over, taking a good look at Coop, "I have to say, I think he has a bit of a thing for you."

I shook my head as I watched Coop from the window, "No, he doesn't. He's like that with everyone. He's flirty and fun away from the job, and serious and controlling on the job. Somehow he makes it fun still, even when he's serious."

His tone changed to angry, "I dare say, you have a thing for him as well."

I looked up at Servario's stoic face, "I'm sorry I ran." I needed the subject changed.

He turned, "Are you?"

I swallowed and nodded, "I am."

"We'll see."

He made me shiver.

He didn't speak to me as we drove. I continued to look at him, to try to catch a glimpse of how he was feeling or what he was thinking.

We arrived at the airport and the door was opened. He climbed out and walked to the plane. Roxy was startled to see me. She looked down as I boarded. I assumed that was bad.

My heart was in my throat. I sat in my seat from before and fought the nervous tears that were threatening me. I was cooler than that, a better spy than to cry from his possible anger. I would take what he would dish.

He didn't sit beside me, like before. He went to the cockpit.

Roxy brought me a glass of wine and quickly left again. Her eyes never met mine.

Steve nodded at me as he took his seat.

I laid the seat back and closed my eyes. If he was going to beat or torture me, I would have to take it. I needed answers; they were worth whatever happened to me.

I closed my eyes and saw my kids' faces. Jules smiling at me and looking so much like her father it was painful, and Mitch trying so hard to be grownup.

At least they had a ninja granny to protect them. I made it out unscathed, they would too.

"We're about to take off, you should at least hold the wine," his voice was detached as he took his seat.

I sat up quickly and held the glass. The jet started right away and began the taxi to the runway.

I glanced nervously in his direction. I was having a hard time seeing the cruel man and not the curve of his lips or the thickness of his fingers. I sipped the wine at first and then finished in a gulp, "Why are you so angry?"

He focused on the laptop in front of him, "I'm not."

I frowned, "You are. I was married, remember? I can tell when a man is angry."

A smile played with his lips momentarily, and then it was back to stoic. He looked at me for a second, "I was crossing the line before. It was wrong. I'm not your husband, Evie."

I unbuckled the seat belt and walked to the bathroom. I closed the door and sat on the closed toilet lid. He always had me in knots, whenever he was around. It was like walking on thin ice, constantly.

The jet started to take off, slamming my side into the sink. I tried to grab ahold of the bar next to me, but the force was too great. I gave in and let it squish me into the counter. I needed to think anyway.

I wanted answers and details from him, but he was no longer interested in me sexually. Why had he been so interested before, or at all? Nothing was making much sense and without the womanly wiles to get him talking, I didn't know what else to do. I could try to spin it around in my favor. I could do what I did to James, and act like I was the angry one. He hated that.

It was an idea. When the plane got to cruising altitude, I stripped naked and cleaned myself in the sink with the hand towels, which was awkward and familiar. I opened the door and looked down the hall. He was no longer in the chair. I tiptoed to the very back of the plane to the dressing closet. I dropped my clothes on the floor and looked through the racks of clothes.

It was a sea of designer labels and soft fabrics. I pulled on a white lacy bra and matching panties. They still had tags, making it slightly less weird. Settling on Armani, I went with the most coverage I could get. I looked very comfortable in the long black, side-slit maxi skirt and mocha sleeveless, tie-waist tunic. I looked around for sandals. Instead, I found a suede pair of black Manolo Blahnik mules with a pointed toe. It was an elegant choice and made me look like a wife.

I pulled on a couple bracelets and pulled my long, dark hair up into a bun.

"That tan tunic compliments your dark skin," Roxy said with a soft smile.

I grinned, "Thanks. My dad was half Black Irish and half Icelandic. Dark hair and golden skin. It was a good thing to inherit. My twin sister and I aren't identical and she looks more like our mother."

She grabbed my hand and whispered, "Are you insane for coming back?"

I nodded, "I need him."

She rolled her eyes, "Oh my God, if you knew how many times I'd heard that from girls about him. He's a bigot player. You need to run."

I forced the fake smile to remain on my lips, "It's not like that, I assure you."

She gave me the up down, "Really?"

I blushed, "I wanted to look professional, not the other kind of professional. All your clothes are more twenty-three and hitting the clubs. This suits me and my other clothes were covered in garden dirt."

She waved her hands, "This is exactly what he bought for you. He brought it on board yesterday. Jesus, you played right into his hands, calling him. I lost ten bucks in the bet we placed on you showing up and putting this on."

I folded my arms, "What? He knew I was coming back? He bought this?" Was I that predicable? "What is he fucking psychic?"

She shrugged, "Sometimes I think he is."

I pursed my lips, "You sure it was for me?"

She sighed, "Does it look like it belongs to me?"

"Shit."

She pressed her lips together and nodded, "Yeah, dumbass."

I looked down at the tags I'd removed and winced, "He's gonna know I took the tags off."

She pulled back the curtain, "You owe me ten bucks and a new pair of Christian Louboutin ankle boots."

"Fair enough," I muttered and walked out of the room to the seats out front. I almost sat in a different one, but I remembered I was the one who was angry. I needed a reason. I sat down and looked at the plate of prawns and sauce in front of me. My stomach gurgled. I rubbed it and picked up a prawn by its tail. I dragged it through the still warm sauce and moaned when I took the first bite. "This is good, Roxy."

She grinned as she passed me, "You like it?"

I nodded, "Wow."

She winked and walked to the front of the plane.

I ignored his existence and enjoyed my meal, as I broke off a piece of bread and dragged it through the sauce on the plate. The crusty bread was still warm. I moaned again.

She cleared it and placed a plate of seared white fish, with a creamy sauce and roasted vegetables. The sauce was a lime and cilantro.

"When was the last time you ate a proper meal?" he finally spoke.

I shrugged and drank from my wine glass. I knew when it was, but I wasn't in the mood to admit the last thing I'd eaten was picks and nibbles of random foods. I wished I'd eaten the entire fruit salad at Fritz's.

I hoped they were okay.

I glanced at my clutch on the table. I would need to call when we landed.

"You need to take better care of yourself."

I looked at him, "I need the stability back in my life. I need you and the CI, and CIA, and James to leave me alone. I was eating regularly before. I was drinking water and eating five meals a day and going to yoga. Now I'm hopping on planes and eating food from convenience stores, and I still don't know that my kids and mom are safe, or if my husband is really dead."

He looked at me, "I knew you would look nice in that outfit."

I shook my head and turned back to my plate of food, gulping back the last of my second glass of wine.

"Why are you angry with me? You think I caused all of this?"

Giving him my death stare and then letting it slide into indifference, I shrugged, "I don't know what to believe. There are too many versions of you to possibly know."

He smirked, "You know me; you just don't want to admit you like what you see."

I laughed and turned back to my dinner. We landed just after Roxy cleared our food.

I hugged her as I left the plane, "I'll get you those shoes."

She pinched, "You better not, but I want my ten bucks."

I laughed and kissed her cheek, "Another magnificent meal. I don't even know how you can get the fish so perfect on a plane."

She rolled her eyes, "You flatter and then I have to make sure it's out of the park next time too." I could see her eyeballing Servario nervously. He was stoic. I decided that should be his new name.

I shook my head, "I doubt that will be an issue," and followed Steve.

His broad shoulders and thick back made me wonder how he stayed so fit. He seemed pretty lazy. He was probably one of those guys who stayed fit, no matter what they did.

We walked to the SUV waiting for us. I had noticed we weren't back in Boston. We flew into San Diego.

My stomach was a ball of nerves. I looked a Servario, "I thought we were going home."

He gave me a blank look, "When did I say that?"

"I need to call my cat sitter and get her to drop by and feed the cat. I've been gone for days."

He watched my face for a second, "Fine. Make it fast and speaker phone."

I pulled out the cellphone he gave me and dialed her, praying Coop traced my calls. I wanted him close in case this was a huge mistake and I needed an evac.

"Hello?" she answered on the first ring.

"Beth, how are you? It's, Evie."

"Evie, how are you doing? Are you okay?" she sounded sad still.

I rolled my eyes, "I'm fine."

"How are the kids?"

I nodded, "They're good. Sad, but good. Anyway, the reason for my call is I need you to stop over and check on Ralph and make sure he's okay. I'm in San Diego for a couple days. We're in San Diego. We decided to take a trip and I forgot, in all the chaos, to call you."

"Yes, of course. I'll see him once a day and check on the house."

I glanced at Servario, "That should be great. You have a key still, right?"

"Yes I do. Have a great trip out west!"

I smiled, forgetting what I was doing, "Thanks sweetie. Say hello to your mom." I hung up the phone and shook my head, "So weird. Her world is normal and mine is destroyed," I muttered, before I could stop myself.

He said nothing. When the truck stopped, the door was opened. I climbed out, ignoring everything around me. I was overcome with the strangest feeling I'd had since my husband died/ran away.

I was lost.

He grabbed my hand and pulled me in a door. I caught a warm breeze, loaded with the smell of the ocean and frowned, "Are we at the beach?"

He pulled me inside and closed the door. He looked at me, "Don't try anything. They will hurt you, if you try to leave." He pressed his lips against my forehead and walked away.

"Where are you going?" I asked, like I had a right to know.

He waved, "Out for the night," and vanished down a long wide corridor. I looked around at the splendor. Everything of his was beautiful. My home was amazing and in all the right areas, whereas his was all luxury. Luxury I was completely alone in and not in the mood to enjoy.

I turned and walked into the large sitting area off the front room. A bottle of Apothic was already opened and poured into the carafe next to the empty bottle.

I poured a glass, sighing.

The walls were covered in art. It was rich and warm Spanish-styled home. It suited the sexy version of him I wanted to see again.

I slumped into a leather, burnt-orange sofa and drank.

"Out for the night?" I muttered and pulled out my phone, tapping it against my palm.

My head game of being the one who was pissed off, didn't work. He didn't come crawling and beg to know why or brought me flowers. Of course seeing it now, the reason for James' constant worry about my moods was obvious. He had a guilty conscience.

I stood and grabbed the carafe and walked down the other hallway. I clicked on light switches, only to discover an array of stunning rooms. Finally, I reached a room with a large fireplace and fabric couches. I curled up on one with my wine and dialed 9-1-1.

Luce answered, "Hey?" She looked worried.

I put a finger to my lips, "Hey."

She frowned, "You okay?"

I nodded, "Yeah. I just need answers. Did Fitz get away?"

She cocked an eyebrow, "Yeah. He woke us up and dragged us to some safe house. We stayed for two hours, then got in a helicopter, and then a private jet. He dropped us in Boston."

I felt confusion all over my face, "Jet?"

She nodded, "Yeah. Jet."

In the background I heard Coop yelling. The phone went crazy and then refocused on his face.

He looked savage, "What did I say, Evie?"

"I need answers, Coop."

He made a face, "Don't give me that shit. Fitz filled in a lot of blanks. We were getting somewhere. You fucking bailed, because you wanted to see him again and don't bullshit me."

I shook my head, "No, I swear. Fitz was never going to tell us anything useful. What more do we know? We know what the Burrow is and that's it. We don't know where it is, or who's there, or what to do with the information. We still don't have any resources." I sighed and looked down shaking my head. His sentence hit my ears, "Wait, what? Did you say jet? Where the hell did Fitz get a jet?"

Coop's look matched mine, "He hasn't always had that?"

I snorted, "Uh no. The buyout for people like us is about half the value of a pension."

He paused, "Weird. He seemed pretty comfy in it. The pilot knew him."

I wriggled my nose, "Was the pilot gay?"

Coop scoffed, "How the hell should I know?"

I rolled my eyes, "Ask Luce."

He turned, "Yo, was that pilot gay?"

I could hear her response, "Almost as gay as you."

He frowned.

I ignored their banter and replied, "He might be dating the owner. Gay people hire gay people, so they don't get fired for being gay."

He frowned harder, "Gays don't get fired for being gay, it's not the fifties, Evie."

I raised my eyebrows, "Coop, a teacher got fired in Idaho last week, because her dead mother's obituary had her partner's name in it. She's a lesbian."

His jaw dropped, "Are you for real?"

I nodded.

"That's sick. Okay, but back to brass tax. I'm coming to get you."

I winked, "This is what's wrong with the world. Stay close; I'll let you know when I'm ready to get picked up."

He scowled, "Try not to have too much fun."

I laughed, "I think you need to head back to Sweden for the week. You seem tense."

He flipped me the bird and I pressed it off.

I dropped the phone and looked around the room. The huge wall-mounted TV looked like something I would be able to use, without too many problems. Of course, I had to search high and low for the remote. It took me twenty minutes to turn it on. I couldn't get sound but I watched the picture. It was Casablanca. It was at the part where she walks into the bar and sees the piano player. I almost tear up, as I see her ask him to play the song they liked. Seeing the anger and the way Bogart storms across the bar to stop Sam from playing the song, makes me think of Servario.

The look on Bogart's face, was the same one he got. Mostly it was the fake smile, with the heartbroken eyes. Almost like his lips couldn't convince the rest of his face, he was happy.

I wondered if I was easy to read or if I was more stone-faced.

I finished my glass of wine and curled into the pillows and cushions. The couch was soft. I closed my eyes, but they opened almost immediately from fear. I didn't like being in the wide open.

I got up and stumbled down the hall farther. I opened door after door until I reached a set of double doors.

I opened them, instantly smelling him in the air. I searched the wall for the light switch. When I clicked it, rope lighting in the ceiling and windowsills lit the room up.

The room was ridiculous. I couldn't even imagine him ever needing a room like it. I closed the doors and crossed to the extra-large king-sized bed. It was made and pristine, like every inch of the unlived-in home.

I turned to find another set of double doors. I opened them to discover the walk-in closet. It was the size of a bedroom. Ladies' clothes, in a few different sizes, filled a tiny corner of the closet. That disturbed me. I closed the doors and looked around at the clothes. He had so many suits, it looked like it was a department store.

I kicked my shoes off and noticed how plush the carpet was on my toes.

I flopped onto the floor and curled up under his suits. The room smelled like him. I reached up and jerked a suit free of the hanger and laid it down, taking in deep breaths of the smell of him.

My mind played tricks on me. It lied to me about what it would be like, if a man like Servario loved a girl like me.

It would be more like Romeo and Juliet and less like Casablanca. We would both end up dead.

I closed my eyes and felt safe in the small room, no one would look for me in.

Chapter Thirteen

Three's a crowd

I woke to a sound I didn't recognize.

It sounded like people but then it didn't. It was muffled and then it was loud again, like it moved in waves. I blinked and opened the door a tiny crack. Figures moved in the dark. I heard moaning and a girl making a sound, I was certain I had made with him.

I stopped breathing, closing the door silently.

With it closed, I pressed my hand against the back of the hardwood and waited for my stomach to drop back down. He was having sex… in his bed… with me in the house. Did he know I was there, in the closet? Was this purposeful?

The reality of the whole situation didn't filter in slowly, it slammed my brain hard. I was his prisoner, his captive, his pawn. I had fooled myself into believing he might have cared about me. Instead, he was setting me up again, only this time he wanted me to hurt. I had let the mission become getting him to dominate me again, instead of finding the Burrow.

It dawned on me that I could have stayed with Coop, Luce, and Jack. I could have made it work with them as a team finding answers. Deep down, I had wanted to come back.

I wanted the things he made me feel, fear… anger… shame… desperation… pleasure. The pleasure was the worst.

The rhythmic sound of the girl got louder.

I took a breath and ignored my basic human senses, which told me not to look, and put my hand on the knob again. I wanted to see it.

I turned the knob and opened the door a crack.

My eyes had adjusted to the dim light, making it easier to see them. The tanned complexion of his broad back and rounded shoulders, looked stunning in the moonlight. He thrust and I could almost feel him inside of me. The door was open only wide enough for my one eye to see through, and yet, I saw it all. Her legs lifted to his shoulders, pressing against his chest to arch her hips better. He sat up, pumping wildly. The sounds escaping her intensified with the slamming of his body against, and inside, of hers. His firm, rounded ass flexed with each mighty strike as his fingers dug into her thighs, dragging her back to him. His head dropped back as a slight moan escaped his lips. I barely caught it, over the spasms going on inside of her body, making her scream and writhe. I was jealous of her but for the wrong reason. I envied her, the release she was getting.

He chuckled and patted her thigh, "Steve will see you out." He climbed off the bed and walked, still erect with a condom on, to the bathroom.

She climbed off the bed, and pulled her mini dress back to its rightful spot.

She tousled her long, blonde hair and walked from the room, holding her pumps.

I heard the shower turn on and knew it was my only chance. I waited for the water to sound like it was hitting his skin. The suspense of it all made it feel like a real mission. I knew he liked long showers. I waited until I heard the jets kick in, he liked them to massage his back.

I slipped from the closet, tiptoeing to the door. I turned the handle slowly. My breath was silent, but my heart was beating wildly.

I opened the door very deliberately, trying not to make a sound. Just as I had it open half an inch, it slammed shut and his soaking wet, dripping body pressed into my back.

"I saved the best for you," he whispered into my neck. I shuddered, "Don't fucking touch me." The right kind of jealousy hit when his dirty hands touched me.

He chuckled, "I figured you were used to sharing your men with other women." That stung.

Cold hatred crossed my face, shutting my body down, "You're clearly not my kind of man."

"And yet here you are, my woman," he growled and pressed my face into the door, lifting my skirt, "I just have to know."

The fight came alive in me. I spun, pushing hard against his chest. He staggered back. I threw open the door, running as fast as I could. In the dark, and disoriented feeling of being in a different house, I was lost instantly.

A light down one of the hallways beckoned to me.

My bare feet slapped against the tiles, as did his.

He called out to me, taunting me, "I like hunting, Evie. I like chasing the things I want to be on top of."

I started running on my tiptoes when I realized I couldn't hear his footsteps anymore. I opened a door when I rounded a corner. I ran hard and rounded another corner. I was back in the main sitting room. The house must have been built like an octopus.

I sprinted across the foyer and down the hall he had gone down for his night out. I opened the first door I found and slipped inside. I closed the door and flicked on the light. It was a games room. Billiards and other tables lined the massive space. I flicked the light off and ran for the back of the room. I remembered where the tables were and hid underneath one.

My breath and heartbeat were my only company.

The wait felt like it was an eternity but it was seconds. The suspense was built so high I didn't think it possible to be more afraid or paralyzed than I was.

I heard the door open but no light came through into the room. It was pitch black, even in the hallway. He must have turned off everything.

I stayed perfectly still, listening for breath or steps but he moved silently.

I crawled farther under the table as my eyes had adjusted to the lack of light, I hoped I would be able to see him. I needed to make it to the door.

"I can hear your heartbeat," he whispered and I couldn't figure where it came from.

I held my breath, frozen in fear and a sickening sort of anticipation.

I waited before creeping forward again.

My left foot was grabbed mid crawl. I screamed and kicked but he dragged me back on the carpet so fast I didn't stand a chance. I scrambled but he was on me instantly, pressing me into the floor with his weight.

His hot breath licking at my nape.

I didn't give up the fight until he star-fished my body, pinning my arms and legs out from me.

Somehow he was still able to free one of his hands, dragging it down the side of me.

He lifted my shirt, tickling the side of my body.

"Stop!"

He kissed the back of my neck, "You don't mean that."

He was right. I was horrified at myself and the fact I was growing excited as his hand slipped down my thigh. The fabric of my skirt rustled as he dragged it up my body. He slid his thick fingers up my spread legs to my ass cheeks and then down between my thighs.

"I need to know."

I shook my head, whispering into the carpet, "Don't touch me. I don't care what you have to know. Why don't you go find yourself another whore, if you're not done?"

I could hear the smile in his reply, "Evie, I want to know if you liked watching me with that whore."

Shame filled me. I knew what he would find inside of my panties.

He let go of my body slightly and arched my ass up with his other hand. He pulled my underwear to the side, dipping his finger between my lips. I felt him slipping in the wetness there, the wetness caused by my watching him fuck someone else.

He moaned when he discovered my shameful secret. "I had a feeling, what I might find."

I hated that he was pleased by the perverse thing I had done, and proud of the things he had made me like, and want. My body was trembling in frozen delight, waiting for the fingers inside of me to move.

But they didn't. He kept them there, completely still and began kneading my ass with his other hand.

My hips tried to rotate against him to try to force him to move, but he pressed me back down with his free hand.

When I stopped moving, he lifted my shirt up to my shoulders. He planted hot kisses along my back ribs and spine, still not moving his fingers.

My breath picked up, my body was ready to convulse. His kisses lowered to my ass cheeks. He dragged my underwear between the cheeks.

His words on the plane about fucking my ass started to play over and over in my head. He wouldn't, would he? I would fight him to the death on it. No matter what.

I jumped when I felt his teeth on my ass. He bit, not hard but enough to make me tense.

"Relax," he spoke softly and then bit again.

I didn't like the biting, I wanted the fucking but he refused to do the thing I wanted.

He murmured sweetly to my ass cheeks, "You liked watching me, didn't you?" His breath caressed my skin.

I shook my head, "No."

He jerked his finger inside my pussy. I cried out into the carpet as he thrust, pumping his fingers in and out.

He stopped just as I was about to orgasm.

"You liked watching me fuck her. Say it."

I shook my head but I couldn't speak. The sounds that threatened to leave my lips, were not words.

Sweat started to form on my brow.

"You want me to let you cum, Evie?"

I trembled, near tears but never spoke a word.

"Then, you say it." His voice was no longer a whisper in the dark. He was commanding me.

My weakened voice quivered when I tried to speak, "N-n-no."

He slowly dragged his fingers from me, but when he was just at my opening, he thrust back in. He held them there momentarily before repeating. On the third time I shouted, "I LIKED IT! FUCK YOU! I FUCKING HATE YOU!"

His hand instantly picked up in speed. He inserted a second finger, stretching me and pumping rhythmically. I gripped the shag carpet, crying into it as my entire body went pins and needles, and then burst into orgasmic flames. Beads of sweat covered every inch of me. He pumped until the twitching stopped. I was about to sigh and possibly cry a little, when he lifted me off the floor, flipping me over. He laid me on the billiards table, spreading my legs and burying his face between them.

He licked my swollen slit in flicks and sucks, starts and stops. I felt his tongue enter me as his fingers rubbed my clit. He sat up, slapping my pussy a few times softly. I was startled by it at first, but then the vibration was nice, I had no idea.

Just as I was getting into the groove of the soft slaps, he would replace his hand with his mouth, and begin the licking again. I could feel the second orgasm building as he flipped me over, dragging me back down so I was bent over the table. My feet barely touched the ground. He slapped my ass hard. My legs being spread as far as they were, made the vibration tingle everywhere.

I gasped as he crawled a hand up my back, nestling it at the base of my head, and pulled my hair. He lifted my head up and spanked again. I cried out. I wanted it to be a cry from pain but it was not.

"You going to let that little fucker touch you again?" he asked menacingly.

I didn't know what he meant. "The fat man?" Who else had touched me?

He spanked and pulled harder, "That young man."

Coop.

I shook my head, struggling against the hair pulling, "He never touched me."

I heard his belt rustle, making my eyes bug out. Was he going to whip me with the belt?

Instead of a lash, his cock entered me hard.

His hand left my head and planted on my hips. He gripped my skin, like he had hers. He pulled my ass back, fucking me.

He reached forward amid thrusts and rubbed between my legs, circling my clit.

The felt of the table scratched against my cheeks and palms. The sound left my lips, like it did hers. I could see him, thrusting into her the way he had done to me. I came again, seeing her feet in the air and his strong ass flexing. His thrusts had slowed to make my orgasm deliciously paced.

Flipping me on my back again, he grabbed my ankles and placed them on the same spot hers were.

I didn't notice until his cock was buried deep inside of me. I tried to kick away but he held me there. Only when he had filled me with his orgasm, could I tell the difference between what he done to her and what he had done to me. He cried out, making a sound I hadn't heard in the room with her, but that I recalled from the hotel.

He slapped against me one last time and collapsed on top of me, forcing my legs apart again. I wrapped them around him as he breathed into my breasts.

"You set me up," I whispered into the heavy, dank air of the giant room, we had somehow managed to pollute with our filth.

He nodded, "I didn't force you to like it though."

I shook my head, "I hate you."

He kissed my belly and stood up, "I need you to hate me, Evie."

He left the room and I didn't feel afraid of him anymore.

I showered in a spare room and found a smaller room to sleep in.

When I woke, I looked around the room for something to put on. The other clothes felt wrong, on a bunch of different levels.

I wrapped in a blanket and made my way back to his room. I could see his foot sticking out of the covers. I snuck into the closet and stole a pair of shorts for jogging and a t-shirt. His clothes hung off me, like they would a kid. I left the blanket in the closet and made my run for the door.

I found the kitchen from the smell in the halls. It was waffles. My mouth watered.

A small man in a chef's outfit grinned at me, "You hungry?" he asked through a thick French accent.

I nodded and sat at the breakfast table.

Everything was oversized, marble, and expensive. His house was like something out of a magazine, including the chef.

He brought me a coffee and a plate of fruit.

I looked at the fruit and then back at the kitchen. "Can I have some of the waffles?" I asked.

He shook his head, "Not yet."

I didn't know what to say, he was like the Soup Nazi on Seinfeld. He was holding out on the waffles, until he was ready to give them to me.

I picked up a chocolate covered strawberry and bit down. I was starving.

The coffee was perfect. I stirred the cream in and sipped. Even with the strawberry taste in my mouth, it was oh-my-God good. My kids would love this house. I wondered what the cost of the chef was? I couldn't help but wonder, if I had enough money in James' sneaky-whore account to have a chef or even a house like this?

I picked the newspaper up off the table, where it was no doubt placed for him, and gasped when I saw the front page.

"PRIVATE JET CRASHES ON MOUNT WASHINGTON"

"Are you reading my newspaper?" Servario interrupted my reading.

I didn't look at him. "A jet crashed on Mount Washington, after taking off from Boston," I muttered. I paused a moment, as I thought about how possible it was that was Fitz. I felt the burning in my eyes, "Did you do this?"

He looked confused, "What are you talking about?"

"Fitz left Boston after dropping everyone else off. He was in a private jet; did you kill him? Is this his jet?"

He sat and shook his head, "No. I don't know whose jet that was. What am I psychic?"

I narrowed my eyes, "Fine." I stood up and walked away. I could tell he was lying to me.

The End of Me

"Are those my clothes?" he asked after me.

I spun around, feeling sickening anger at the possibility that Uncle Fitz might have been in a plane crash. "I'm done with this. This sick, twisted version of playing house with you. Last night was really fun and I have to admit surprising. I have new things to talk to my shrink about now; that's always good. But I am done. You either level with me, or I am walking out the front door, and I will kill whoever decides to get in my way."

He grins at me, "You feel that confident in your abilities?"

I shake my head, "No. I feel that confident in my anger at the things that happened last night."

He watched me and then sighed, "Come and sit and eat breakfast. Pierre makes an incredible Belgian waffle."

I walked over to the counter and stole a waffle from the steaming plate of them Pierre was plating. I walked away, "Screw you, Servario. I'll leave you two alone. Thanks for the waffle, Pierre."

I nearly ran to the room where I had slept and grabbed my clutch. I left the room, but he was right there, "That was incredibly rude and I've asked you repeatedly not to swear."

I looked up into his stormy expression and chewed the stolen waffle, "You're right. These are the best."

His mood didn't improve, "If I tell you what I know, will you stay?"

I shook my head, "No. I'm here because my vagina wants to be. I need to focus on my kids. You need me to hate you—well, you know what? The feeling is mutual."

A grin toyed with his lips, "You say that word with no apprehension. I find that odd. You are too forward with the things you'll say."

"What word?" Had I sworn again?

"Vagina."

I crossed my arms over my clutch and snickered, "One of my kids got stuck in there for like twelve hours, before the doctors figured it out. I had been in labor for thirty-nine hours, before I got a cesarean section. I pushed for two hours and got two—yes two hemorrhoids, hence the reason I won't ever have anal sex. I have a deep amount of comfort with the lower half of my body because of it all. I recovered with mineral baths, Epsom salts, and rectal suppositories. I didn't have sex comfortably for one whole year, and even then, it was annoying. Yet, I still had another baby. The second was much easier. I just booked the surgery and out she came. Then on top of all of that, I breastfed both my kids the full recommended eighteen month minimum, earning me horrid looks from everyone, even other women. I was the pervy hippie who breastfed for too long."

He looked like he might get sick.

I nodded, "And voila, you no longer see me as a sexual object you get to toy with." I stood on my tiptoes, dragging his cheek down to my level, "Thank you for making me feel things I haven't felt in a long time, shame and perversion included." I brushed my lips against his rough cheek and walked past him. I knew he was still stuck in the hemorrhoid story. That truly was a cock blocker.

"Say goodbye to Steve and foxy Roxy for me," I looked back and walked to the foyer, then strolled out the front door. I had zero idea where I was, but the good thing about iPhones was the map. I decided to steal his iPhone. I didn't even care if he tracked me down. I was never letting him in my panties again.

"Dirty bastard." I muttered, and turned the phone on as I walked to the gate. It didn't open. I sighed and looked back. Servario was walking down the very, long driveway.

"Great." My clutch vibrated at the same time he shouted something at me. I ignored Servario and took the FaceTime call. It was Coop, not Jack.

"We have a problem."

I could see the seriousness on his face, "What?"

He closed his eyes and pinched between his eyes.

"What, Coop?"

He looked at me and shook his head, "The protection team has gone missing. They have hourly check-ins with someone, and it's been five hours since a check-in has happened."

My breath was stolen. I shook my head, "No."

He nodded, "I know. Your mom, more than likely, got the kids away, but...I still want to know. We need to figure out what's happened."

It was my worst-case scenario. There was nothing I could do, from where I stood. "I need to find them. Come get me."

He nodded and the call ended.

I turned and looked at the gate; there was no way I was climbing over it.

I turned my back and waited for Servario to hurry up and come drag me back. The defeat and fear were all consuming. How could I find my family, if he was holding me captive?

Servario chuckled, "You're taking my clothes again. I think you've forgotten the deal we have about you taking the things I bought you."

I looked down, grinning, hiding the terror I was feeling. I shook my head, "You didn't buy this for me. I stole it."

"Same thing. It's mine. You're mine."

I fought the tears in my throat, "Fine, have them back but I'm not yours."

I pulled down the shorts, luckily the shirt was long enough to cover my bare ass. I noticed a guard in the guardhouse across the huge driveway. He looked confused.

Servario shouted at him, "Take a break and turn off the cameras!"

The guard closed the blinds.

I bit my lip and lifted the shirt up. It was pulled down hard and fast, dragged against my skin. His huge hands pinned it to my sides, "Stop that," he scolded.

I shook my head, "You are distracting me on purpose. I see it now. Your role in this, from the beginning was to distract me. Tell me the truth. My kids are missing. You tell me the God damned truth." I was shaking from the bad things rolling through my mind.

I stared at the massive wrought-iron gate that dwarfed even him.

His words came slowly, "You were so wrapped up in them at first, it was so easy. You missed so many things, running here and there and everywhere with the kids. Then you got bored. I was scared you would see the truth then. I was about to intervene, when you found hot yoga."

I turned to face him, shoving him, "ARE YOU HIGH? WHAT DOES THIS HAVE TO DO WITH MY KIDS?"

He kissed the top of my head, looking grim, "The secret must be kept at all costs."

It hit me like a ton bricks in the head, "You're the Master Key…" The words left my dry mouth. I felt him nod against the top of my head, "Who better, than a man suspected of a thousand bad things."

Chapter Fourteen

Why mommy, what BIG shoes you have!

We hadn't spoken in hours.

He wouldn't answer a single question or tell me where we were going, so it didn't matter. I didn't want to talk, unless it was Q&A time, anyway.

My foot tapping was getting on his nerves, I could tell.

I looked down at the outfit I was wearing and shook my head, "Why don't you have normal clothes for women on the jet?"

He gave me a sideways look, "You're the only normal girl, ever to come on here. You could have stayed in the other outfit. Lord knows, all you care about is comfort." His tone was mocking.

I rolled my eyes, "Yes, maybe you could have found me a piece of cord to hold the shorts up. Look, I don't dress like I'm homeless, all the time."

He coughed, "You aren't exactly a sex kitten either."

I glared, "The other outfit would have suited the house slippers of yours I stole."

He gave me another look, "You make sure those get back to the house. They were a gift from my mother."

I sneered, "You have a problem."

He looked hurt, "What? My mother bought them for me."

I tapped my heel and tried not to look down at the sexy heel, or think about the fact they were spiciest shoes, I'd ever donned. I wished the tight pants were half as comfortable, but they cut into my slight mommy tummy fiercely.

Steve looked back at me, "For the love of God and all things holy, stop tapping your damned foot."

I scowled, "No."

Servario snorted, "We land in eight minutes, children. Shut it."

Steve scowled and turned back around.

I wanted to tap louder. My nerves were on fire. I needed to hold my babies.

I distracted myself with a question, I assumed he would actually answer, "Why are we always flying? Is this really how you live?"

He laughed, "We need to keep moving. I can't afford a mistake right now." And that was it.

I rolled my eyes at him, "Fine, be aloof."

We landed and I forced Steve and Servario to run to the car. Well, as fast as my heels would go. The salty smell of the Boston harbor made me relax a bit.

I watched out the window as we drove to wherever we were going.

"So you called young Cooper and explained we would meet them tomorrow?" he asked distractedly.

I nodded, "I gave them my word, that you meant them no harm and were not working with the military or government; I told them you just wanted the Burrow."

He chuckled, "Have I ever worked with them? I like nothing better, than to watch them squirm."

My stress levels were too high. I didn't want to listen to him speak, but I needed answers, "Where are my children?" I pestered again.

He shook his head, "I'm not in the position to tell you that."

I growled, "No one is ever in the position to tell me anything."

He cocked an eyebrow, "Do you know much about your mother, Evie?"

I swallowed and looked back out the window.

He laughed, "You do know. I was wondering, when they would let it spill. Now that you know, I can tell you, your children are safe. I can also tell you, no one would care for them the way your mother will." His eyes sparkled, "She has kept you alive."

"You know my mother?"

He nodded, "I do."

I felt sick. An arms dealer, who was secretly the Master Key for the covert op my father had dedicated his life to, knew my family better than I did.

"Is my sister safe?"

He chuckled, "Never. She is a walking disaster."

What didn't he know?

The car stopped in a neighborhood I didn't recognize. The houses were smaller and older. "This doesn't really look like your type of neighborhood."

He gave me a blank stare, "They're inside, smartass."

I frowned, "How do you do it? How do you know everything?"

He laughed, "I know people, who know things."

"Like what?" I crossed my arms and got comfy in the seat.

He shook his head, "Go inside and tell them to hurry up. We have ten minutes."

I noticed the darkness of his eyes; they were missing the green altogether.

I unbuckled my seat belt and crawled across the seat to him, climbing onto his lap and straddling him. I lowered my face and licked along his neck to his ear. I bit down on his lobe. He was a sex addict, there was no doubt taunting him would get me information. I ground my pelvis into his and sucked his lobe, "What do you know?" I whispered.

His hands roamed my back, settling on my hips where he gripped me hard. I made my way, kissing and sucking, to his cheek and placed feather-light kisses on either side of his face. "If you tell me what you know, things between us could be different," I muttered and brushed my lips against his.

He was frozen, either terrified or about to attack.

I kissed him once more, "You want me to play along next time, Servario? You want me to suck things? Bite things?" I leaned to the other side and whispered into his other ear, "Stroke things?"

He shifted us both, nestling his erection between my legs better.

I sat back, grinning ear from ear, "Maybe you want me to put on a show for you? Let you pick the outfit, the shoes, and the toys?" I bit my lip.

He swallowed; the darkness had overtaken his eyes in a dangerous way.

"We'll see," I muttered and opened his door, climbing off of him and walking up to the house.

I winced at the thought of him forcing any of that.

If ever there was a bluff, that was it. I didn't have a show or any sexual talents. I could cum and hold my legs up. James wasn't seeking it elsewhere, because I was too much in the sheets.

I just prayed Servario didn't know that yet. The terrible blowjob I'd given him in the shower, might have ruined my chances at seducing him. But I was willing to try. I needed him hard, weak, and under my spell. I just needed to learn how to cast one first.

Luce opened the door to the dingy house, looking confused and cautious. "How the hell are you here?" she asked.

I shook my head, "He must have known you took the phone and bugged it. He's onto your every move. He's a savage stalker."

I could hear Servario walking up behind me on the gravel driveway, "Except fleeing the hotel. I wasn't aware you would actually do any of that, not naked anyway," he said flatly.

I looked back at him and noticed he was walking funny. Luce looked down at his groin and nodded, "Welcome to casa del dumpo."

We entered and instantly, I was hit with the smell of fried food. Servario looked like he might throw up. I felt like I might.

Coop came around the corner with a gun out, "What the fuck? You said we were meeting tomorrow."

Servario sighed, "Yes well, that was for the benefit of the government agents tracking you with those cell phones you buy illegally. Please feel free to leave those here. We need to hurry. We have four minutes before they're here. I wanted them to think that we were picking you up tomorrow. They aren't as smart as they think they are."

I looked back, "It was ten minutes."

He shook his head, "That was before your display in the car. Let's move."

He turned his back on Coop, who was still pointing his weapon on him.

Coop shook his head, "You played right into his hands, Evie."

I shrugged, "He's all we've got right now. I need to find my kids." I didn't want to tell them, he was the Master Key.

Servario shook his head with his hand over his face, "Well, that's all the poverty I can take. Let's, shall we." He pointed at the doorway. When Coop didn't speak Servario turned and left with Luce following him. She smiled back, "He's sexy. I'm game. It's better than this shit hole."

I scowled at the dingy insides, "What is this place?"

Jack came out with a plate of food, "My old roommate's mom's house. She died and he travels a lot, so he hasn't sold it yet. He isn't here. He's in Thailand. He said we could stay, and apparently, he's rented the basement out to a nice couple of chubby people with their own deep-fry machine. It's in the house. She made this fish and chips right downstairs."

I laughed and stole a fry, "Those have been around since before you were born, whippersnapper."

He beamed, "I'm getting my mom to buy one."

"You eat whatever you want and stay skinny, don't you?" I asked.

"Yup." Jack laughed and took the plate of food to the car. He sat up front.

I looked at Coop with the gun in his hands still, "Let's go."

He holstered it and sighed, "This is a mistake. Later when he sells us down the river, you remember I said this was a mistake, and that you were thinking with your dick."

I closed the door behind him, "I will. Don't worry, I already have my apology planned out. Have you heard anything about the kids and my

The End of Me

mom?"

He shook his head, "Nope."

I almost sobbed a tiny bit. He walked with me out to the car, "You okay?"

I shook my head, "I hardly know. I need my kids." I didn't trust Servario's word that they were fine. Not yet.

He looked concerned, as he squished into the back seat. I sat up front with Jack and made him share his food.

"Good God, I wish we had brought a larger vehicle. That stinks. Please throw it out the window," Servario asked, sounding snooty. He clearly had never had to stuff a bunch of people into a car before.

I shook my head, "No. Steve's eating some now too."

Servario opened his window and made a sighing noise.

"Is the tartar sauce homemade too?" Steve asked with a big mouthful.

Jack nodded, "Yes. I watched her make it, while the fish was frying. Amazing woman."

Coop snorted, "Size of a damned Buick, you mean."

Jack looked back, "You hush your mouth. That woman was a chubby angel. She made me homemade donuts yesterday. I'm marrying a chubby woman. I decided this just yesterday."

I laughed and dragged a fry through the fatty-mayonnaise tartar sauce, "Never trust a skinny cook."

Steve glanced at me, "I thought you were a good cook."

I beamed, "Are you calling me skinny?"

He nodded, "You are skinny. Don't be one of those skinny girls, who doesn't know she's skinny."

I gave Coop a death stare, "It doesn't help when people call you fat, all the time."

Coop looked less than impressed, "I never said you were fat. I said lazy and old."

The same homicidal look I usually had on my face when I was with him, appeared. I turned around, crossing my arms.

Servario muttered, "Say something rude like that again, and I won't need to leak your location."

Coop laughed. I glanced back at him, "Yeah. Look who has the arms dealer on her side? This old, lazy bitch, that's right."

Coop's eyes gleamed with the things he wanted to say. He gave me a grin and a wink instead. I shook my head and turned around; it wasn't the response I was expecting.

We drove out of the city to a small, private airport.

Steve parked the car and walked ahead. I climbed out and followed him. Servario hurried along, "Hurry. They're close behind us."

"Who?" Coop asked running for the plane. I cursed my choosing the sexy Christian Louboutin platform, patent-leather jade-colored pumps. They were so pretty. I was never parting with them. I forced Servario to give Roxy money, so she would stop complaining when I tried them on.

"You look like a Bratz doll," Luce said with a smile.

I laughed, "His planes have clothes on them. They're all designer and amazing. It's a fun distraction."

Her eyes lit up, "What sizes?"

I shrugged, "Fours and a couple things in six. Shoes are all size seven. I can squeak into the fours, if I don't eat or breathe."

She wrinkled her nose, "I'm a six for sure, but I can definitely fit the shoes."

I whispered, "You have to sneak them past Roxy. That girl has a problem."

We were all huffing when we boarded. Everyone put on seat belts as the jet took off.

I glanced at Servario, whispering, "How did you know they were coming?"

He nodded, "I have a friend. He keeps tabs on CI, CIA, MI6, the UN, and Homeland Security. Thus far, they don't know we have them." He looked at Coop, Jack, and Luce sitting up a few rows from us with Steve. "They just think I have you for all the fun I can handle."

I grimaced, "What?"

He nodded, "They sold you to me for information. James found documents linking me to the Burrow. It's what I have been terrified, you would find. I don't know how James did it. The man was a bumbling idiot. But, even a broken watch is right twice a day."

I gulped, "They knew you were asking for me for sexual purposes?" Horror was smeared across my face. "Why not just kill me? Why do that to me?"

"Luring your dad." He gave me a stern look, "The only stipulation was the fat man and Derringer. CI wanted something on you, something they could lure your father with."

"They told you that?"

He shook his head, "No. I know because of sources."

I frowned, still whispering, "CI knows he's alive?" I'd barely had time to register it myself.

"Yes. It was in the documentation James must have found. You must have had something at your house, something that linked me and your father to the Burrow. Information that was from after he had died. I played along and said I had been working your dad over all along, because I had to have the Burrow. I acted like I was willing to do anything to get it. They wanted to make your life so hard, that your dad would be forced out of hiding. They were trying to frame you for a variety of things. Mob ties and other unsavory things. Prostitutes and murderesses lose their children."

I gasped, "You let them humiliate and frame me?"

He laughed so quietly, I barely caught it. He shook his head again, "No. I only let them humiliate you. I own the casino and the hotel. I would have faked the recording, before I let them frame you. You ran when I was trying to help you. Fortunately, I didn't have to. You are a bit of a genius when it comes to spy work."

I looked at Coop and shook my head, "No. It was them. They set it up perfectly." I looked back at him, "You still let everyone believe you were having sex with me, against my will. How could you do that? And why did they believe you wanted the Burrow so badly?"

He gave me a look, "Really? I'm a gunrunner, Evie. I always want anything to do with weaponry. Your pride is nothing, compared to the secrets I keep. I'm sorry you were embarrassed to be with me. Now you know how I manage. But if it makes you feel better, I also told them that I wanted you, because I wanted to avenge the death of my father, more than anything."

My brow knit, "Is that true?"

He nodded and whispered, "I told them I wanted to work out a few weeks of fun with the daughter of the man, who had destroyed my family. Your running, only made me look like a monster. I suppose I owe you a thanks for keeping up my appearances."

My insides started to tingle, "My dad killed your dad?"

He gave me a look, "It was the bitter end of the Cold War and the Star Wars were out of control; everyone's dads were murdering someone. Mine caught wind of the Burrow. He wanted it. Your father, being the Master Key, was dispensed to remove the interest in the Burrow. It's our job."

"I'm sorry."

He shook his head, "Don't be. Your dad saved my life. I was eighteen and on CI's payroll, not to mention, given the freedom and finances to do whatever the hell I wanted. I ran the family business the same as I always had, to avoid suspicions. Only I didn't have to worry, the way my father did. I was given resources. I was able to develop the business and make my family more money, than we could ever spend."

I pointed at his face, "You've got a bit of arrogance in your teeth."

He chuckled, "You Americans have a saying for that... don't hate the player, hate the game." A sickening amount of disgust was filling me, as I processed the fact he'd told me such nice things, and yet, had bargained to have me.

The jet hit cruising altitude and Coop was out of his seat and back with us, within seconds. He knelt in the seat in front of me, looking us both over, "What the fuck?"

Servario sighed.

I nodded, "He doesn't like swearing, unless it's referring to sex."

Coop rolled his eyes, "I care about the terrorist's feelings."

Servario's gaze lowered, "I am not a terrorist."

"Arms dealer... terrorist... same shit, different pile of shit."

I laughed, "Wow, this could be fun but let's not do this. Not on a plane."

Coop tilted his head, "Your call."

Servario scoffed, "I'm comfortable with my cock's size and how far it can piss, Cooper."

Coop's look didn't improve. His steel-blue eyes didn't get less intense, and his jaw didn't ease up on its clench. He looked ready to go.

I put a hand on his arm, "When we land, we will talk about it. Right now, we need to remember that none of us can win this alone."

He nodded and placed a hand over mine, holding it to his arm. He squeezed, "Keep telling yourself that it's all going to work out, and that he doesn't have an ulterior motive. It'll make banging him, that much easier."

Servario growled.

Coop got up and left for the seats at the front.

I swallowed and looked at Servario, "He shouldn't be able to bother you, if fucking me was the only thing you and I had going."

He gave me a look, but I couldn't see the answers on his face.

Then something else occurred to me. "Why did you actually make me have sex with you? I get that you lied about wanting revenge for your father's death to appease the CI and CIA, but you didn't have to actually do it. You could have just taken me to the hotel and made me kill the fat man, and that would have been the end of it. Or we could have run from the beginning, like we've been doing. You could have told me the truth."

He smirked, "Evie, I wasn't lying to them; I wanted you. Not to mention, I needed to keep up the façade of sex-addicted arms dealer."

I shook my head, "You are addicted to sex. I can tell. I think you did all of this to use me, even if it was just a little. You haven't told me anything, or utilized the time we had to help me, or my father."

He raised his eyebrows, "No, I utilized it to fuck you, a lot. I've always wanted to have sex with you. Well, before you were married. With James you were so sad and lonely. I saw you before, when you were twenty-one. You were full of life and excitement, and piss and vinegar. I didn't know that girl was gone, until I saw you about six months ago, when I discovered James had knowledge of the Burrow. I started watching you the same time this lot did." He nodded towards Coop and continued, "When James died you seemed even worse, until you found out about the affairs. That's when I saw it. There it was—a tiny spark of the girl who was once there. She resurfaced for a moment and I knew she wasn't lost, only buried in your sad existence."

The tingle in my belly grew, "You made me have sex with you for fun?"

He shrugged, "I didn't make you do anything. You did it all on your own. I needed to keep up my reputation, and I needed it to be hard on you, or they would have suspected something. Guys like me don't fall for or help girls like you. You wanted everything we did."

I shook, "No. I did it because I thought I had to. You scared the hell out of me. You made me kill someone. We could have run. I thought I needed to keep my children safe. I thought I was…oh my God." I unbuckled and walked to the back of the plane. I closed the door to the bathroom and sat on the toilet.

I did it, because I wanted to. I wanted him. I was an idiot and slowly becoming a ho.

I shook my head. There was no room left for the things still floating outside, waiting to be dealt with.

My throat got thick. I turned and threw up lunch from the plane ride to Boston.

I flushed and washed my face and fled for the safety of the dressing closet.

I sat there, dumbfounded, until Luce came into the back.

"This it?" she asked, already pulling her shirt off.

I laughed because it was better than crying.

She started pulling things on. Her tight, fit body was leaner than I thought.

She fit the four perfectly.

She made a face at the tightness and plucked at it, "See, too tight."

I sighed, "It's perfect. That's how it's supposed to fit."

She looked at it and wrinkled her nose.

Roxy pulled back the curtain. Her expression was fierce for thirty seconds until she clapped, "Makeover!"

I laughed and Luce moaned.

Roxy pointed, whispering savagely, "You bitches want to try on my clothes and steal my shoes. Then I get to make over the lesbian."

Luce looked wounded, "I'm not gay."

I laughed harder and got a better seat for the show.

Roxy nodded, "Yes, you are. You just didn't realize it yet. Here, feel these." She grabbed Luce's hand and placed it on her perky breast. Luce shook her head and attempted to pull her hand back, "No... no... this is wrong. Please, don't make me."

Roxy frowned, "I have very nice breasts. Lesbians always like them."

Luce looked at me, pleading for help with her eyes. I shrugged, "I seriously thought you were gay."

"Hah!" Roxy started massaging her own breasts with more vigor, of course still using Luce's hand.

Luce scowled, "You guys suck. I had a boyfriend named Lance, up until three weeks ago. I'm not gay."

Roxy and I burst out laughing, "Lance is such a gay name. He's a closet gay too."

Jack walked into the back room grinning, "I suspected this was what the girls change room looked like. One girl watching, while the other two made out."

I threw a tissue box at him. He laughed and ducked back out. He folded his arms, staying in the entryway.

Roxy closed the curtain, "No. You can't see her, not till we're done."

I folded my arms around myself and hugged, holding me together.

Roxy set to work. I felt myself withdraw from them. They chatted and laughed. I didn't have it in me.

"You okay?"

I looked up at Luce and smiled, "No."

Roxy shook her head, "I tried to warn you. He's a pig."

My smile grew, "He is. I like him, I don't know why. I can't make myself hate him. He's lied from the start, hidden my children away from me, used me." The last part of the sentence was nearly silent. I didn't want to face that part because he was right when he said, I let him do it all. I wanted it and him.

I hadn't even worried about my children, not properly.

Roxy vanished through the curtain and came back with a fishbowl-sized glass of wine.

I smelled it, "Thanks."

I sipped and looked down into it, like it was a magic crystal ball and would tell me my future.

Sighing, I drank and watched as Roxy made Luce, into something I never imagined possible, delicate.

She wore an asymmetrical navy Marc Jacob's dress that hit mid-calf and had only one arm. The line of the dress ran across her tight and perky chest. She had cleavage and even a little side boob with the bare arm and shoulder. She lifted her delicate-looking foot with the Jimmy Choo glittery platform sandal and shook her head, "They look and feel like ankle boots, but they're sandals. They're really comfy."

I laughed, "That's because they cost a grand, no doubt."

Roxy nodded, "Yeah, that's about the price. The lace-looking shoe is what makes it a sandal, but the lace coming all the way up to your ankle, gives you the sturdiness of boots. Jimmy Choo is a genius." She handed her a small, blue Coach shoulder bag and I marveled.

"You look amazing."

Luce smiled at me, "I look pretty."

It wasn't the response I expected from her.

I nodded, "Roxy, you have done an amazing thing here."

She beamed and clapped again, "I love it!"

Luce took my hand as I put down the empty fish bowl. I could feel the bottle of wine I'd drank. We walked out to the front of the plane.

Servario looked back, taking a double take.

Coop's jaw hung open and Jack dropped his iPad onto the floor.

Steve looked over and grinned. He looked hungry.

Luce's dark eyes were smoky and sexy. She looked almost Egyptian with the makeup.

Her dark hair, that I had imagined was short, was actually very long. It hung in a side ponytail over the bare arm in tendrils and small curls. Her lips were red, Russian Red.

Her nails were navy to match the dress but tipped with stark white, also matching the trim of the dress. The hem and neckline were lined with stark white. The navy and white almost had a mariner look to it.

She was a model with her tanned, tight skin and zero body fat. The curve of her arm was still thicker, but in a lean and sexy curve.

She made Roxy look plain, which was a feat.

Servario turned back around, "We land in half an hour."

Luce looked down, blushing. The other three men were still standing and staring.

Coop closed his mouth, "You look hot."

Steve nodded, "Too hot."

I went to my seat and buckled in.

Luce walked to hers and instantly Jack was sitting next to her. Steve sat on the other side.

Luce shook her head, "There are plenty of other seats, you two scram."

Steve got up, but Jack stayed.

Steve sat in his regular chair. I looked down and tried to focus my eyes. I was drunk.

Servario didn't talk to me. I was stewing inside.

I glanced over at him, "Are you trying to push me away still? Is that why you said those things to me?"

He looked up from his laptop, "What?"

I whispered, "Are you trying to push me away? Is that why you said that?"

He looked confused, "Which part?"

I felt disgust slither down my throat, "You just wanted sex?"

He licked his lips, "No. I had to protect myself, and I couldn't let anything happen to you. Your father saved me once, I owed him that. I had to keep you and your children safe. Pretending to be interested in the Burrow and you, made it possible for me to protect you and not risk myself. Yes, I risked your reputation but that was the cost. There is always cost with me, Evie. I did try to warn you... As far as the sex was concerned, it was an added bonus. You wanted it too. It had been ages for you; you seemed receptive to it."

I couldn't fight the fury making its way to my face, "I have a hard time believing you went to that effort to fuck me. Why me? Why not just the whore from your room?"

He shrugged, "I told you, I had always wanted to, and then after seeing you so angry and desperate, I knew you would be into some fun."

I almost gagged, "What about the bank accounts, and the payroll, and the money James had left behind?"

He pointed at the computer, "It's there for you and your children. You may have it, if and when, I am safely back to being a scummy arms dealer, and you are back to being the prudish mother you were."

I looked forward, "What about them?"

He shook his head, "I don't know."

"What about me?"

He looked grave, "I don't know."

I felt sick, "You said I was yours."

He gave me a grim smile, "I said a lot of things to get in your pants. Like you said, I really am a sex addict. It's more fun if you give yourself to me, than if I am forced to take what I want."

"Will you let us live?"

His eyes narrow as he thought on the answer, but never spoke.

I unbuckled my seatbelt, needing to be away from him.

I walked to the front of the plane and sat next to Jack. I buckled my belt and tried not to think about how sick it all was—how sick Servario was.

I needed to warn them that he was going to kill them, but I needed my kids more.

Chapter Fifteen

Silent as the grave you promised me

When we landed it was dark and humid. I wasn't excited about the tight pants I was wearing in the heat. We walked to the limo waiting for us on the dusty tarmac. Looking back, the sleek, white jet and stretched, black limo looked out of place at the tiny rundown airport. I slumped into a seat and closed my eyes, blocking the world out.

We drove for what felt like an eternity. The limo bumped along the road, until we reached our destination and the vehicle came to a stop. I opened my eyes, seeing a look of worry on Coop's face. I nodded subtly.

The doors opened. My heart started to pick up pace as we got out into the damp heat. We were outside of a villa of sorts. There was a huge gate. As it opened Servario leaned in, "You will be sleeping in my room tonight." Chills ran up my spine.

We entered the courtyard of a beautifully lit home. Torches lit the way down the courtyard. "The way to the sea." Servario pointed.

The home was massive and every room was lit, making it warm and inviting. We walked into the house, greeted by a small woman in a maid's uniform.

Servario held his hand out to everyone, "Pick rooms in the wing to the right, shower and rest up. We leave again tomorrow."

Luce stepped out of the heels, "Night." She walked down the hallway. Jack followed her but Coop watched me for a second.

"You coming?"

I glanced sideways at Servario speaking with Steve, and shook my head, "You know how us agents are, always thinking with our cocks."

He saw it. He knew what I meant. "Fuck," he mouthed and walked down the hall, "Night, Evie."

I nodded, "Night, Coop."

I was almost trembling when I looked at the men talking, "Which way to your room?"

Servario pointed down the hall the opposite way my team went. I walked past his arm and headed for the room.

Of course it was ridiculous. It was oversized and lush. If I hadn't seen his cock I would assume he was trying to make up for things with the extravagance in his life. I closed the double door and found my way into the huge ensuite. I started a bubble bath and stripped down, tying my hair up. He had salts and bubbles and soaps, all in a dish. I climbed into the steamy tub, nearly moaning. The tub was an oversized, corner unit.

I closed my eyes and planned my next move. I would seduce him, tie him up maybe, and get them out. But was that risking my kids? Did he have them or did my mother or did he have them all? Where had Fitz gotten the private jet? Why was my father in hiding and did my mother know? What did I know for a fact?

Nothing. Everything was up in the air.

James might be alive, or not.

Servario might be the Master Key, or not. My team might be murdered, or not.

My kids might be safe, or not.

I might be kept alive, or not.

Nothing was left, nothing was a guarantee.

I heard a zipper and opened my eyes. Servario dropped his pants and pulled his shirt off. I closed my eyes, but he didn't have a shower like I thought he might. He stepped into my tub, pushing me over to a side, to accommodate him.

The water level rose, nearly touching the top of the tub.

"What are you doing?" I asked, not raising my voice.

"I am enjoying my last night with you."

My stomach sunk. "You're going to murder me tomorrow?"

He didn't answer me. I opened my eyes, startled by the look on his face.

"Just promise not to hurt my kids." The words weren't a plea. They were a demand. My life for theirs.

He nodded, "I will guard them with my life."

Tears leaked from my eyes, "Why are you doing this?"

His lip quivered as he mouthed something and I read his lips, "The secret must be kept. There is no price too high. No matter what it is, I will pay it to protect the world from the chaos it could bring."

He didn't speak aloud in his own home? Were we ever safe? He was always mouthing and whispering. He was always silent, unless he was showboating his bad qualities. Then he was loud and slightly demented.

He turned on the loud jets as he picked up one of my feet and started to rub, "Tell me something you don't want to."

I frowned, barely hearing what he'd said, "I like you. I don't know why, but when it's just you and me, and say, some bubbles or a bed, I like you." I spoke in the same low whisper he did.

He nodded.

"Tell me something you don't want to."

He grinned, "I joined the mile-high club with you. I have never had sex on my jets, ever."

I laughed silently, still too-near tears for it to not sound like crying, "Didn't see that coming."

"If you could do anything in the world, for the next year, what would it be?"

I frowned.

He chuckled murmuring, "Humor me."

Arching an eyebrow, I spoke softly, after thinking for only a second, "Take my kids to an ashram in Thailand and learn to be a Yogi. Let them homeschool for the year and run around on a private beach, like Swiss Family Robinson, only the Thai edition. Then I would rent a house in France and I would take them to museums and galleries, and the ruins of France. I would winter in the Alps and ski. And I would probably finish the year off in Australia, or Greece, or somewhere completely different. Maybe on a yacht." The words each brought a different flash of images, I could imagine every moment. I could see their faces.

He nodded, "I knew you were high maintenance, deep down."

I laughed bitterly, still leaking tears.

His eyes looked the same as mine, devastated.

"What about after that? Would you go back to Boston?"

I searched his face for where it was all going, "You mean if I could and be safe?"

"Yes."

I nodded, "I would. My kids are in an amazing school. They love their friends and sports. They excel in the things they do. I would go back. I would need a different house though, maybe neighborhood. James fucked some of the neighbors as well."

He coughed, "That man makes me look like a preacher."

I gave him a look, "Yeah, maybe one of the ones who they have to keep moving 'cause he is always in the paper for bad things."

He pinched my toes.

I pulled back my foot. He grabbed the other one and started to massage it.

"Evie, if things were different and you were just a girl and I was just a guy, would you go to the Alps with me for Christmas?"

The question hurt my insides. I shook my head, "No."

He nodded, "I see." He paused, "May I ask why?"

I blinked a tear down my cheek, "I don't think I can ever forget the conversation we had on the plane."

A soft smile grew on his face, "Fair enough."

We lay in silence until, finally, I stood up, dripping water on him, "I need some sleep. Do you have some pajamas I can borrow?"

He shook his head, "No, you may not wear any."

I climbed out and dried myself with, what was probably, the softest towel on the planet. The queen probably didn't have as nice of a towel. I walked naked to his bed and climbed in.

He got out and walked across the room in the dim light coming from the bathroom.

"Should I sleep in the closet or are you not having company over tonight?"

He chuckled, "You stay right where you are."

My stomach tensed, "Gustavo, you can't be serious."

He turned sharply, grinning, "You never call me that."

I tilted my head, "I should sleep in clothing. I just…I can't—, not with you. Not ever again."

He laughed and fiddled with a drawer of things, "All I ask is for five minutes to persuade you otherwise."

I shook my head, "No."

"Don't say no to me." He pointed at me and walked back across the room to turn off the light in the bathroom.

He climbed into the bed, dragging me across it to him. He wrapped himself around me and whispered in my ear, "You want to know my perfect year, assuming I had another one to live?"

I nodded. I was scared of him. Not the right kind of fear though. It was a fear he was going to break my heart, after only a week of knowing each other.

His words were breath only, tickling my ear, "It would start with spooning you for a whole night, like you deserve to be. Then I would do everything in my power to ensure your life was the way you wanted it to be. I would say that I would die for you, Evie, but that won't guarantee your safety. I would spend my whole year in your shadow, protecting you and earning the place I want to be in your heart. So that you would invite me for Christmas in the Alps." He kissed my cheek, "I need one last show out of you tonight. Someone is watching me and I don't know who. Please, let me play bad guy. Can you do that?"

Tears were streaming down my face, I gave myself the moment and then shut it off. I turned to him, speaking loudly, "You have five minutes to make me want it. But you have to stop whispering that dirty shit in my ear."

I could see the glossiness of his eyes in the moonlight, filtering in when he nodded, "I knew you'd come around."

I woke hours later and looked over at him. He was sleeping still. I cuddled in and let everything he had said be more than it probably was.

Flashes of the night before crept in my brain, making me blush. I'd ridden him for the first time. It was amazing. My body was clenching just from remembering.

"You're making me sweat," he uttered, not opening his eyes.

I smiled, "You made me sweat last night."

He grinned, "You liked it."

I bit his arm lightly, "You liked it."

He opened one very green eye, "I did."

His smile was infectious. I dragged my hands across his torso, "I'm hungry."

He chuckled, "I'll see is Matilda has any raisin bran for you."

I swatted him and climbed off the bed. "I want more of Pierre's waffles."

He lifted his head and watched me pull on clothes, I stole from his drawer, "Stop stealing my clothes and no more waffles for you. You aren't even allowed to come over anymore."

I rolled my eyes, "Whatever."

I looked down at his shorts and black t-shirt, "These almost fit. Were you slimmer before?"

He shook his head, "I called ahead a few days ago and asked Matilda to get you some of my clothes, from when I was a boy, out of the old bags. I was shoving them in there last night, when you were being rude to me."

The End of Me

I folded my arms, "How am I so predictable to you? How do you guess my every move?"

His eyes sparkled, "You military people are all the same. You follow orders. I knew if I told you to do something, you would."

I snorted as I left the room in search of food.

I found Coop instead.

He gave me a grave look, "You okay?"

I nodded, "Yeah. We're fucked, but I'm okay."

"Why? What did he say?"

I shook my head and walked down the hall, "Nothing. That's the problem. He hasn't told me anything. He doesn't talk to me about James, or the Burrow, or anything. I told him whatever happens, to keep my kids safe and that's the only guarantee I've gotten from him."

He swallowed, "Martin's team hasn't checked in since they went silent."

Worry snuck in, where I had told myself not to. I sighed, "What can we do? Realistically, what are our options?"

He shook his head and led me to the bedroom where Luce and Jack were sitting on a huge bed.

"Morning," Luce smiled. I could see the fear on her face. She looked like herself again, no makeup, or fancy clothes, or big hair. I pointed to their outfits, "Where'd you get clothes from?"

Jack shrugged, "There were laid out already. The lady, who doesn't speak any of the languages I have tossed at her, did it."

I snorted, "How many do you speak, Jack?"

He looked down, "Counting Elvish and Klingon, nine."

I smirked and looked at Luce who was shaking her head, "Dude."

He blushed, "What?"

I crossed my arms, "We need a plan."

Coop made a face, "This place is bugged to fuck. I found seven between my room and this one. I'm assuming we didn't get them all. We've been pretty careful of what we said."

I pointed at the clothes, "And we all put on clothes from here. Probably sewn in the damned hems."

Luce sighed, "Go for a swim?"

I nodded, "Let's."

We walked back out into the main room and out the front door.

There was no one around, "Creepy how there is no staff, huh?"

Coop looked around, "Super creepy. Not to mention, Steve took our guns before we got on the plane."

The path to the ocean was bricked with sand and rock gardens the entire way. The ocean was beautiful and turquoise.

"Where the hell are we?"

Jack smirked, "We are in Mexico, just North of Veracruz."

I frowned, "How the hell did he get us in Mexico without passports or shit?"

Coop picked up the pace, "Not a clue."

We started to run, as we got closer to the sandy beach. We all dove into the waves. They weren't too rough, there was a rocky break, out in the water, not too far from the beach. It got the worst of the moody Atlantic. The beach near the house was more of a pool. The water was warm, and yet refreshing. We swam out against the current, each of us dunking and soaking ourselves thoroughly.

I flutter-kicked and looked back at the house, "He's trying something. I don't know what, but I think he wants to help us."

Coop pointed, "Well, here he comes, swimming trunks and all. Maybe he'll just offer it up."

I laughed when I saw, he truly had on Bermuda shorts and was carrying a stack of towels.

He dropped them on the beach, far from us and jogged for the water. We all watched in silence as he jumped in and swam out.

Servario bobbed and looked us all over before speaking softly, "I was hoping you would come out here. Let's all pretend to swim and be playful. Whoever is the mole, is watching. Unless of course, it's one of you."

My jaw dropped, "What?"

He nodded, "I have a mole. I didn't know, until recently. My staff is unaware of a lot of aspects in my life, and when I made inquiries about the Burrow, like any arms dealer worth his salt would, I had James up my ass, instantly. My plan was to put it out there and see who bit. James bit instantly."

I looked at Coop, "One of ours, maybe?"

He shook his head, "If there is, it's over my head."

Jack frowned, "Wait, who was Derringer to all this?"

Servario shook his head, "The patsy, your people wanted to blame a lot of things related to all of this on. It's not him. It's someone in my employment. My houses are not safe. My planes weren't safe."

I frowned, "Is the plane safe now?" I asked thinking on the conversation we'd had.

He smirked, "I had something installed, it alerts to issues of that nature. The plane starts and an alarm goes off, it only works in planes and vehicles."

Coop looked confused, "Does anyone know you installed it?"

He shook his head, "No. Impossible."

Coop looked lost, "So you're on our side?"

Servario shook his head, "I'm on her side. Whatever side you choose, will dictate if I'm on your side or not."

I could tell Coop wasn't buying it. Jack nodded, "That actually makes sense. You must have been friends with her dad, and that's why the information James found, tied you together."

Coop's eyes widened, "Her father killed your father when you were what, eighteen?"

Servario's eyes had no green in them, "Let's drop it. It's my business, not yours. Yours is staying alive. Your government has a few key members in it, who won't rest until they've got the Burrow. Those same people, by now, think you all are involved. Running with Evie, when you were told to keep her with me, didn't help your cause. You don't stand a chance at surviving the next forty-eight hours, unless you off them and hide the evidence linking you."

My teeth started to chatter as we floated in the water, "We know the commander is involved."

Coop nodded, "He's been my only contact throughout the whole thing."

Luce nodded, "The eyes on the house. We know for sure that's gonna be one team, following along. They wouldn't risk the information getting out."

Servario licked his lips, making a face from the salt, "Don't forget, there has to be a politician in on this. There is no way the commander got involved, without someone higher up putting it in his face. The only people who really knew about the Burrow were very high in the CIA, UN, MI6, and CI. One of them has opened this can of worms."

I thought and nodded, "We split up and take them out?"

Coop gave me a look, "This is a top breach if we do it. We can be tried with espionage, treason, terrorism, and a variety of other really chargeable offenses. You in for that, with your kids?"

I swallowed and looked at Servario. He shook his head, "She's out. She isn't negotiable. She is a civilian."

My eyes narrowed, "Are my kids safe?"

He shook his head, "Doesn't matter, you aren't in."

I searched his face, "I'm in. This is my father's work, my country's work, my mother's work, and if this ends, my kids can have normalcy again."

"You could die and leave them orphaned—or worse, get caught and shame them with the lies they charge you with."

I swam to shore, "We leave here in an hour. We need to figure out your situation first."

I knew who it was.

I knew who the mole was.

He came out of the water after me, "You aren't in."

I looked back, "You ever sleep with Roxy?"

He sighed, "I told you I won't have you disrespecting her. I truly hired her for the cooking and the OCD. She is very clean. Yes, she's pretty but I don't like to mix business with pleasure."

I put my hands on my hips, "You mixed it with me."

He shook his head, "You have never been anything, but pleasure in my mind."

I bit my lip, "Roxy doesn't know that."

He picked up a towel and dried himself off, "You think it's her?"

I dried off and walked up to the house, "She is it. She's jealous."

He looked back at Coop, Luce, and Jack in the water, still plotting. He sighed, "No way. I never brought women on the plane, and I've never been that way with her."

I shrugged, "You fucked how many chicks on that yacht?"

His eyes burned.

I pointed at him, "I know what it's like to see you with your whores; you're a sex addict. What did you think? You think she was never gonna get tired of the constant, hardcore sexathons you had on board. She told me about them. Women coming on board to cum. She hates you for never picking her, and your obsession with me has only provoked it. I guarantee James got to her, she's the weak link."

He looked sickened, "You are better at this, than I am giving you credit for."

I laughed at him, "No, you were blinded by the tight piece of ass, who you could pay to cook and clean and not have to spoon in the morning."

He didn't laugh. He looked like he might actually be sick.

Chapter Sixteen

Blood debt

We boarded the plane and, instantly, I felt sick. Roxy smiled and waved. Luce, Coop, and Jack were in the dark, but they were still cautious.

"The pilot said he didn't know where we were going?" Roxy said with a smile.

Servario smiled at her softly, "No. I wanted to keep it our secret." He walked past her to the pilot, who I had yet to see.

A brief look of confusion crossed her face, as she went to the back of the plane. I liked her. I hated that she had betrayed a man she suspected of doing horrid things. She knew he was bad and, no doubt, feared quitting. Then James had come along and threatened her, using his government ties to bribe her into working with him. I can only assume it was how it happened, but I was willing gamble on it.

Technically, she had made the right choice, the just choice. But my kids were part of the things that prevented me from helping her.

I let her go to the back of the plane.

I took my seat, my usual seat, and waited for us to take off, and for the shit to hit the fan.

Luce gave me a grave look.

I winked subtly.

Steve hadn't come. Servario had put him to work elsewhere.

It was just Roxy, the mystery pilot, and us.

I stopped paying attention to anything and everything. I had a sickening guilt twisting inside of me.

I was sacrificing another person for my family.

Coop was staring at me when I looked up. He mouthed, "You okay?"

I twitched a no.

I wasn't as good at mouthing things as he and Servario were. I could still read lips as fast as ever.

Coop mouthed again, "You want me to make you feel better?"

I laughed and nodded.

He came over and sat in the pod next to me, Servario's usual spot. I wondered if Servario would care if Coop was sitting there?

Coop leaned in, "You have to let it slide. Just think, she made her bed."

I pressed my lips together and then whispered, "I can't. I have a terrible feeling."

He got up and went to the front of the plane. He came back a minute later with a tray.

I laughed when Coop put it down.

I licked my wrist and held it out. He shook the salt on mine and then his and poured the shots. He poured four instead of two.

He nodded at Jack and Luce. They were sitting beside each other up front, but both got up and made their way to us.

"Oh yeah." Luce laughed and licked her wrist. Jack shook his head, "I'm not good at this one. Tequila makes me throw up."

Luce shook her head, "What is your deal?"

Jack hesitated and licked his wrist. Coop salted and passed out the shots.

He held his up, "To our families, wherever they are. May they be safe, wherever they are."

Jack added, "And may they never know about how close the world comes to ending or what we really do for a living."

I snorted, "Cheers to that."

We clanked, licked, drank and sucked.

Jack walked away, with his glass and a sour face. Luce laughed, "I'll go make sure he's okay."

I looked at them walking back to their seats and gave Coop a look.

He looked at me like I was insane, "Duh."

"What? I didn't know."

Coop shook his head, whispering, "That dress made everyone see her differently. Jack may never be the same."

I laughed and whispered, "I seriously thought she was gay."

He gave me a look, "Why?"

I shook my head, "She seems like one of the boys…."

Servario interrupted my sentence, "You used to be like that." I glanced up at Servario standing next to me. I hadn't even noticed him coming back.

I squinted, "I was not."

Servario folded his arms across his chest, "You were. You were the sharpest shooter, and had to be the fastest runner, and could drink everyone under the table. You were."

Coop laughed, "I heard the same reports."

I looked at him, blushing, "I must have forgotten."

Coop smirked, "The best agents are 'one of the boys'. They fit in; first rule of being an agent, F.I.F.O. It means Fit In or Fuck Off."

I put my hand out for another shot. I looked up at Servario, "What if it isn't her?"

He gave me a look and walked to the back of the plane.

We took off but Roxy never came back, neither did Servario.

Coop poured me a third shot. I couldn't stop my eyes from darting to the back.

I drank the shot smoothly, fighting the shudder I wanted to do.

My belly rumbled.

Coop laughed, "I'm starving too."

I looked over at him, "How are we going to clean this all up?"

He shook his head, "This mess is huge. I don't even know. Right now we're riding with enemy number one. Me, Luce and Jack all went off the reservation, so we're as guilty as you now. They'll find a way to pin this on us too. Being with Servario is only making it easier for them to do it."

I closed my eyes and sighed, "I know, and yet, I have the feeling that he is the only person we can actually trust."

I opened one eye when he didn't say anything. He looked stricken, "I agree," he whispered.

For the strangest of reasons, Coop's words didn't make me feel better.

I closed my eye again and let the comfy pod take me away.

I woke up with a start. I looked around the plane, Luce and Jack were leaned up against each other. Coop was sound asleep next to me.

I heard a noise.

It must have been the thing that woke me up.

I unbuckled and walked to the back of the plane.

"Stop, we shouldn't be doing this here," Roxy said, in between ragged breaths.

My stomach clenched, "Oh God," I whispered to myself.

He was fucking Roxy.

He was betraying me.

I froze and prepared myself for what I was about to see.

Did I want to see it?

I didn't, it didn't feel the same as before. The conversations we'd had since then, changed everything.

But had they? Had I fallen for his smooth lines and sexy ways?

Christ.

She moaned again, "Oh my God, Gustavo... please!"

I reached for the curtain to the dressing room and ripped it back fast.

Her hands were tied to the roof with blood trails running down them. Her face was beaten. Servario's hands were cut from hitting her. He looked back with a savage expression, "Get out."

I shook my head and fought the motherly urge to dive in front of the blow he gave her, with the back of his hand. She cried out again, shaking her head and sniffling. "Please, Evie, help me. Please. I swear, whatever you think is missing or whatever, I didn't do it. I wouldn't do that to you, Gustavo."

Servario shoved me back and closed the curtain. The look on his face was scarier than anything I had ever seen. His eyes were completely black.

She cried out moments later.

I jumped, stepping away from it. My back pressed against the wall.

She was innocent. I was wrong. I had a terrible feeling.

I sunk to the floor, shaking and forcing myself to listen to each strike.

He could beat a woman that badly?

I didn't know him.

She screamed in a long series of shrieks and bleats like a sheep. Whatever he was doing, was bad.

"FUCK YOU!" she screamed.

I could hear him speaking in low, hushed tones.

"EVIEEEEEEE! EVIE, SAVE ME!" she screamed and sobbed.

I didn't know I was shaking, until I felt the still of Coop against me. He wrapped around me, holding me tight to him. Instead of stopping the madness, he carried me to a row of seats and sat, holding me like a child. I was cradled against his chest. But even the distance couldn't stop the screams.

"We have to help her. I was wrong. I was wrong. Please," I pleaded.

Coop shook his head, "You didn't do this, Evie. If he suspects her, then we have to let it play out. We need to know who we're against. Without her, we've got nothing."

The End of Me

I felt tears streaming down my cheeks, "What if she's innocent?"

He shrugged, "There is no magic pill to determine that. Torture is the best way. You've been trained, you know that."

I crawled off of him and sat in the chair next to him, "I haven't been part of this world for a long time. And technically, I was never part of anything like this."

The screaming never died down for a long time.

It started to dull in my mind though.

We flew for a long time before Servario came out. He had blood spatter all over him. He sat next to Coop and I.

"I have a list of names and a location for James." Servario's voice was distant and disturbing.

I looked at him, "Is she... dead?"

He shook his head, "No. I'm not done with her. He stared forward at the wall in front of us with the huge, blank, flat-screen TV on it.

Coop was the one to talk first, "Sorry man, that's rough having to do that to a girl."

Servario clenched his jaw.

I looked down and waited to get off the plane.

We touched down in the dark again. It felt like we were always in the dark.

Servario never tried to touch me or talk to me.

When we landed, a helicopter was waiting for us on the tarmac. We were boarded on it, when I got my first glimpse of Roxy. Her eyes were swollen shut. She was a mess—fat lips and cuts. Her hands were wrapped in soaked bandages. He dragged her from the plane and shoved her in the back. Her blonde hair was ratty and missing in parts.

Luce and Coop shared the same blank expression, whereas I imagined Jack and I were both horrified.

He looked at me, terrified.

I nodded.

We were somewhere warm still. We flew down a coastline, rocky and beautiful. I was lost, completely.

I forced myself to see the stunning things, and not the dying girl in the back, who used to be stunning.

The helicopter circled a huge house. It landed on a large, cement pad.

James was walking down the path from the huge house. My breathing stopped completely, as my heart pounded out of my chest. I felt my face flush. Coop covered my hands with his, "No."

I looked at him.

He shook his head, "No—to what you're thinking or feeling. Shut it off."

I tried, but my kids' faces were all over his. My kids, who I hadn't seen in, what felt like an eternity. My face pinched and balled. I fought tears so hard it hurt.

I sniffled and sighed, "I can do this," I whispered.

We landed. James didn't look up. He walked until the door opened.

Then he stopped, stared and then frowned. His girlfriend was tossed from the helicopter first. Servario had a gun drawn. He passed one to Luce and Coop, as he stepped down.

James put his hands up. He was completely lost and confused.

The End of Me

He hadn't even seen me yet.

I climbed out last, following Jack.

His eyes darted as the helicopter turned off, making a huge wind surround us all momentarily, until it finally stopping spinning.

James' eye caught my face. He put his hands out, "Evie!"

I shook my head and snatched the gun from Luce's hand. I fired at his left kneecap.

He screamed out as crimson started to seep out from this beige, linen pants.

Luce reached for the gun, but when she saw my face, she stopped.

"How could you?" I asked just barely audible.

His face crumpled as he held his knee, "Evie, please let me speak."

I shot at the other knee, missing. He dropped to the ground anyway.

Servario walked away from the nearly falling-over Roxy and came up to me. He looked down, lifting my face up. He brushed his lips against mine, "Let me. You don't want this memory when you look at your children," he whispered into my lips.

I nodded and stepped back. He pulled the gun from my hand and passed it back to Luce. She gave me an understanding look but Coop looked psychotic.

"Is Mel here?" I asked past Servario's back. He wasn't looking at me, he was trying to crawl to his girlfriend, Roxy. She swayed as blood dripped from her bandaged hands.

Finally James looked at me long and hard, "Your father did this, Evie. Not me."

I pointed, "Just kill him. I want him gone for real."

I turned and walked back to the helicopter.

I heard the shot fire but I didn't look back. Then the second one.

I sat in the seat and waited. I wanted to look inside of the house. I wanted to know his secrets. I wanted it all to become clear to me but a voice, probably my father's, told me I didn't really want that.

It told me that I wanted to let this one go. I would find answers in other places too. I didn't just need these answers. These ones would haunt me for all my days.

Chapter Seventeen

Princess Evie

The jet felt haunted as we crossed an ocean. I could only assume it was the Pacific. We were going to Asia. I wondered if he was taking me to an ashram. I needed it.

I looked at Servario, trying not to see the sadistic fuck I'd seen in that room. He looked like I'd killed his cat, when he glanced over at me. "I'm sorry, Evie."

I nodded, "Me too. I'm sorry it was her."

Coop glanced over from the notes Servario must have taken while torturing her. "So Mel is dead. She was the one in the car." That hurt. Mel too, had been used by James.

I shook my head, "He didn't need her anymore, because he had Roxy. Roxy, who wanted to find herself a millionaire like Servario."

Servario stood and walked to the front of the plane.

Coop continued, "James was helping frame you to get your dad out of hiding. He had asked Roxy to take pictures of every meeting Servario went to. After your dad was dead, he and Servario met. Roxy got it on her cellphone so it must have been recent. It was the proof CI needed to use you to bring him out of hiding."

I frowned, "They knew he was in hiding all along? He's been dead for a long time."

He shrugged, "Must have suspected something. Anyway, Servario beat her and broke her and she confessed. The plan was to take the money, leave you screwed and leave the kids with your mom. She actually said James never really cared what happened to the kids. He just wanted his easy life in his beach house with his blonde."

It didn't even hurt anymore. Not even for my kids. I didn't even care a little. I couldn't. If I cared about one thing, all the emotions I was shutting off would find their way in.

I sighed, "He was a douche nozzle."

Coop snorted, "Yeah. Dumb fuck. Who does that to their own family? Anyway, Servario used Roxy's cell to text James and send the helicopter. James was expecting her to get off alone. They were going to start their new life together. Roxy had been letting him in on the progress of the fuck-Evie campaign. Apparently, he was quite satisfied with how it had turned out. You were a fugitive and Servario was forcing sex on you all the time and humiliating you." His tone was filled with disgust.

I blushed at that. My lips curled into a grim smile, "She was thorough."

Servario brought a tray to Luce and Jack and then one to us. It was filled with snacks and things. He smiled at me, "I'm so sorry, Evie. I had no idea it was her. I assumed Steve."

I shrugged, "They got the death they deserved, then I guess." I smirked, "The account is still there right?"

He nodded.

My eyes flashed, "Excellent."

We landed hours later in smoggy Tokyo.

I frowned, "Japan?"

Servario bowed, "Yes, Princess Evie."

The End of Me

We climbed into another helicopter. I shook my head, "It's too much. I need to be away from all vehicles—all. I need a vacation from this vacation."

Jack moaned, "Not another flight."

We sat in our seats and instantly started for the mountains.

Servario grinned, "This is going to take about two hours. So buckle up and try to enjoy the ride." He seemed tense.

I supposed I would too.

I, on the other hand, felt a renewed sense of freedom. My marriage had never had confines that I was aware of. Looking back, I could see the sense of freedom I was feeling was stemming from a lack of confines. Ones I had gotten so used to that I didn't see them.

The money in the account freed me from worry, guilt, and obligation.

The kids were mine. I had never considered divorce, seven months without sex and I never considered divorce. I knew why that was. I never wanted to battle it out like our friends had.

I glanced at Servario and smirked. He was a savage and a complete fiend, and yet he made me feel like a woman. I finally understood the damned song, "A Natural Woman." Looking at him, I would swear I could hear the bloody lyrics.

He scared me.

I liked that. Was there shame in my feelings for him, after everything? I couldn't find any.

We would never fall into a routine. We would never go seven months without sex. I would never be truly safe with him.

I liked that a lot.

Clearly, he wasn't the only freak in the relationship that would never be a relationship.

Looking out over the city, I wondered if he was taking me to my kids? I was scared we were never going to get them back. I couldn't let myself dwell or I would cry.

I closed my eyes and laid my head back.

The next thing I knew, I was being shoved. I opened my eyes with a start.

Jack grinned at me, "We're here."

I looked around, he was waiting for me. Everyone else was outside stretching their legs.

I smiled, "Where are we?"

He beamed, "I could cry. It's genius. It actually makes perfect sense."

I rolled my eyes, "You are such a nerd."

He nodded, "I know."

I climbed out to see nothing but forest.

"What is this?"

Servario gave me a look. I wasn't sure what it meant. "This is where I leave you."

I frowned, "No. What? No. I don't want you to leave."

He nodded, whispering, "I have to. I can never set foot in there. It's a rule. The Master Key may never set foot in the Princess's temple, once he has taken on the role. I know I'm safe right now but they don't know that. They assume I could bring the bad people down on them. I take the role of Master Key and I walk away. Always leading the suspicious people away from this spot. This temple."

I looked around, "What temple?"

He pointed to a small black cave-looking thing, "That's the entrance. You have to go in there and walk until you see the light again." He held a hand out, "I need all of your clothes, and phones, and every piece of electronics." I looked down at the others. When they looked up at me, they could tell something was wrong.

It didn't matter that we griped.

We eventually got naked, one at a time behind the helicopter, and left everything with him. We put on the robes he left us. They were stunning Japanese traditional-looking robes.

Luce smiled when she came from behind it in the robe. It wasn't her usual smile, but it counted as effort, after everything we'd been through.

"It's nice, huh?" I asked.

She nodded, "So pretty."

"You look pretty." I read Jack's lips as he leaned over and whispered it to her.

I gave Servario a pleading look, "Please just come."

He shook his head, "I've broken every other rule for you, Evie. This is one I cannot."

"I can't be strong without you."

He laughed; it was fake, "You are stronger than you think."

"No, I'm not. You have to say that."

He leaned in and kissed my forehead, "Consider inviting me to

Christmas. Please, baby. I want to see you in all your glory, pajamas till noon and everything."

I felt the dam breaking. The tears were winning.

He kissed each of my eyelids, "Go now."

He turned and walked to the helicopter.

The pilot started it up.

I started to sob.

Servario pointed at me. Coop grabbed one of my hands, dragging me to the cave entrance.

We stepped into the darkness and all I could think about, was the light behind me.

We walked for a while before my eyes adjusted. The dark of the tunnel was annoying and never ending. My eyes were sticking from the tears.

Coop never let go of my hand. He squeezed tight, pulling me through.

My CI brain switched on about halfway. Our pace slowed and I knew what was happening.

I never doubted for a second, that each one of us assumed it was a trap of sorts.

We didn't trust Servario, not completely.

We never heard Roxy's story or James'.

We took everything Servario had said at face value.

In the dark, Jack whispered, "Is anyone else seeing that last scene in the movie The Usual Suspects rolling around in their head? You know where Kevin Spacey leaves the police station and his limp slowly leaves."

I nodded, "I have that same bad feeling I had on the plane."

Coop nodded, "I don't know what to expect on the other side of this tunnel."

Luce laughed bitterly, "I'm waiting for him to shoot it with bombs and collapse it."

That was it.

We all started running.

I tripped but Coop dragged me up.

"Light!" Luce shouted back.

We slowed when we saw it get brighter.

It was a door.

When we got closer we could see the light around the edges.

Coop went to the front. He ran his hands on the metal of the door, making an almost-silent scratching noise against it.

"No handle."

I shrugged, "Knock."

He banged lightly.

Something made a grinding noise, and instantly, dust moved in the beams of light we had around us from the door.

It pulled back and light filled the dank space.

My eyes needed a second to adjust, but when they did I didn't believe what I saw.

My father.

"Daddy?" I whispered.

The man looked much older, grey-haired and more wrinkled than before, but he was my father.

His face split into a grin, but I could see the panic in his eyes.

His smile was fake. He wasn't happy to see me.

I wanted to cry but the commander didn't like crying. At least I didn't think he did, but tears leaked from his old, green eyes.

He held his arms out for me. I leapt into them. He wrapped and squeezed and I couldn't breathe but I didn't care.

"Mommy!" I caught the word being screamed from beyond my father and I.

My ears caught it in the distance.

Dad kissed me on the cheek and pulled me back, "Go see them. They've missed you, something fierce."

I nodded and felt the collapse of the walls inside of me.

I broke free of him and ran along the cobblestone. I dropped to my knees and they jumped me.

I cried as hard as they did.

"You took too long!" Jules squeaked at me.

I cried and sniffled, "I'm so sorry. It was more work than I thought."

Coop ruffled Mitch's head, "Hey, kid."

Mitch stood up and crossed his arms over his chest, "Hey, Coop."

I smiled at the way he tried to be a big boy around Coop. They seemed to hit it off the moment they met, back at the house after James' funeral. Jules clung to me for a second longer and then pulled my hand, "Come see. There's a real princess."

I smiled and looked back at Luce and Jack. He mouthed, "I knew it. Ise Grand Shrine temple."

I nodded and gave him the thumbs up, "I don't know what that means?" I mouthed back.

Jack made a face, "What?"

I laughed and said aloud, "Nothing."

I looked back at my dad, "How?" I asked, being cryptic because of the others around us.

Dad grinned, knowing I meant how had they fooled me all along. He shrugged subtly, "A hell of a lot of work."

I nodded, "I bet. So Mom and you both?"

He laughed, "Your mom more than me."

I shook my head, still baffled, "How?"

Dad laughed again, "A hell of a lot of work!" He linked arms with me as Luce and Jack introduced themselves to Jules. She dragged them up the road. Coop and Mitch walked behind them.

"You were right about James, Daddy."

He nodded, "I know, princess. I tried to make him do the right thing by you and I made a bigger mess. I'm sorry. I should have been honest with you. I liked to imagine my rank had an effect on him. The guy was a wiener."

I laughed.

He gave me a sideways glance, "A dead wiener?"

I nodded quickly, knowing he would want full details when we were completely alone.

"Suffer?"

I nodded again.

He sighed, "I take you and Servario met?"

"Yup." I missed him already.

"He's a strange kid too. I like that one though. He came to me when he was twenty-two and asked my permission to date you. I kick myself now for telling him no. I told him the secret was more important. I think he liked you because you were so good at all of this, but telling him no, seemed to make him obsess about you. Well, fat lot of good that did me. Look at where you are. You've met him anyway," he chuckled and I understood something new about Servario. His infatuation with me had been genuine from the beginning, and the challenge of being told no by my father, had only made things worse.

I decided to save that one for later and looked around, changing the subject, "What is this place?"

He glanced around in awe, "This place is perfect for our purpose. It's a Japanese temple that's dedicated to a Goddess. There are 123 temple shrines here. This particular one is forbidden access for regular visitors. No one may enter, and then there's the fact they renovate every twenty years. Anyway, the legend is that a daughter of some guy wandered the woods for twenty years, trying to find the perfect place to worship this goddess. She ended up here in Ise. It's all rebuilt, every twenty years, to maintain the respect of the order of things. The natural decay cycles. So we can be here, moving in amongst the shrines, staying hidden."

I shook my head, "Why would the Japanese ever agree to this? They hate Americans, rightfully so."

He looked down on me intensely, "The Fat Man and The Little Boy. After the Second World War they were dedicated to the preservation of the world. Few cultures care about nature and balance like the Japanese do. Once we dropped the bombs on Hiroshima and Nagasaki, the Japanese royals were in. They wanted the immediate control of the weapons that ruined so much of their country. They gave us their most sacred temple as a show of their dedication to the Burrow. They don't hate Americans, they hate disrespect."

I looked around at the people walking past us. They were multicultural. "So everyone here is a threat to the world in some way?"

He nodded.

"Wow."

He nudged me, "You have no idea. You guys coming here is a huge mess. I'll be lucky to get out alive."

I looked around, "I can imagine. What have you told the kids?"

He laughed, "That they're in Thailand, going to an ashram for meditation. They're pretty mad at you for picking this as a vacation. I told them it was James' idea."

I laughed.

I looked up to see my mom walking down the road. I started to cry again. I ran to her. She wrapped around me, "My baby."

My sister was close behind. She wrapped around mom and me.

"Sissy."

She shook when she hugged me. I knew she would be in the dark. She wouldn't know and wouldn't want to. She was a typical hippie from a typical commune on the West Coast.

"Are you in some kind of shit," Sissy whispered.

Mom gave her a look, "No swearing in the temple."

Sis scowled at me, "How did this happen? We're prisoner here and Dad's alive? What the heck?"

I shrugged, "I got nothing."

She laughed, "I see." She grabbed dad, "You—old man, are in trouble. You broke my heart."

He sighed, "It was all for you girls. I needed to keep you safe." He looked at me, "Speaking of which, you have a date with some people."

I held my robe to my body and nodded, "I figured something would come of it."

He put a hand out for me. I took it and smiled at my mom and sister, "Be back in a bit."

Mom smirked.

We walked up the road, I smelled the blossoming trees and looked around at the beauty of it all.

"They will make you clean this up or die. That's the only option."

I looked up, "What?"

He nodded, and the grim look I saw on his face when he first saw me, was back.

"Dad!"

He shook his head, "My hands are tied. James screwed you hard kid. He put you a pickle, I'm not positive you'll get out of."

I started to panic but he grabbed both my arms, "But I do know, if anyone is going to get out of it, it's you."

I looked at him, "You think so?" My faith in my survival was dwindling.

He nodded, "One hundred percent. If anyone can, it's you. That Coop kid is intense but I really like him. He reminds me of me I think. Luce seems reliable, and Jack is a genius. The kid speaks fake languages."

I laughed weakly, "I know."

"You four are going to have to do something, that no one has done before." His eyes sparkled.

He turned and dragged me up the short hill. We entered a small building that became huge inside.

I saw everyone else in there. Jack laughed, "It's like the Harry Potter tents, way bigger inside."

I sighed, "Let's face the music."

Dad led the way into another room.

We stepped into an elevator. It went down.

I started to get nervous. We stopped and got out into an intense-looking laboratory or tech building. He brought us to a door. He put his hand on it, "Say yes to everything," he whispered.

Coop glanced at me and grinned.

Dad pushed on the door and when we entered I nearly had a heart attack. The room was bright and huge, and set up like a senate. It was filled with people from everywhere.

We walked into the middle and voices started from all sides of the room.

My palms started to sweat. We followed my dad to the center of the circle. He put his hands in the air.

A woman with dark hair, and an evil sort of sparkle in her eyes, spoke, "You have a choice. You will end the threat to the Burrow, or you will forfeit your lives. We have hidden you and your families long enough."

Jack and Luce looked a bit surprised, but Coop seemed like he was expecting it.

"Our countries will offer you support, financing, and intel, but you will have to do the work and clean up the mess. You must stop whoever is looking for the Burrow and get whatever information they have gathered."

I looked at my dad, "Aren't we fugitives as of now?"

He shook his head, "No, something is being done to make it look like Servario took you all captive and hurt you. You will walk from this still unaware and clear of any suspicions." I didn't understand how that was possible at all."

The woman looked at my father, "You and Servario know your jobs?"

He nodded once firmly and turned to me, "I love you more than anything on this planet. There is a custom here on this island." He kissed my forehead, "I give you all my hope and love and strength." He lifted the locket and smiled, "I gave it to you a long time ago."

He kissed the locket and my cheek and turned on his heel in true, military fashion, walking away from me.

I knew then, whatever he and Servario were going to do, he wasn't planning on coming back.

I didn't let myself have the second I needed. I shut it off and looked back at the lady. Her eyes shone when she spoke, "I am sorry for your loss."

My face was strong and brave, and I didn't let the tears flowing down my cheeks affect that.

"You will leave here tomorrow. You will begin something incredible and intense. We are doing something we have never done before. The world is a different place, than it was when we started, and we feel like this is the best way to keep up with the change."

I looked at Coop. He looked lost. That was a bad sign.

She cleared her throat, "Welcome the new Master Keys! Commence the swear-in ceremony."

My stomach dropped. Coop took my hand in his, squeezing it hard.

I wanted to protest. I had kids. I was a single mom. It wasn't fair. Just as I opened my lips, I noticed a man in the background. He was incredibly old. He smiled at me and waved. He had no fingers on his hand. He looked at me with an awe and respect I didn't deserve. Not yet. But I imagined I would one day.

I just needed to figure out how to do it all.

I smiled at the man and looked down at the floor, when I felt my heart attempting to leave my chest.

I put my right hand in the air and spoke the words, but my heartbeat distracted me.

The lady came down and hugged me, "They have made such a sacrifice for you to be able to leave here and live normally; well, to the outside world you will be normal. Even to your own military operation you will be innocent. For that they died."

I looked at her, "They?"

She nodded, "They both had to die. They had to clear the suspicions from your name and the temptation to harm you. Servario will not be suspected as the Master Key or linked to the Burrow. He will look like another greedy arms dealer looking for another weapon. Your father's remains will be found in Mexico and Servario's in Boston. That will be where you lot escaped from. The true Master Key will kill him and help you escape the madness and torture. You must be grateful for the sacrifice they're making."

My breathing picked up, I nodded, "Yes, I am a lucky girl." She smiled and missed the heartache and sarcasm in my voice.

He smiled, "You must leave here tomorrow and you may never come back. The Key must never come near here again. Your father was granted special privileges to come and live here, during his faked death, but that is not something we ever do. This whole mess is because we let him live."

I looked at Coop, Jack, and Luce; that statement didn't sit well with me. Was she going to have us killed when our usefulness ran out?

We walked from the circular room.

"Did anyone else feel like we were just given a death sentence that we're supposed to feel grateful for?" Jack muttered.

I pushed the elevator button but my heart was burning, "Pretty much. Like this is a huge honor, they're bestowing on us." I felt all the floors above me threatening to come down on me. The avalanche of bad things was back. This time it was real. The elevator dinged and we all stepped in like mindless zombies.

We left the next day.

I didn't remember the flight.

I tried to accept the fact we had to be tortured and left in the hotel parking lot, where we were locked in the back of a van. We managed to escape and flee to another hotel where Coop called us in. We were brought in for questioning and cleared, when it became obvious whoever was the Master Key had killed James and Roxy, and possibly Servario. The commander came down and requested we start back after we all healed. We would be the Burrow task force, to stop this sort of thing from happening again. We needed to know what it was, so we could protect our country from it.

The End of Me

It didn't matter to me.

I still needed to give myself the moment I had been denied at the temple.

An agent drove me to my car, which was still parked at the Boston airport.

He dropped me off and drove away. I lifted a bruised hand up into the midday sun and looked at it. It was real. I could feel the dam about to burst inside of me, so I got into the car and drove home quickly.

When I got to my driveway, I looked up at my house. My family, what was left of it, came running out to greet me. They had been returned home from their lovely getaway in Thailand.

After we hugged on the lawn, and my kids got past the bruising, my mom wrapped her arms around my neck and whispered, "He loved you so much." She sobbed and walked into the house. I felt a sickness, I couldn't let in. He had to be dead for her to act like that.

I went directly to my room. I needed a shower. I needed to really cry in the shower.

I opened the bedroom door and then the bathroom.

I gasped and dropped to my knees.

In Russian Red my bathroom mirror read, "**Best week of my life xoxo**".

The lipstick was on the counter next to a pair of black, patent-leather Christian Louboutin ankle-boot pumps.

Had he done it before or after? Was he dead? I didn't know.

I sobbed into my carpet.

What if he was dead?

I had nothing...no feeling...I was numb.

Chapter Eighteen

The end of me

His death was the end of me.

The end of sad Evie Evans. The mom who made everyone more important. The hockey/soccer/every damned sport-under-the-sun single parent. The yoga-pant wearing, mortgage poor, stressed to the hilt, and sex-deprived wife.

She died.

She died the week her dad was shot down in Mexico. Her ex-husband and his girlfriend had been there as well. The house was torched and the helicopter pilot was murdered savagely.

She died the week the only man she had ever been able to be a real woman with, was murdered. He died in a hotel room of a heart attack, but they suspected poisoning. Maybe potassium chloride pills. No one knew. His body had vanished from the ME's office before they could be sure.

In dead Evie's stead, there was a new Evie. She was strong and fun, like a girl she once knew.

She still cried sometimes at night, when no one was looking, but that stopped when she got a postcard in the mail from a stranger. All it said was "See you at Christmas". She stopped crying then.

She stopped being broken at night when no one could see. She started counting down the days till Christmas. And until the damned house sold, so she could stop looking over at the neighbors' house and wanting to kill the home-wrecking slut that lived there.

The End

Stay tuned for book two in the Single Lady Spy Series, **The End of Games**

ABOUT THE AUTHOR

Tara Brown is a Canadian author who writes Fantasy, Science Fiction, Paranormal Romance and Contemporary Romance in New Adult, Young Adult and Adult fiction. She lives in Eastern Canada with her husband, two daughters and pets.

Other Books by Tara Brown
The Devil's Roses
Cursed
Bane
Witch
Hyde
Death

The Born Trilogy
Born
Born to Fight
Reborn

The Light Series
The Light of the World

P.I.'s Like Us

The Blood Trail Chronicles
Vengeance

Blackwater Witches
Blackwater

Imaginations

My Side
The Long Way Home
The Lonely
LOST BOY

Made in the USA
Charleston, SC
24 November 2013